Nowhere Man

Deborah Stone

Nowhere Man

First printing September 2024

Stone, Deborah
Paperback ISBN: 9798338511510

Edited & Interior design by Eva Myrick, MSCP

Printed in the U.S.A.

"The trust of the innocent is the liar's most useful tool."

- **Stephen King**

Table of Contents

For Jonathan

Part I

Chapter One

———

Patrick was keen to ensure that he got this, his final project, exactly right. He had always been a stickler for intricate details and this in particular had to be executed correctly and on time. The layout of his house was not hugely helpful for this endeavour. For maximum effect, he would have preferred the lounge to be visible from the front door, but of course, most houses were not designed this way. The whole point of the entrance hall was to shield visitors from the main living spaces, in case of unexpected or unwanted callers, or the occupants themselves being caught in various degrees of undress. It was merely that, frustratingly for him in relation to this exercise, the location of the lounge did not suit his purposes. So, his only other option was to shift the furniture he required into the hallway. Actually, he would not need to move too much. His armchair and a side table would suffice, but the lighting would be critical. This special tableau must be the very first thing she would see as she came through the front door. His requirements were most specific.

Moving the armchair - Patrick's own chair, which he had sat in most evenings for the past forty odd years - was more challenging than he had expected. He wondered how they had ever got it into the lounge in the first place. It was large and cumbersome, with splayed arms that stuck in the doorway whether he tried to take it forwards, backwards or turned it on its side. The crocheted arm protectors, placed there by his fastidious wife to keep them from fading, kept falling off, but as he had always hated them anyway, he left them behind where they fell on the green patterned carpet, next to the pile of dust that had accumulated under the chair. He reflected on the fact that Diana was so fussy about the possibility of him marking the arms of the chair with his sweat, yet she was not house proud enough to have moved the actual armchair to hoover underneath it. *Out of sight and out of mind*, he mused, a phrase that could possibly sum up most of his life, at least until now, when he was simply out of his mind, having lost sight of any other solution other than the one he was about to adopt.

Patrick paused, wrestling his crumpled handkerchief from his pocket, and using it to wipe his damp forehead. He was not a fit man, having long ago succumbed to the numbing effects of alcohol, fatty food, and spending too much time in cars and sub-standard hotels. A thousand years ago, he had been reasonably lithe and handsome. In fact, he had been quite the athlete at school, but life had sapped him of the will to care. He could not pinpoint the exact moment when he began to let himself sag, but his body had gradually piled on the pounds to mirror the sheer weight of his disappointment at not having lived the life he had really wanted. He glanced down at his belly and sighed, the lower buttons of his shirt straining against its bulk, while large sweat patches had stained his armpits. Stuffing his handkerchief back into his trouser pocket, he took a deep breath and lunged at the armchair one last time. This final wrench succeeded in pulling it through the doorway, although it did bring a sizeable chunk of the doorframe with it.

But that's no longer my concern.

Patrick dragged the chair into the centre of the hallway, lining it up so that it would be immediately visible from the front door. He stood back and considered its positioning, nodding with satisfaction. Then, he returned to the lounge and unplugged the standard lamp, which he carried into the hall and placed next to the chair. Picking up the plug cable, he hunted around for the socket, but quickly realised that there was no such thing. It was amazing how long you could live in a house and yet not realise its electrical shortcomings. The nearest socket appeared to be back around the corner of the lounge door. He would have to dig out an extension cable, which was irritating, as it would leave a trailing wire, but there was nothing else to be done at this juncture.

He ran his fingers through his hair - which was still thick and wavy at the age of sixty-five, even if it was somewhat whiter than brown these days - before shuffling off into the kitchen at the back of the house to search for the extension. The grey Formica table where he ate most of his meals was badly chipped, as were the majority of the cupboard doors. His wife had begged him for years to allow her to remodel it, but it was such an expense, and he could never quite see the point. The units served their purpose just as they were, and Patrick saw no reason to spend a fortune on a new kitchen just so that his wife could boast to her friends that she had an island and an American fridge-freezer. He had suggested that they could change the handles on the cupboards, but this had been dismissed as a paltry effort.

He rummaged in the 'everything drawer'; the only one that he was allowed to use as his own. Old fuses, loose batteries, and two screwdrivers fell out onto the black-and-white- chequered linoleum as Patrick bent down to search for the cable. He located one at the back, leaving the rest of the stuff on the floor where it had fallen. *She can clean it up later*, he reasoned. *It will take her mind off things, poor dear.*

Back in the lounge, he succeeded in plugging in the standard lamp and then spent some minutes moving the lamp closer and then further away from the armchair in the hall to assess which position might provide optimal lighting for the chair once he was sitting in it. After fiddling with it for a while, he decided that it was the large lampshade that was the main problem, as it was simply too efficient at its job. He removed the shade and stood back. Harsh white light was exactly what was required here. Patrick returned to the lounge and retrieved the small side table, which he would need to place next to his armchair to hold his drink and his letter.

Having sorted out the hall, Patrick heaved himself upstairs to the bathroom, where he scrubbed at his face with a flannel and sprayed deodorant under his armpits. Moving into the bedroom, he changed his shirt, lifting the gold crucifix around his neck to kiss it for one final time, before straightening it and buttoning his collar over the top. He knotted his favourite, blue-striped tie in the Windsor style and combed his hair, so that he would look presentable. *You don't look too bad, all things considered*, he complimented his sceptical reflection, which stared back at him, defeated and resigned. He sat down on the bed, removed his grey felt slippers and replaced them with his black leather brogues, which he polished quickly with the same damp flannel he had brought with him from the bathroom after washing his face. *You'll just have to do*, he remarked quietly, hauling himself back off the bed and walking back downstairs to the kitchen.

He picked up a letter simply addressed *Diana* and a small glass of colourless liquid that he had prepared earlier and left next to the kettle. He carried these two items into the hall and placed them on the side table, ensuring that the letter was face up and clearly visible, before settling himself into his chair. He blinked hard, took a deep breath and then swallowed down the contents of the glass in one gulp. Placing the glass back on the table with a decisive thump, he rested his hands on the arms of the chair and closed his eyes, his mission completed.

Chapter Two

Diana did not have the best start to her day. Just after she arrived at work, she received a call on her mobile from her mother's neighbour, Belinda.

'Diana, sorry to bother you so early, but I've just had to rescue your mum.'

Diana, holding the receiver between her teeth while attempting to open a box of gift cards that had just been delivered to the shop, sighed audibly. 'What's she done now?' She ran the scissors along the Sellotape that held the top of the box together.

'Well, she appears to be stuck underneath the garage door. I think she was trying to put her bins out and she must have pressed the wrong button, so that the door came down on top of her. The problem is, I can't release it, because I can't get inside the garage. The door is wedged, and so is she. I don't have a key to get into the bungalow and she's obviously quite distressed.'

Blast, thought Diana. She kept meaning to sort out a key for Belinda, but had never got around to it; only partly through laziness, but mostly because her mother was vehemently opposed to the suggestion.

'Is she OK?'

'She's upset. Brian is sitting with her.'

'I'm on my way.'

Diana slammed the receiver down and grabbed her bag. She turned the sign on the front door of the shop back over to Closed, locking the door from the inside, before exiting at the back of the shop where she had a small parking space for her car. Her heart was racing with both anger and frustration as she reversed out of the alley and onto the main road, narrowly missing a young mother who was pushing her baby's pram into her path. It would take her at least half an hour to reach her mother and then who knows how long to sort out this latest accident. She would lose half a day of trade at the very least and it was coming up to Christmas, so it really mattered. She gripped the steering wheel so tightly that she almost lost all feeling in her fingers.

Her mother was becoming increasingly impossible. She refused to move into sheltered accommodation where someone could be on call to help her, never mind the thought of an actual care home. She definitely refused to have any help in her own home, claiming that they would only serve to get in her way. The situation was completely unmanageable.

'And anyway, Diana. What would I do if I had help? Sit there staring at this stranger all day long? I don't think so!'

The only other option was for her mother to come to live with Diana, and that was never going to happen. Diana and her mother had always had a strained relationship to put it mildly, and Patrick would never contemplate having her as a permanent resident. Their resentment of each other was entirely mutual; her mother still believing that Diana could have done a lot better for herself and Patrick being fully aware of this fact as she mentioned it to him on almost every occasion. Yet her mother was obviously no longer capable of living alone. She was forgetful and often confused. In the past year, she had drunk surgical spirit by mistake and alternately taken too many pills in one day or too few. She called Diana several times a day asking her to pop to the shops and bring things over, never recognising or remembering that Diana actually worked and had her own home to run. It was truly hopeless.

The heavy traffic finally cleared on the main road, and Diana managed to cut round the side streets to reach her mother's bungalow. She stopped her ageing white Fiesta with a screech of the brakes and leapt out of the car. Running up the drive, she saw her mother's feet sticking out from under the garage door like the Wicked Witch of the East in *The Wizard of Oz*, Brian and Belinda crouched down by each foot.

'Thanks so much, guys,' Diana panted as she came up the drive. 'I really do appreciate you calling me and staying with her.'

She made a mental note to drop yet another bunch of flowers over to them later on.

'Mum, it's Diana. What have you done this time?'

'Argh, Diana,' her mother wailed. 'Where've you been?'

Diana ignored her and marched to the front door, rummaging in her bag for her mother's keys, which she always carried along with her own.

'Brian, Belinda, you go. I know you've got to get to work. We'll be OK now.'

'Are you sure?' they chorused.

'Yes, thank you so much as always.'

Diana fiddled with the key in the lock and once inside, closed the front door behind her. She was at the same time grateful to but also annoyed by Belinda and Brian, who she knew judged her and the way that she cared for her mother. She did her best, but she intimated from their sidelong glances that they thought

11

otherwise. All it served to do was pile on the guilt Diana already felt like a lead weight pressing down on her every day.

She dashed through the kitchen and opened the door on the other side of the lounge which led into the garage. The top half of her mother lay on the floor, ashen, her legs trapped by the electric door. Diana pressed the button on the side of the wall and the door slowly rose, releasing her.

Diana knelt down.

'Are you alright, Mum?'

She glanced up to see the neighbours lingering at the end of the drive and she waved her thanks, muttering 'bugger off' under her breath.

'Of course I'm not alright!' her mother cried. Huge, fat tears coursed down her face. 'I've been trapped here for hours.'

'I don't think it's been hours,' Diana replied gently.

'How would you know? It took you long enough to get here. And those two were bloody useless. Asking me every five seconds if I was OK.'

'They were very kind, Mum. If they hadn't seen you as they were leaving for work, you might have been lying here for a lot longer. Come on, can you sit up?'

Diana placed her hand behind her mother's back and helped her into a sitting position. 'Do your legs hurt?'

'Yes, of course they bloody hurt. The door fell on top of them!' she shrilled.

'OK. Let's try to stand up slowly.'

Diana gritted her teeth and placed her arms under her mother's armpits, helping her to stand. Her mother was so light to move, just bones and skin these days. She had been statuesque in her prime, but now had withered to almost nothing, like a wilting houseplant.

Her mother screeched in pain as Diana hoisted her up.

'Come on, let's try to get to you into the lounge and I can take a proper look at your legs.'

Slowly, they limped across the garage and into the lounge – a very short distance, yet it took an extremely long time - where Diana lowered her mother onto the sofa, while her mother continued to sob.

'Now, let's assess the damage, shall we?' Diana soothed, talking to her mother as if she were a three-year-old child. She knelt down, willing herself to stay calm, and pulled up her mother's nightdress above the knees. The skin was badly cut and already bruising.

'I'm going to lie you down.'

Her mother nodded, sniffing, allowing Diana to lift her legs.

'Stay there while I get some wet cloths and the first aid kit.'

Diana rushed to the bathroom and grabbed a couple of flannels and the first aid kit, which was kept in the cabinet below the sink. She ran the hot water tap and soaked one of the flannels before returning to the living room.

'I'll see if I can clean you up a bit.'

Diana spread the dry towel under her mother's legs and began to pat the cuts with the wet towel. She then retrieved the TCP antiseptic liquid and some cotton wool pads from the first aid kit.

'This is going to sting, Mum.'

Her mother howled as the TCP touched the wound.

'Sorry, but you don't want it to get infected, do you?'

Diana cleaned the wounds and then placed the largest plasters she could find on top.

'The good news is that I think they are just flesh wounds, but we need to watch them and get the doctor out if they get any worse. Now, let's get you into bed.'

Together, they hobbled into the bedroom and Diana tucked her mother in.

'Let me get you some painkillers.'

Her mother had an ample supply, as the doctor prescribed them readily after each mishap and they had accumulated. She could have opened her own pharmacy.

'Here, take two of these and try to get some sleep. Have you taken you other tablets today?'

Marjorie shook her head. She suffered from high blood pressure and took statins and an anticoagulant every day to reduce her risk of heart attack or stroke.

Diana doled out the requisite tablets and handed them to her mother along with a small glass of water to swallow them down with, watching her to make sure that she did so.

'Right, I'll pop back in later to see how you're doing. You're lucky, Mum. You could have broken your legs.'

Her mother rolled her eyes.

'We will talk about all this later when you're feeling a bit better, but this can't keep happening, Mum.'

'You're not leaving me here all alone, are you?' she whimpered.

'Mum, I've got a business to run. I've already had to close the shop this morning and I simply can't afford to be shut all day. You'll be absolutely fine. Just stay where you are, and I'll be back as soon as I can. There's water by your bed, and I'll make you a nice cup of tea before I go. You need to sleep.' She paused. 'But this simply can't go on, you know.'

Her mother made no reply, her eyes already closing. Diana knew she ought to stay; but equally, she knew that she had to go.

Back at the shop, business was slow, but Mondays always were. It would get much busier towards the end of the week, as people were already Christmas shopping and there were always those who realised that they needed a gift for a birthday, or a housewarming present at the last minute. Some would rush in and out, choosing something in moments, including the card and the gift wrap. She preferred these emergency shoppers to the other kind, who dawdled in the small shop for what seemed like hours at a time, examining every item several times and then eventually not buying anything at all. Diana had no time for timewasters.

She spent the rest of the afternoon unpacking the latest deliveries and tidying up the stock room. By four-thirty, it had begun to rain heavily and the high street was dead, deterring any potential shoppers from venturing forth, so she closed up. She popped up the road and bought a fish pie for one and some vanilla ice cream for her mother, as well as some more dressings for her legs. Then she went back to the car.

Just as she was starting the engine, her phone beeped.

Fancy a quick drink before you head home?

I can't. Mum has fallen again and I've got to go back there

She OK?

Not really. Just another trauma!!

Poor you. Sure you don't want to meet on your way home?

15

Diana deleted the messages and lobbed her phone into her tote bag. What she really needed was for everyone to just leave her alone.

Chapter Three

'Is Dad home yet?' Ben shouted as he barged through the front door, knocking over the umbrella stand with his poorly packed sports bag.

'No,' his mother replied, righting the stand, and replacing the clutter that had fallen out of it - not just umbrellas, but cricket balls and various mismatched goalie gloves. 'He should have been here a few hours ago, but he must be stuck in traffic. I tried to call him, but I didn't get any reply. He's probably out of charge again. You know what he's like.' She held out her hand. 'Here, give me that bag and I'll put your kit in the wash.' She ran her fingers through the fringe of her blonde hair, pushing it out of her eyes.

Angie had emerged from the kitchen as Ben had arrived home from school, wiping her hands on her apron before reaching up to give him a kiss. He had grown almost a foot in the past year and now towered over his petite mother. She wondered, not for the first time, how she had managed to produce such a tall, if somewhat gangly, child.

'How was your day?'

'I don't know why you ask me that exact same question every single time I get back. It was just boring. School is so boring.' Ben backed away from her attempted kiss, which hit the air with a smack.

Angie bit her lip and headed back into the kitchen. 'Your tea will be ready in five minutes.'

'What is it?'

'Cod.'

'Oh Mum, it's always cod on a Monday. And you know it never fills me up, especially after games. What's for pudding?'

'Brownies, your favourite.'

'Did you make them or are they the ones I really like from Tesco?'

'They're mine.'

Ben huffed ostentatiously. 'I hope you haven't put nuts in them.'

'No, I haven't put nuts in them, obviously. I never do.' She turned and gave him a hug, which he allowed. 'Go and wash your hands.'

'I'm seventeen, Mum, not seven.'

Angie made no reply because she was counting very slowly to ten in her head. It did not always work and eventually, her patience would inevitably expire, but she did her best. She doled out his food and watched it cooling. After a few minutes, she called up the stairs.

'Ben, your dinner is on the table!'

Ben loped back down, taking the stairs two at a time, and sprang into the kitchen, his mobile ringing out on speaker. 'Hello, I am afraid I can't take your call at the moment, but please do leave a message stating your name and number and I will call you straight back.'

'I'm sure he'll be here soon, Ben. What do you want him for so urgently anyway?'

18

Ben slumped down heavily onto the kitchen chair. 'I just wanted to tell him about my game this afternoon.'

'So, how was it?'

'We won,' Ben replied, shovelling the fish and asparagus into his mouth as if he was shielding it from an angry lion who might snatch it at any moment.

'That's great, Ben,' Angie replied rather over-enthusiastically. 'Did you score?'

'I'll tell Dad all about it later when he gets here,' Ben snapped, stuffing his headphones into his ears. 'Let's face it, you're not that interested in football, are you?'

She found it hard to disagree with this fact.

His father travelled for the latter half of every week and often at the weekend too, so Ben really looked forward to the days when he was at home. They talked about sport non-stop. His father worked at the Ministry of Defence, and he could never be contacted when he was working away. It meant that the time Ben spent with him was even more precious. He was proud of his father and his secret job, assuming that he was some sort of spy like James Bond or Jason Bourne, given that his father never gave anything away about his exact location and what he was actually doing. Ben hoped that one day he could follow in his footsteps and get away from this dull, small town where nothing exciting ever happened.

They lived in the small village of Abbotts Ripton in Cambridgeshire, which was, in Ben's view, the absolute middle of nowhere. It was quiet, with a population of just over three hundred people. Its only claim to fame, apart from having one shop, garage, and post office, was that the village hall had been opened by John Major in 1988 when he was MP for Huntingdon, which as far as Ben was concerned was ancient history. Ben commuted to school for an hour each day by bus to Cambridge, having won a scholarship to the prestigious Perse School, where he had a good group of friends. However, the fact that he lived so far away dramatically hampered his social life. He could not wait until he could drive, because currently he was mostly housebound and hugely frustrated. The only real highlight of his week was seeing his father. The downside was that his dad was only around sporadically to spend time with him. They had rarely been to a football game together and his father only ever watched him play occasionally. He envied his friends who had their dads around all the time, although most of them thought Ben was far luckier for not having his father breathing down his neck all the time.

His mother removed his dinner plate and served him his brownies with vanilla ice cream, which he gobbled down in seconds.

'More?' she enquired.

He nodded without glancing up from his mobile, dialling his father again. It was strange, because his dad was usually home on time and if he was delayed, he would usually message or call.

As the evening wore on, Ben became increasingly agitated and so did his mother, although she was doing her best to pretend otherwise.

'Maybe we should call the police and check whether there have been any accidents?' Ben suggested, as his father's mobile continued to ring out.

'It's only nine-thirty. Let's wait and see,' Angie replied. 'He might be working on something which has made him late, and he can't contact us right now. It has happened before, hasn't it? Well, it used to more often when you were very little, and you just don't remember. Sometimes, he was weeks late.'

Angie remembered the anxiety she had felt when he had failed to come home - yet when he did finally arrive, it was always with such gushing apologies accompanied by lavish gifts of flowers and chocolates that she could never remain angry with him for very long.

'You know that I'll never leave you, Angie and that even if I can't call, I'm always thinking of you,' he would whisper into her ear after they had made love fiercely and quickly. 'It's just the job. Sometimes it makes it impossible to call, but you should never worry. I'll always turn up eventually.'

'He will be here by the time you wake up in the morning, love. Don't you worry.'

And Ben allowed his mother to give him another short hug for reassurance, before he remembered that he was far too old for that sort of thing.

But when morning came, his father had still not arrived.

Chapter Four

Diana pulled onto her drive and switched off the car headlights. For a moment, she just sat there: the Christmas songs on the radio mercifully silenced. Even though it was only early November, sheer exhaustion pinned her to the driver's seat. She rubbed her eyes and grabbed her handbag before opening the car door and hauling herself out into a gust of cold air.

She had just come back from her mother's where she had been for almost two hours. The cuts on her mother's legs were relatively superficial, but she was clearly shaken up, bruised, and sore. Diana had helped her wash and made her some supper, watching to make sure that she ate some of it. Always a healthy eater, now she merely picked around the edges of her food like a fussy toddler. The only thing that kept her going was her love of vanilla ice cream. She would always eat a scoop or two of it, so at least that was something. Diana had tucked her back into bed and promised to come in again on her way to work tomorrow. She had resisted the temptation to have the care conversation again. Neither of them had the energy that night. Inevitably, she felt guilty as always; torn between the belief that she should really stay overnight to watch her mother and her desire to go home to sleep in her own familiar bed.

Diana fumbled her way towards the front door. Oddly, Patrick was clearly in, because his car was parked outside and there was a light on in the hall. She thought that he was away for a couple of days on his usual buying trip that he took at the start of each week, but maybe it had been cancelled at the last minute.

He could at least have switched the outside lights on, she thought with irritation.

She could not see to get the key in the lock. Eventually, she managed to open the door, calling out, 'Patrick, are you home?' as she bent down to collect some leaflets on the doormat. When she looked up again, she saw him immediately, illuminated like a ghoul by the standard lamp. For a split second, she was confused. What was the armchair doing in the hall? Why was Patrick just sitting there? And then she focussed on him and began to scream.

Diana dropped her handbag and raced over to him. He was sitting ramrod straight in the chair: his eyes open, staring straight ahead. She reached out her hand and touched his arm, but he did not move. A small pool of vomit had congealed on his chin, staining his favourite tie. 'Patrick! Wake up!' she screeched, shaking him now, but his body already felt stiff and cold. Diana fell to her knees, her body folding in on itself like poorly constructed origami. She knew she should call an ambulance, but she was paralysed, and anyway, she could see that it was far too late. She knelt at his feet and stared at him, her husband of almost three decades.

'Why? Why, Patrick? What the bloody hell have you done?' was all she could sob.

After some minutes, she managed to right herself and, as she stood up to retrieve her handbag and search for her phone, she spotted an envelope addressed to her on the side table next to the armchair. She turned it over. It had not been sealed. Her hand shaking, she drew out the letter, which had been typed on a plain sheet of A4 - she assumed for clarity as his handwriting had always been atrocious.

Diana,

I have never been completely honest with you and I can't go on living a lie.

I am sorry to have disappointed you like this, and hope that you can find future happiness.

I have made full provision for you.

Please forgive me.

Your loving husband

Patrick

He had not signed it by hand.

Diana sank to the floor and scanned the note several times, her hand wobbling so violently that she could barely read it. He had seemed absolutely fine that morning, ready to go on his work trip as usual. A wave of nausea washed over her as she read the note again. Then she crawled across the floor to retrieve her phone from her handbag before slowly dialling 999.

Chapter Five

Marjorie woke up and tried to lift her head off the pillow. 'Jesus Christ!' she cried out. She rested her head back down again and called out. There was no reply. 'Diana, where are you? I can't move,' she warbled, but the house was silent, and her cry merely echoed back at her. She was sure Diana had been here a couple of minutes ago, but maybe she had gone home. She was so inconsiderate like that, always putting her needs and those of that dull husband of hers above her own.

Marjorie turned her head very gingerly to try to read the digital clock. Its enormous numbers blinked back at her - 4.30 a.m. So, it was still the middle of the night, and not yet morning. She needed the toilet, but did not appear to be able to move. She attempted to shuffle to the edge of the bed so that she could reach for the grab rail, but even that proved to be impossible.

She could not hold it any longer and she relieved herself, her nightdress soaking up the hot wetness. She let out a shriek of frustration, disgusted with her ageing body, which continually let her down. She was appalled at herself and with what she had become, a decaying old lady with no purpose and no ability to help herself anymore. She wondered how it had come to this, when she had always been so robust and capable. She lay there, waiting for rescue, weeping fat tears, which coursed down her face and trickled down the crevasses of her crepey neck. She just wanted to know when it was all going to end.

Chapter Six

Angie was beginning to feel quite agitated now. Ray had neither appeared, nor called or messaged. She had tried repeatedly to ring him and sent more than a dozen texts, which she knew would irritate him, but she could not get through. It occurred to her, as she stood by the breakfast bar in the kitchen at two in the morning, that she had no other way of contacting him. She had no work number for him, as he had always told her that under no circumstances should she contact the Ministry. It was not even as though he had any other family or a best friend she could contact. Ray's parents had both passed away before she met him, and he was an only child. His work effectively meant that he could not develop meaningful friendships because he could never really tell anyone who he was or what he did for a living. They told people in the village that he worked for the Foreign Office. Ben believed he was in defence and that the Foreign Office was code for his real job. Only she knew that he was MI5. This was almost fine, but at times like these Angie realised how isolated it made them.

She moved over to the fridge and refilled her empty glass with white wine, taking a hearty slug, before immediately castigating herself and throwing the rest of it down the sink. Who drinks in the middle of the night? Her mother used to do it, particularly after her father had died, and she had no intention of turning into her mother. And anyway, she needed to be sober enough to drive just in case she suddenly received a call and it turned out that Ray was injured, or sick, lying somewhere alone. She knew deep down that this was highly unlikely, but there was always that possibility.

In fact, Ray had warned her early on in their relationship that there might come a time when he would simply not return and if that happened, she must simply accept it and carry on, as if he had been a mere figment of her imagination. He had made provision for all eventualities. He had assured her repeatedly.

She tried to gulp away the solid lump that had been stuck in her throat since early evening, but it merely tightened, and she shivered involuntarily. She knew that there was very little she could actually do at this time of night, so she pulled her quilted dressing gown around herself before tiptoeing back to bed, taking care not to wake Ben. She grabbed one of Ray's pillows and inhaled deeply, hugging it to her. It did not help her to go back to sleep.

Chapter Seven

———

Ian kept messaging Diana, but she did not reply. She had met him when he was looking for a birthday present for his sister. Apparently, he had left his gift buying very late and had dashed into town in a desperate hope of finding something, anything, at the last minute. The little gift shop on the corner of the high street in the small Hertfordshire village had lurked next to the butcher's for years. He said he had walked past it many a time, but he had never stepped inside before. Normally, he got away with giving gift vouchers, but his sister was turning forty and had asked for something special that she could keep, whatever that meant. When he asked her to be more specific, she unhelpfully told him to surprise her - which was self-defeating as she would inevitably be disappointed. So, in this fog of confusion, he had entered the world of *Gifts and Glamour.*

Diana had hung the inside walls with pink twinkly lights and displayed small knickknacks artfully on tables and shelves of differing heights. One of the walls was devoted to a tasteful display of greetings cards and gift-wrap, whilst at the back of the shop was a small desk housing the till. As you opened the door, an irritating bell tinkled above your head, but it served to alert her to customers if she was in the back.

'Can I help you?' she had asked from behind the door, startling Ian.

'I have absolutely no idea, but I really hope so. It's my sister's birthday and I am rather at a loss as to what to get her.'

'Well, what kind of things does she like?'

Ian cocked his head to one side, which was something he did unknowingly when he tried to think.

'I really have no clue what my sister likes. She's lived up in Scotland for the past fifteen years with her husband and four children. Whenever we do try to chat, one or more of the little pests usually interrupts within the first minute of our conversation, so we rely mostly on texts, which are cursory at best.

'Well, why don't I show you a few things?' she suggested as Ian stood looking at her blankly, making no reply. 'I have some lovely new cashmere gloves, which are perfect for this time of year and are super soft. Here, feel.' She held out a pair of pale grey gloves for Ian to stroke, which he dutifully did.

'Are gloves something she can keep? That's my brief, you see.'

'Well, most definitely. Cashmere is always a good investment – as long as you can keep it away from moths.'

'Hmm, maybe. I rather suspect that there might be a prevalence of moths at my sister's place.' He glanced around, but was finding the fairy lights quite distracting. 'Do you have any other suggestions?'

'Well, if it's something special and lasting that you are after, I've got this gorgeous vase.' She moved towards a shelf on the left and gingerly picked up a small glass vase, handblown with a swirl of deep reds. 'It's rather beautiful, don't you think? It's from Venice, Murano, in fact.'

Ian had taken it from her hands and as he did so, a small electric shock passed between the two of them. The woman smiled and glanced away. At a guess, she was in her early to mid-sixties, very well-preserved, as his father used to remark about various female newsreaders on the television when he was growing up. He had had a particular fondness for Angela Rippon, especially after seeing her long legs revealed on *The Morecambe and Wise Show*. Today, the shopkeeper wore very flattering flared, navy trousers topped with a cream jacket. Her blonde, streaked hair was tied up in a neat ponytail. Her skin was clear and relatively unlined apart from her eyes, which crinkled pleasantly when she smiled.

'It is charming, but she has four rampaging brats at home, and I suspect that one of them would knock it over and break it within moments of it being put on display.'

'I understand,' she replied, taking the vase from his hands in case he did the same, and replacing it with care back onto the shelf. 'Maybe, if you're looking for durability, a leather jewellery box might be the thing?' She turned and picked up a square, cream leather box. 'It's perfect for necklaces, earrings, rings etc. You can see that it has various useful compartments. She can keep it on her dressing table, which would hopefully be well out of harm's way.'

Ian breathed a sigh of relief. 'Now that looks perfect. I'll take it.'

'Not a problem. That's what I'm here for. Would you like it gift wrapped? And are you giving it in person or posting it?' she enquired, carrying the jewellery box over to the counter.

'Posting it. The thought of visiting my sister fills me with horror if I'm being perfectly honest. We never had anything in common even as children.'

Diana ignored this remark, unable to think of a suitable reply. 'I can gift wrap it and then cover it in bubble wrap and brown paper as a second layer if you like, so it can go straight to the post office, and I also have labels here. Do you need a card?'

'Yes, thank you for reminding me. Do you have one for a fortieth?'

'I have a wide selection. Would you like me to show you?'

'Could you choose one for me? I feel you would be a far better judge. I'm not great at these things, to be honest.'

She plucked a card from the display, which featured a glamorous woman lounging on a sofa sipping a glass of wine and read *40 and still fabulous!* 'Will this work?'

'Perfect, although fabulous is significantly over-egging it for my sister, but I suppose it is a special occasion.' He paused. 'I really can't thank you enough. I was in a real panic about getting this present.'

'Not at all. I have so many men who come in here with exactly the same predicament. Here's a pen. You can write it out now if you'd like and then I'll package it up with the jewellery box.'

'You've been a real godsend, um, sorry I don't know your name.'

'I'm Diana,' she replied, concentrating as she totted up the bill on the till.

'Ian.' Once again, he paused. 'Look, you've been so very kind and helpful, can I buy you a quick cup of tea to thank you properly?'

She hesitated, glancing at the clock on the wall. 'Well, I am about to close up for the day, but I must admit that I could murder a coffee. Maybe we could grab one next door at Costa for a few minutes.'

'Terrific. Let me pop this parcel over to the post office before they shut, and I'll meet you there in ten.' He took the packaged box from her.

'Great, see you then.'

Since then, Diana had met up with Ian occasionally for coffee. He would pop into her shop around five and hang about until she closed, which she was beginning to find quite irritating. Sometimes Diana took ages fiddling about and often tried to make an excuse not to come. She had her mother to visit or her husband to cook for. But Ian was infinitely patient. When he did manage to persuade her, they would wander up to Costa or Starbucks, depending on where a table was available. He always offered to pay, but Diana was very strict about paying fifty-fifty for everything. She had a thing about being beholden to people.

Diana often moaned to him about her mother and how much she was stressed out about her stubbornness when it came to admitting that she needed any help.

Ian was always happy to listen.

'Look, I'm always prattling on about myself. Tell me more about you,' Diana insisted the third time they met up.

He told her a little more about his own job. 'Not much to tell really. I work from home as a customer services agent for a clothing retailer, so listening is my job, I suppose. My hours are completely flexible. Quite often, I work mornings and early evenings, and I don't go out much.'

Diana was not really concentrating on what he was saying, despite having asked the question. She was still wrapped up in her own parental troubles.

'I just worry that something catastrophic will happen one day. I mean, recently she has fallen over, and she drank the antiseptic which was supposed to be used to treat her cuts and bruises.' Diana smiled weakly and leant back on the armchair.

'Well, on the upside, she's survived it all so far. She's obviously tough.'

'Yes, I suppose so. But I dread the phone calls. It's all so draining and more often than not, I have to close the shop to sort it out.'

'Can't you get an assistant?'

'I can't afford it. I barely break even as it is. But the place keeps me busy and with Patrick travelling during the week, it keeps me out of mischief, I suppose.' It turned out that her husband was the head buyer for a white goods company, so he had to visit his suppliers to hammer out the deals.

'I can always be around to help you out if you ever need it.' He leaned towards her as he offered this.

She crossed her legs away from him. 'That's very kind, Ian but really, it's fine. I'm fine.' She drained her coffee and placed the mug back onto the table. 'I'm so sorry. I always seem to be complaining to you.'

'Not at all, Diana. That's what friends are for, isn't it?'

She made no reply, but picked up her handbag. 'Look, I really must run. I've got to go to Mum's and then get back home.'

'Already?'

'Yes, you know I've only ever got half an hour or so, and not even that usually. There's really no need for you to call in as often as you do. It's always nice to see you, obviously, but at the moment, I always seem to be pressed for time. Bye, Ian.'

She stood and turned to go, disappearing onto the uninvitingly wet and cold high street.

'Thanks for the coffee, Diana. My shout next time,' he called to her back as the door closed.

Chapter Eight

The ambulance and the police had been and gone. The paramedics had recorded Patrick dead at the scene. Diana had not expected the police to come, but they explained that it was standard procedure in the case of all suicides. They asked if Patrick had left a note and Diana said no. She felt that the letter was personal and even possibly implicated her in some way, - even though she had no idea why she thought so - and that the police might misunderstand it. She did not even begin to understand it herself. It was currently tucked away inside her bra.

'We will have to ask for a post-mortem to be performed and then the coroner will give a verdict on the death,' a policewoman young enough to still be at school explained to Diana as she sat opposite her at the kitchen table. 'I think, given the nature of his death, we will be able to categorise this as an apparent suicide and pass that on to the coroner.'

'Apparent? What else could it possibly be?' Diana whispered, her voice hoarse as she pressed her nails deep into her palms as if checking that she was still alive and that she was not stuck in the middle of some terrible nightmare from which she might wake up at any moment. She glanced up at the PC, her eyes bloodshot and sore from weeping.

'Probably nothing, but as your husband did not leave a note and the location was slightly strange - given that he moved some of the furniture into the hall - it will need investigating. Had he ever had suicidal tendencies that you know of, or had he been depressed recently?' She had her notebook and pencil poised at the ready.

Diana swallowed hard. 'No, not at all. Patrick was always so steady. My rock, really. He worked hard and otherwise we led a pretty quiet life. Quite boring, really.' She hesitated. 'And he was very religious, Catholic in fact. He believed that suicide was a mortal sin.'

'And you?'

'Am I Catholic or do I believe in mortal sin?'

'Either or both.'

'Neither I suppose. I went to church on Sundays sometimes to accompany Patrick, but I struggled with it all. I mean, with all the horror in the world, it's hard to comprehend a loving God.'

The policewoman nodded vaguely and looked back to her tiny notebook. 'And did he have any problems at work?'

'Not that I was aware of.'

Patrick had never talked about his work in much depth. He had always told Diana that it was not particularly interesting. One model of washing machine was very much like another, and it was just a process of negotiation in the end. He travelled a couple of days a week to meet suppliers and visit the stores, but that was it. She had stopped asking about it years ago.

'I just haggle for a living,' he used to say, 'which is why I like a nice quiet life when I get home.'

'Well, you've told us where he worked, so we will check in with them and see if there were any issues. What about any other family?'

Diana tugged another handful of tissues out of the box on the kitchen table, which was strewn with ones she had already soaked, and blew her nose loudly. 'His parents are dead and we never managed to have any children, which was a source of regret to both of us. We tried, you know, but it wasn't to be. And I never felt comfortable with the idea of adoption.'

The policewoman nodded. 'And was there any family history of depression?'

'No, no, I don't think so. Patrick's parents both died of cancer. That was obviously hard for him, but it was a very long time ago.'

'Was he a drinker or a gambler?'

'No!' Diana replied a little too sharply. 'Sorry, I mean no. Patrick was temperate in all things. He might have a beer after work occasionally, but nothing other than that, and he only ever had a bet once a year on the Grand National. When he did, he mentioned it in confession and said his appropriate number of Hail Marys in repentance. He was really very risk averse.'

Diana just wanted the police to go away now. Her head was pounding, and she felt as if her body would not hold her upright in her chair for very much longer.

'Look, I don't know why you're asking me all these questions. I don't understand why he would do something like this. I thought he was happy, I thought we were happy. I don't understand why you can't see that I can't help you.' She began to sob again.

The policewoman patted her arm. 'Is there anyone I can call to be with you?'

'No, no, thank you, I'll be alright. I just need to lie down, I think.'

'The ambulance will take your husband to the hospital now and the coroner will be in touch. If we need anything else, we will let you know.'

'I keep telling you that don't have anything else to tell you. I don't know why he did this. I can't tell you anything else because I don't get it. I just can't imagine why he would do something like this.' She lay her head onto the table.

The policewoman waited silently until Diana recovered herself slightly and then helped her upstairs, so that she could lie on her bed. She fetched her a glass of water and finally left her alone.

Diana lay there, staring at the painting of the Madonna that hung over her dressing table, listening to the creaks and groans of the house. It also seemed to be moaning the same question.

Why?

Chapter Nine

Two days had passed since Ray had been expected home and Angie had been doing her best to keep busy. She worked part-time as a blogger for a number of online companies, which meant she could work from home with flexible hours. It suited her in many respects; but as Ben had grown into his teenage years, she felt more alone because inevitably he needed her less. She often thought back to the frantic years when Ben was small, and Ray was away. At the time, she had felt exhausted and frazzled, complaining to herself and other mothers at the school gates about how tough it was to try to have it all as she tried to manage her part-time job, the house and for most of the time, single-handed parenting. But now, as she sat alone writing a blog about salad recipes for the local garden centre with only the loud ticking of the kitchen clock for company, she realised how much she missed all the hustle and bustle of never having enough time or energy. Sometimes she felt as if no one really needed her that much anymore.

She stared at the three sentences that she had managed to write since breakfast. Even that pitiful output read badly and would have to be rewritten. She rose from the kitchen table to make her third coffee of the morning, groaning like an arthritic octogenarian, and as she did so, she heard the clap of the letterbox. Even the post was something to look forward to these days – well, at least until she picked it up off the mat and was inevitably disappointed that it contained either bills to be paid, or leaflets which went straight into the recycling basket. Did anyone ever read those flyers, or were all those trees felled in vain? She wandered slowly into the hall and retrieved the bundle lying on the mat. There was a Vodafone bill, - she really ought to switch to digital - a letter from the council about the electoral register, a double-glazing leaflet, and an actual letter with her name and address typed on it. She carried the meagre stack back into the kitchen and switched on the coffee machine before opening the letter.

It was typed, but using a handwritten font. There was no address at the top of the letter.

Angie Baby, it began.

So, it was from Ray. He always called her that after the Helen Reddy song, which was well before her time, but Ray had introduced her to it and now she loved it.

'It's about a crazy girl with a secret lover who keeps her satisfied,' Ray would grin as he spooned her in bed, nuzzling the back of her neck.

'I'm not crazy.'

'No, but we are kind of secret,' he would shush into her ear. 'And I'm a great lover, don't you agree?'

'I think you're paraphrasing,' she giggled, kissing him.

Angie Baby,

Sorry for the letter, but you know that sometimes SMS etc. cannot be trusted. I'm going to be away for a while. Things are hectic here. You know I can't say more.

I don't know when I'll be back, but usual rules apply. My phone will be off, and I'll be back as soon as I can.

Send my love to Ben and tell him to be good. Remember our song. No one asks you to explain.

Love you, Angie Baby

P.S. Shred this

And so here she was, all alone once more, Angie Baby.

Damn Ray, she thought, as the kettle boiled. She was tired of being a part-time wife and mother and of never really knowing where he was. When he got back, she would sit him down and force him to discuss everything properly. It was time to make some changes to their lives so that they could be together for good and live a normal life, rather than everything being constantly in limbo.

Chapter Ten

——

Diana felt as if she was floating above herself, watching remotely as she went through the motions of her life. She observed herself washing her face and brushing her teeth, her skin and gums numb. She made coffee, but did not drink it. She heated up soup, but could not eat it. The television hurt her eyes and the radio made her head throb. She kept the curtains closed and simply lay on the sofa in the living room in her pyjamas, opposite the space left by Patrick's empty armchair, which still stood sentinel in the hallway, the carpet new and bright in the space it had left behind. She had neither the strength nor the will to move the chair back again, half expecting him to be sitting there when she drifted into the hall, asking her what was for his dinner.

And in her head, the same questions circled and tormented her. Why would he have taken his own life? And why in such a mystifying manner? She thought they had been happy, or at least as happy as most married couples could be who had been together effectively forever. They had rubbed along well enough, hadn't they? And they were kind to each other, rarely arguing. They might have bickered on occasion when he did not fluff up the cushions on the sofa, or if he put his plates in the dishwasher unrinsed. He would get narked when she ordered too many things online. Patrick always worried about money, even though they were fairly comfortable. Without children, they had more disposable income than many.

The only calls Diana had made since his passing were to her mother.

'Mum, there's something I have to tell you.'

'What? I can't hear you, Diana. Hold on. Let me turn the telly down.'

The television was blaring so loudly that Diana could have heard it at her house three miles away. Her mother had shuffled away from the phone and when she returned to it, she put the receiver down.

Diana had called again.

'Mum, can you hear me now?'

'Diana? Is that you? You sound funny.'

'Yes, it's me. I'm just, well I'm quite upset.'

'What about?'

'Well, I don't know how to tell you this, but Patrick has died.' Her voice cracked as she mentioned Patrick's name.

'Did you say *died*?'

'Yes.'

There was silence for a moment on both ends of the line.

'So, he's dead?'

'Yes, that's right. He died last night.'

'Oh, Diana, I'm so sorry. Heart attack, was it? Mind you, I did keep telling him to watch his weight. He had a real spare tyre on him. Hang on a second, Diana. I'm just going to sit down.'

She put the phone down and cut Diana off again.

Diana called back and they continued as if there had been no interruptions.

'Hi, Mum. So, no it wasn't a heart attack. He, well, I don't know how to say this nicely, but he seems to have committed suicide.' She felt bile rise into her mouth. It was the first time she had said the word out loud.

'Suicide? Patrick? Well, I never. I wouldn't have thought he was that brave. Mind you, he might have been selfish enough. He was always a little tight, wasn't he?'

Diana rolled her eyes at the wall.

'Mum, how can you even say that at a time like this? And what has that got to do with anything anyway? All I know is that he's dead and I don't know why,' she howled down the phone, beginning to sob.

'Well, there's no point in asking me, love. I don't know why either. Maybe he had just had enough. I know that I have some days, and we all think about ending it at times. Was he depressed?'

'No, no, well at least, I don't think so. That's what the police asked me.' Diana blew her nose loudly on a tissue and pulled another handful from the cardboard cube by the phone.

'They always ask that question in those police shows, don't they? I watched a good one the other evening. Now, what was it called? You know, the one with the handsome man with the moustache. Who do I mean, Diana?'

Diana made no reply.

'Diana?'

'Look, Mum, I have to go. I might not be able to come round for a couple of days, because I have things to sort out here, but I'll ask the neighbours to pop in and see if you need anything.'

'I don't want those two nosey parkers over here. They always want to look in my fridge.'

'Only when they help you to put your shopping away, Mum.'

'You don't know the half of it, Diana. The other day, one of them stole my butter.'

'I think that's highly unlikely.'

'Your problem is that you are just too trusting, Diana.'

Diana sat in the dark and wondered if her mother was right.

The following morning, the doorbell rang. Diana was sitting at the kitchen table in her dressing gown, staring into space and nursing a cold mug of tea, despite the fact that it was almost noon. She could not see the point in getting dressed at the moment. She picked up her mobile and pressed the Ring app. There were two men standing outside and behind them on the road she could see a large delivery truck. She put the phone down and ignored them. She had not ordered anything, and she certainly had no intention of taking anything in for the neighbours. She was not ready to see anyone quite yet.

The bell trilled again. Diana opened the Ring app and reluctantly said hello, her voice hoarse.

'Delivery from Magnet,' a distant voice shouted.

'Magnet?' *What was Magnet?*

'I think you must have the wrong address, sorry.'

'Are you Diana Whitlock?'

'Yes.'

'Well, it's for you.'

'Hang on a moment.' Diana stood up and the room span for a second. She steadied herself on the back of the chair before shuffling into the hall, shuddering as she passed the armchair. She opened the door and a large man, scruffy and more than slightly sweaty, stood on the doorstep. His colleague was propped against the van smoking.

'So, love, where do you want it?'

Diana stared at him. She was aware that her mouth opened, but that no sound emerged.

'The kitchen. Where do you want it?'

'The kitchen?' Diana echoed.

'Yes, it's on the truck.'

'But I have a kitchen.' She was starting to feel quite nauseous and wondered if she could sit down on the doorstep to continue this bizarre conversation.

'Well, most people do, love, but I assume you've ordered a new one. I've got your name and address here, and all your cabinets are on the truck. So, do you want us to bring them through or shall we leave them on the drive?'

'But I never ordered any new cabinets.'

'Look, I only deliver the stuff and all I know is that I have to drop these cabinets to a Mrs Diana Whitlock at this address, which we all agree is you. I've got seven other deliveries to make before I clock off, so I need to get on with it.'

'Well, you can't,' Diana stammered. 'Please take it all away. There's obviously been some sort of dreadful mistake.'

'No can do, love. Everything's stacked in order, you see, and if I don't drop your load off, I can't do the rest. So, what's it to be? Inside or out?'

Diana shivered involuntarily, despite the warm winter sun flooding the porch. 'Can I see your paperwork?'

The man thrust an A4 sheet at Diana.

Diana scanned the order, the list swimming before her eyes. But when she turned the page over, she gasped and lost her footing, stumbling into the arms of the delivery driver.

'You OK, love?'

Diana stared at him, ashen-faced, and then back to the paper. Patrick's signature was at the bottom. He had placed the order two days before he died.

Chapter Eleven

Marjorie was standing next to the kitchen phone. She had been trying to call Diana all morning, but had received no reply. She wanted her to take her into Harpenden so that she could go to the supermarket, but she could not get there without Diana. It was so irritating that she had just gone AWOL. Marjorie assumed that she was busy with that silly little shop of hers and sorting stuff out after Patrick's theatrical demise, but it really was disappointing that she had been left alone for days now. Those bloody neighbours had been over, but she did not let them in. They were always poking about in her stuff.

The doorbell rang, making her jump, and she shuffled over to the kitchen window to see who was there. Maybe Diana had finally bothered to come. But it was a man in a dark suit holding a clipboard. She did not recognise him, but he spotted her peeping at him and waved, so she ambled slowly to the front door, holding onto the strategically placed grabrails that Patrick had screwed into the walls to help her to move around.

'Hello?' Marjorie warbled through the keyhole. 'Who is it?'

'St Albans council, Mrs Barnes. I just need to ask you a few questions if that's OK. Would you mind opening the door?'

Marjorie knew at this point that there was something else she should ask. Diana was always droning on about it, but she could not remember what.

'Just a minute.' She fumbled with the lock and pulled the door open. It stopped short because the chain was still on.

'Can you undo the chain?'

ID, that was it. 'Do you have any ID?'

'Of course, Mrs Barnes.' He flashed a card hanging on a lanyard around his neck. Marjorie could not quite see what it was, but he seemed like a well-turned-out sort of man, so she undid the chain and opened the door.

'Mrs Barnes, good morning. My name is Thomas Maloney and I work for St Albans council as I said. This is just a courtesy call to see if there is anything we can do to make your life a little easier as one of our more senior residents. I hope you don't mind me using the word senior. It's not my choice, if I'm honest. And in your case, it hardly applies.'

Marjorie felt her face flush and she brushed her hand through her hair.

'Not at all, Mr? Sorry, I've already forgotten your name.'

'Thomas Maloney, but just call me Tom. Everybody does.' He smiled broadly.

'Why don't you come in for a cup of tea, Tom?'

'Well, if you're sure, Mrs Barnes, that would be most kind. And it will be easier to chat if we can sit down and I take appropriate note of any of your comments.' He stepped through the door, closing it behind her, as Marjorie wobbled slowly in front of him leading the way into the lounge.

'Sit down and I'll make tea. How do you take it?'

'As it comes, please, Mrs Barnes.'

'Sugar?'

'Two please. It's my one vice, I'm afraid.'

'Well, you're a very slim. You can afford it.'

He placed his clipboard on the coffee table and followed Marjorie into the kitchen. 'You have a lovely home. Have you lived here long? Here, let me get that for you.' He took the kettle off her and began to fill it under the tap.

'Thank you. Biscuit?'

'Oh, if you're offering, go on then.'

'I've got some custard creams.'

'Ooh, my favourite.'

Marjorie arranged the biscuits on a plate and fetched two cups and saucers from the cupboard by her knees while the kettle boiled. Tom poured the hot water into the teapot and carried the tray back into the lounge. 'Shall I be mother?'

'Thank you.'

Tom poured and placed a cup of tea and two custard creams on the side table next to where Marjorie had lowered herself down into her armchair. He sat on the sofa opposite her.

'So, Mrs Barnes, can I ask you a few questions if I may? Are there any particular aspects of day-to-day life which you find more challenging than you used to and that we might be able to help you with?'

Marjorie bit into a custard cream, crumbs littering the front of her cardigan. She brushed them off with her hand. 'Well, the bins are a bit of a problem. I struggle to take them in and out of the garage and I don't like to leave them outside.'

'That's a common issue that we come across. The wheelie bins are a pest, aren't they? I'll have a think about how we might be able to help with that. Anything else?'

'Well, I don't drive any more. My daughter insisted that I stop after I had a couple of minor accidents, although to be honest, I think she was over-exaggerating as usual. It's not as if I actually hit anyone or anything. But anyway, now I have to wait for her to come over and she's not been over for the last few days. She did tell me why, but I can't quite remember the details. Anyway, I get a bit stuck in the house.'

'Is this your daughter?' He lifted a photograph frame from the coffee table.

'Yes, that's Diana. She's older now, obviously.'

'Good genes obviously run in the family, I can see that.'

'Oh, you are a terrible flatterer, Mr?'

She raised her teacup to her lips to hide her pleasure.

'Tom.'

'Oh, that's right.'

'Anything else?'

'The neighbours are always a bother.'

'Really, in what way?'

'Well, they're always pretending to try to help, but actually they just want to root through my stuff. I try not to let them in.'

'Very wise, Mrs Barnes. You really can't be too careful these days.'

Tom ticked various boxes and scribbled a few notes.

'I couldn't help noticing that you have a few cuts and bruises on your face and arms. Have you suffered a fall?'

'Oh, it was nothing.' Marjorie waved her second custard cream in the air. 'I stumbled with the bins. They are awkward to handle, as I told you. That's all.' She paused. 'Why? Has anyone reported me? I'm not leaving this house unless they carry me out in a box!'

'No, no, not at all. I was just concerned when I saw them, that's all. Safety in the home is our primary concern after all.'

Marjorie breathed heavily and popped the second biscuit into her mouth. Still chewing, she replied, 'That's very thoughtful. To be honest, I never thought the council cared that much, but you have been very helpful.'

'Not at all, Mrs Barnes and *thank you* so much for giving me so much of your precious time. I will take all of this away, and I'll see what I can do for you. Would it be alright if I pop back in a few days to update you on my progress?'

'Of course. It will be lovely to see you. I don't get many visitors.'

'Great. Well, I will see you then. In the meantime, you take care of yourself.' He rose and shook her hand. 'No, don't get up. I can see myself out.'

What a nice, polite, young man, she thought to herself as she polished off another custard cream which Tom had left uneaten. *If only everyone could be like him.*

Chapter Twelve

———

'Ray is away for a while then, is he?' Julia lowered her ample frame into one of Angie's rickety kitchen chairs, which creaked ominously as she did so.

'It would appear so,' Angie replied, cutting into the Victoria sandwich cake that her friend had brought over. 'This looks delicious, Jules.'

'I picked it up at Tesco on my way here. I thought we could make a decent dent in it, and still leave enough for Ben when he gets home from school. How's he doing?'

Angie sighed, running her fingers through her ash-blonde bob before handing Julia a generous slice of cake and a mug of tea. They were in the kitchen, which was brightly lit by the mid-morning sun streaming through the opened blind and hitting the white painted table.

'He's a bloody grumpy sod if I'm honest. Most days just saying hello to him seems to be a capital crime. You know better than anyone how teenage boys are a pain in the neck! And it really doesn't help when Ray is away for so long. Ben really misses him and then he gets even more bad-tempered. I could deal with the tantrums when Ben was small, but it's a bit different when he's a foot taller than me.'

She took a large bite of cake and wiped a glob of cream from the corner of her mouth with her finger.

'I sympathise. If Sam wasn't around, I'd find my two very hard to control. It's good to have someone to play good cop, bad cop with, isn't it? But you must be used to it by now, Ange. I mean, Ray's worked for the Foreign Office for years.'

'I know, but it doesn't seem to get any easier. I've decided that I'll talk to him when he gets back and see if he can't get himself out of this ridiculous job and into something a bit more nine-to-five and definitely more local. I think he deserves a break after working so hard for so long.'

'Do you think he'll agree to that? I mean, he's so used to travelling and I know sometimes it's not hugely glamorous, but it must have its perks.' Julia raised her eyebrows to herself and slurped her tea rather too loudly.

'Yes, maybe for him, but not for me or for Ben. And I think at some point he needs to start putting us first.'

'Hmm, well I hope you manage to persuade him. It hasn't worked so far.'

'More cake?' Angie asked, dangling the knife above it, marginally irritated by Julia's bluntness.

'Oh, go on then. I'm going to try to go to the gym later. Mind you, I say that every day and I haven't managed it for over three months!'

'You look great, Julia,' Angie lied. As far as she knew, Julia had never made it to the gym. She cut Julia another large slice. 'I'll put the rest in the tin for Ben. It'll be a treat for him.'

'It's my twenty-fifth wedding anniversary next week. I can't believe how I've put up with him for so long!' She bit into her cake and chewed. 'It's funny how fast time flashes by without us even noticing, isn't it? Quite scary in fact. How long have you and Ray been together now?'

'Coming up for eighteen years, I guess. We knew straight away that we were meant to be together. And it was just as well, because I got pregnant within a few weeks of us meeting.' She laughed and sipped her tea, folding her legs underneath her on the chair. 'It's hard to believe that we got married within three months of saying hello and that it has worked out so well. Strange, isn't it?'

'It's definitely lucky. And the age gap has never bothered you?'

'No, not really. I mean, my mother was extremely unhappy about it. I was only seventeen and she had hoped that I would go to university and make a good career for myself. But I've never regretted the way things turned out because I love him. And it's only a decade or so in age terms. I just wish he was around more. It's always been so part-time.'

She took the cake back out of the tin and cut herself a small sliver.

'Give me another piece, Ange, will you? Don't hog it all to yourself.'

She cut Julia another slice.

'Maybe that's your secret. You know, absence makes the heart grow fonder and all that crap. If he was under your feet all day every day, you might not be so lovestruck. Sam annoys the shit out of me most days.'

'You might be right! But we still need to talk. Ray's not getting any younger and every time I see him, he appears a little bit more exhausted. I just want to get more time with him before he's too old.'

'I get that. Maybe when he's back you could take a holiday together?'

Angie picked up her mug and stared out of the kitchen window across the fields at the back where the cows were grazing absentmindedly.

'You know, we've only ever managed a handful of proper holidays together, because he always had commitments at work or gets called away at the last minute. I think our last trip was five years ago when we went to Cyprus for a week.'

'I didn't think civil servants had to work so hard. I mean, to never get any real time off is a little odd, isn't it?'

'Maybe, but Ray is very senior, and they rely on him. He does some pretty sensitive stuff and he's simply too conscientious to let everyone down.'

Julia made no reply, concentrating on tucking into her cake. 'So,' she asked eventually, 'you have no idea where he is right now?'

'No, he never tells me.'

'So, even when you've just had sex and he's in that sweet spot, you know, where you can ask men literally anything, he still never lets on?'

'What sweet spot? Surely that's just before they, well you know, not after. More tea?'

Angie unfurled her slim legs and stood up to re-boil the kettle.

'I read about it in *Cosmo* years ago. And it really works. Whenever I want Sam to agree to something I know he might be difficult about, I ask him straight afterwards and he always folds.'

'Well, I'll have to try it.' Ange giggled, fetching the mugs from the table to refill them.

'You must. Anyway, you really need to find out where Ray goes. I can't understand why you haven't tried to find out more years ago. The not knowing would drive me up the bloody wall.' Julia paused, eyeing up the rest of the cake. 'We may as well finish it off. Ben never needs to know that it existed!'

Chapter Thirteen

The doorbell rang again as it had incessantly for days, and every time more unwanted stuff arrived. A new washing machine and dryer from Currys, a new dishwasher, a shiny red Dualit toaster, a Nespresso coffee maker - all paid for by Patrick. The items were all top of the range and none of them were things that Patrick would ever have even considered buying while he was alive. He was careful to the point of miserliness, always preferring to make do and mend as his mother had done after the war, rather than replace and buy. He did not hold with the disposable consumer economy despite his job. *Green before his time, I suppose*, Diana often thought. And if he did buy anything, it would have been own label, despite the fact that he worked in the business and could get decent discounts on the best brands.

Diana simply could not understand what the hell was happening with all this gear. Was this some sort of elaborate joke on Patrick's part, or was it some twisted way for him to make amends for removing himself from her life without notice? It was as if she was being given every material object she had ever desired, yet now she wanted none of it. She spent her days on interminable hold, arranging returns and trying to explain a totally inexplicable situation. She wanted to scream at the customer service operatives that Patrick was dead. Why didn't they realise what had happened? But they could not have known, and she had to repeat it all each time like some asinine ritual, explaining that her husband had ordered the goods without consulting her and they were wrong or did not fit or were unsuited.

'Can we speak to your husband? We can only deal with the person who placed the order, or is he there to authorise you to speak on his behalf.'

'No, I'm afraid he's not.'

'Well, can he call us back?'

'No, he can't.'

'Well, we can't help you until we speak to him. Will he be able to call later in the week?'

'No, because he's dead.'

A short silence. 'I am very sorry to hear that.'

'Me too.'

The bank had frozen Patrick's accounts until Diana could provide a death certificate. Diana could not provide the death certificate until the coroner had ruled on his cause of death. She had to explain this to the utility companies, to the credit card people, to quite literally everyone. Some were helpful and some were immensely obstructive. Every company followed a different bereavement procedure when surely they could have standardised how to speak to people in the throes of grief. It was completely exhausting; and more than Diana could bear. Her facial features were bent into an expression of permanent torment, as if she had become a personification of Munch's *The Scream*.

The bell trilled again. Diana had left her phone upstairs and so she could not check it to ask the delivery man to return the parcel to sender or failing that, to leave it on the doorstep. She trudged to the door, seeing the outline of a figure with its nose pressed against the glass. She hated it when people did that. It seemed so rude and obtrusive, not to mention the unsightly mark it left behind. Pulling the cord around her dressing gown a little tighter, she called through the door. 'Hello, can I help you?'

'Diana, it's me, Ian. Can I come in?'

His face was still too close to the door, as if he would fall flat on his face into the hall if she opened it.

'Ian?'

She felt confused for a moment. What was Ian doing here? How did he even know where she lived? She had been extremely careful never to tell him. She was not entirely sure why, but she sensed that she needed to keep him at arm's length. His regular visits to her shop had begun to annoy her.

'Can I see you another time? I'm not feeling too well today.'

She suddenly felt quite dizzy and put out her hand onto the doorframe to support herself.

'Diana? Are you alright? I've been so worried about you. The shop has been closed for days and when I asked around, no one had seen you.'

'I'm perfectly fine, Ian. Really. There's just a lot going on.'

He bent down and peered through the letterbox, causing Diana to jump back from the door.

'Please, Diana. You can talk to me. If there's anything troubling you, you know I'm always here for you. That's what friends are for, after all. Just let me in. Please.' His voice had heightened in pitch a little.

'Ian, go home, please. It's just not a good time for me today,' she called feebly, wobbling away from the door.

He knocked once more on the glass, calling her name, but she carried on walking away, past Patrick's deathly chair and into the kitchen, shutting the door behind her. She slumped into a chair, burying her head in her hands, and wept until her chest hurt. She thought she could still hear Ian breathing outside the front door, but it might have just been her imagination.

She waited and a few minutes later, the house felt silent again. Diana raised her head, wiping her salty face with the sleeve of her dressing gown, something which only days earlier would have appalled her, but now seemed an irrelevance. A week ago, she was living her normal existence, bumbling along a well-worn pattern of daily paths from waking to sleeping, the odd wave created by her mother's antics. But now there was no pattern and no familiarity. She was off-grid with no understanding of how to locate a way forward. Patrick - good, old, dependable Patrick - had shoved her off a cliff and she was falling, falling like Alice down her rabbit hole, but there was no Wonderland at the bottom. There was seemingly no bottom at all.

Diana shivered. Patrick would have known what to do about Ian, not that there had been any similar incidents in the past. Diana had distant admirers, but always managed to brush them away and had never been interested in anyone other than Patrick. She had made a commitment to him, all those years ago, and she believed firmly in the solemnity of her vows - not from a religious perspective, but from a strong, moral one. Patrick was the choice she had made, and she had never wavered from it. She had not even considered it. He had never been one for expressing his emotions, but in a way that was what she loved about him. He was upright and self-contained. He made her feel safe and protected, as if she was inside a glass case that could not be shattered while he was around. But with one draft of whatever it was he had ingested, she had lost her protector and was left

68

totally exposed. She had been confident precisely because Patrick had stood silently behind her, but now her scaffolding had been taken down.

And what was she to think about Ian turning up at her home out of the blue? She had only met him on a handful of occasions for coffee, and now she wondered why she had done so at all. It was something she never would have entertained before, drinking coffee with a perfect stranger. Thinking back, the first time he asked her, when she had helped him choose the gift for his sister, she had gone along as a delaying tactic. She was tired and knew that she had to visit her mother on the way home. A caffeine shot had been required. On the other occasions, she had not wanted to appear rude, but she had quickly realised that Ian was clinging on to her. He was lonely she suspected, although she could not understand why. He was quite tall, well-built, with thick, dark hair and a tanned complexion. Not handsome, but pleasant enough. And he did not appear to be under-confident or shy. He had flirted with the girl in the coffee shop on each occasion they had visited. Maybe he was just in need of a friend and maybe in her, as an older woman, he saw the opportunity for an unthreatening relationship, just someone he could talk to.

However, his constantly popping into the shop, and his assumption that they were already great friends she found rather odd, but maybe she was being a little harsh. It was only that, in her mind at least, building a friendship was something that took time and commitment. She knew this only too well, having only ever had a couple of genuinely close girlfriends, both of whom she had lost in the last few years to cancer: Ginny and Katie. Each loss had winded her completely, like a boxer's punch in the guts. She had known them both since school, where the three of them had fused together like triplets almost from the moment they met in the classroom. They could laugh and cry about almost anything together. And once they were no longer there for her to talk to, she had been left with Patrick and it had been hard, because Patrick did not like to do emotion. They died, he was sorry for her, but he told her that she must not dwell on it. She must move forward and concentrate on the positives.

And to be fair, she had tried. She had worked longer hours at the shop, spent even more time with her mother and volunteered at various fetes and charity walks to support cancer research. But what was the point of all this activity when death was all around her? They say bad luck comes in threes and she had most certainly had her three. She could not believe that there could be any good luck left.

Her mobile rang, startling her, and she began to fumble inside her dressing gown pocket. Just as she retrieved it, it rang off. She slammed the phone onto the table. After a few moments, it rang again. Voicemail.

'You have one new message. Message one.' Beep. 'Mrs Whitlock, it's Shamila from Harpenden Police station. I just wanted to let you know that the coroner has ruled on your husband's death and the verdict is suicide. I am so very sorry. The paperwork will be with you soon and then hopefully you can begin to make the necessary arrangements. Once again, I am very sorry for your loss.'

'Thank you,' Diana muttered to the empty kitchen. Arrangements must be made, and people must be told. It was now official, and she could no longer pretend that it had not happened, and that Patrick might just walk through the door at any moment asking for a cup of tea or whether or not there was any cake. Chocolate had been his particular favourite, but otherwise anything would do. He had had a very sweet tooth.

She screamed aloud in frustration. If only Patrick had told her what he intended to do, she might have decided to join him. Anything was preferable to being the one left behind.

Chapter Fourteen

'Mum, it's only me!' Diana called, turning the key in her mother's door, and letting herself in. The chain was off, despite her repeated instructions to Marjorie to keep it on at all times. She followed the sound of the radio into the lounge; Michael Bublé bellowing out some song from a musical Diana ought to have recognised but could not instantly place. It was so loud that her mother would not have noticed if a herd of buffalo had come rampaging through the bungalow.

Her mother was sitting in her armchair with her back to Diana, drumming away on the arm in time to the music. Diana did not disturb her for a moment, instead walking through to the kitchen to unpack the food she had brought. She tended to buy microwaveable meals for one from Sainsburys or Marks and Spencer, which her mother could easily heat up on the odd occasion that she was hungry, and plenty of biscuits, as her mother could be relied on to munch on those even if she forgot to eat anything more nutritious. Diana reckoned that once you reached your eighties, any food you fancied was better than nothing. She stacked a couple of fish pies and a spaghetti bolognese on the bare shelf of the fridge and put the vegetables in the drawer underneath. Closing the fridge, she took the lid off the biscuit tin, noting that it was almost empty. She tore open a packet of custard creams and one of bourbon biscuits into the tin to refill it. Taking the last bourbon for herself, she nibbled around the edges, but her appetite was still lost, so she threw the rest of the biscuit into the bin. She lobbed the wrappers into the recycling bin, which was oddly completely empty. Her mother could not lift the basket and emptying it into the wheelie bin was one of Diana's many jobs.

Diana turned around to the sink to wash her hands and that was when she noticed the tea tray which housed two used cups and a scattering of biscuit crumbs on a couple of plates. Maybe the neighbours had been round, but her mother was very unlikely to have asked them to stay for a drink.

She walked back into the lounge, pecking her mother on the top of her head with her lips as she did so.

Her mother started in her chair. 'Jesus, Diana. Are you trying to give me a heart attack?' She peered at Diana over her reading glasses, a copy of The Radio Times opened on her lap. 'You look very peaky, love. Are you alright?'

Diana moved over to the radio and switched it off.

'Not really. It's been a very difficult week.'

Her mother frowned.

'You know, what with Patrick and all that.'

'Oh yes, Patrick. I forgot for a minute. I am sorry. It's a terrible thing, suicide. I remember your dad's friend, Harold. Hung himself in a seedy hotel in Brighton and left Doreen with a shedload of debt. Do you think that was it? Gambling?'

'I very much doubt it. You know Patrick never did anything like that, except once a year on the Grand National.'

'Well, it's a bugger's muddle, that's for sure. Have you checked with the bank?'

'Not yet. I can't access anything until I've got the death certificate. I should get it shortly.'

'It's a terrible shock, regardless of why he did it. Mind you, it's always the quiet ones, isn't it? I wonder what he was thinking?' She picked up the magazine and then put it down again. 'To be honest with you, I never believed Patrick did very much thinking. In fact, I never really understood what you two ever had to talk about.' She paused and looked around the room. 'Can you see my knitting anywhere?'

Diana sighed and picked up a canvas bag from behind the sofa and handed it her mother, who pulled out a ball of pink wool and a pair of needles. 'Booties,' she commented, replacing her glasses, and beginning to cast on.

'Who for?' Diana sagged into the sofa opposite.

'Oh, I don't know, Diana. People are always having babies. You know that.'

Her mother had a cupboard full of baby clothes, all of which she had knitted. When it got full, Diana would take some of them away and give them to the charity shop. She never took so many that her mother might notice, but just enough so that there was room for the next batch.

Diana swiftly changed the subject. 'Have the neighbours been over? I noticed the tea tray.'

'Christ no. Those bloody nosey devils can go whistle for my biscuits. No, it was the nice man from the council again.'

'Which man from the council?'

'The one they sent round to see if I needed anything. I have to say, it's the only time in my entire life that the council have shown any interest whatsoever in helping me, but they appear to be bucking up their ideas a bit these days.' She paused over her knitting. 'Actually, how about a cup of tea? Do you fancy making me one?'

'In a minute, Mum. Tell me more about this man. What's his name?'

Her mother stared into the middle distance for a moment. 'Tim something, I think.'

'Did he give you his surname?'

'No, but he was ever so polite. And very helpful. He's offered to come round once a week to take the bins out to the bottom of the drive for me.'

'The man from the council is coming round personally to do your bins?' Diana shifted in her seat and leaned in towards her mother. 'That sounds very odd, Mum.'

'That's you all over, isn't it? Suspicious and can't think well of anyone, can you?'

Diana laughed. 'That's a bit pot and kettle, isn't it?'

'Look, Diana, you should be bloody grateful that someone wants to help me. You've not been about much recently, have you?'

'Mum, I'm always about. But Patrick has just died and I haven't felt able to do anything. To be honest with you, I feel like I'm falling apart.' Fat tears fell unbidden down Diana's cheeks, already raw from so much crying.

Her mother tried to reach across to pat her hand, but Diana was too far away. 'Now then, Diana. None of that. You've had a terrible shock, that's all. I'm sure you'll feel a bit better soon.' She leaned back again in her chair. 'Now how about that tea and maybe a couple of biscuits?'

'OK, Mum,' she sniffed.

'Or do you fancy a brandy? It's good for shock.'

Diana did not enjoy brandy, but right now the thought of something strongly alcoholic to numb her constant pain was quite appealing. 'I'm driving,' she sniffed, rooting in her handbag for a packet of tissues. She took one out and blew her nose loudly.

'Jesus, Diana. You sound like an elephant.'

Diana dabbed at her eyes, which were red and swollen.

'This guy, Mum. How's often has he been round?'

'Which guy?'

Diana sighed with the effort of summoning up enough energy to continue the conversation. 'The one from the council.'

'Oh, a couple of times. He's offered to help me to file my paperwork as well. You know how I never get round to it.'

'Oh, no.' Diana had raised her voice more than she intended to. 'Mum, this isn't right. No man from the council would come round to file your papers. I think he must be a scammer of some kind.'

'Do you think I'm an idiot?' Her mother threw her knitting onto the floor. 'Why do you always have to be so suspicious. Can't you see that he's just trying to do me a good turn?'

'I don't think he is, Mum. In fact, I think he's most probably doing quite the opposite. Let me at least call the council when I get home and check him out for you. Just to make sure.'

Her mother made no reply.

'In the meantime, please can you keep the chain on the door. I ask you every time and it's never on when I come.'

'Because I usually know when you're coming, and it saves me having to get up.'

'Hmm, well, just keep it on, alright?'

'Don't lecture me, Diana. I've got this far in life without your help, thank you very much.'

Diana rolled her eyes to the ceiling.

'Let me get you your tea.'

Chapter Fifteen

———

Angie was seated at the desk in her office, staring at the locked filing cabinet. She had converted the box room years before so that she could work comfortably from home, but in effect, it had become Ray's office almost immediately. She much preferred to work at the breakfast bar in the kitchen, as it provided a far greater level of distraction - she could procrastinate by staring out into the garden at the back of the house, watching the birds hopping on the lawn and digging for worms; or out to the street at the front, where random passers-by strolled along. She also liked being closer to the kettle and the fridge, so that coffee breaks were both more frequent and more convenient. These days, she hardly ever ventured into the office upstairs apart from dusting it occasionally.

It was totally empty apart from a white Ikea desk and a black chair from Staples, that she had bought during one of their sales. It was horrendously uncomfortable to sit on, which was probably why it had been such a bargain at the time. In one corner lay a large plastic folder overflowing with old paintings that Ben had done over the years at school and photographs of his various sports teams, many still in their original cellophane wrappers. In the opposite corner was a silver, metallic filing cabinet consisting of two drawers, which Ray used to store important documents, such as their wills and the deeds to the house. She had never had cause to open it and had never until now been curious about its contents. But after her last conversation with Julia, she had begun to wonder whether she should try to have a look inside it. *What if Ray ever got injured at work? Or possibly worse?* she reasoned with herself. She would need to know its contents in such a situation. And maybe there might be some clues in there about Ray's work. It felt that it might ease her mind to know more than she already did, or alternatively it could terrify her. She had never attempted to open it before because Ray had always insisted that she did not.

'It's my only private area in the whole house. Some men have sheds to retire into. I have my poor filing cabinet. And there's nothing in there that you need to be concerned about. You'll only ever need to hack into it if someone turns up and tells you that I'm dead. And that's very unlikely to happen.' He had laughed, pulling her to him and hugging her tightly. 'You're stuck with me, I'm afraid.'

Angie had never given it much thought. In fact, she never questioned anything very much. She had always trusted Ray implicitly: from the first moment they met to when he talked her into bed a few days later, and ever since. Her mother had been far more distrustful.

'Angela, he's almost twice your age. It borders on paedophilia,' her mother had carped after she first introduced her to Ray.

'Hardly, Mum.'

'And you're just seventeen and he's what? Twenty-six? I mean, it's simply not decent, is it? Why is he preying on young girls?' She had pushed her glasses back up her beaked nose and sniffed loudly.

'He's not preying on young girls. We met and we hit it off, that's all. It's not that unusual to have a such big age gap among couples. Look at you and Dad.'

'That was only five years. Anything over that number is completely inappropriate.'

'Says who?'

'Says everyone, Angela. It's just a fact.'

Her mother was very good at quoting so-called facts that were completely unsubstantiated by any evidence whatsoever, and there was little point arguing with someone who stated things so incontrovertibly. When Angie thought about her mother, she often reflected that she might have been a tremendous asset to any political party given her ability to hold her ground no matter how wrong she was.

'And I dread to think what your father would say, Angela, may his soul rest in peace. He's probably turning in his grave as we speak. He had such big dreams for you, you know. He wanted you to be a doctor or a lawyer, or even an accountant would have been acceptable. I know you miss Dad, we both do, but this guy can't be a substitute for him, you know.'

'He's not a father replacement, Mum. Don't be ridiculous!'

Her mother frowned.

'Look, I just worry, that's all. The way you're going, you will end married to this bloke, possibly pregnant, and then he will bugger off, leaving you with nothing!'

Angie had stalked out of the living room, leaving her mother to continue shouting in her wake.

'You want to get rid of him now, my girl, before you get yourself a reputation.'

Her mother proved to be somewhat prophetic. Ray did get her pregnant within a few weeks of their meeting despite the fact that she only saw him once or twice a week. He had reassured her that he was an expert at the withdrawal method, but it turned out that on one occasion he had been rather slow off the mark in that respect. But he had absolutely no intention of leaving her in the lurch. In fact, it was quite the opposite. Angie had no way of contacting Ray unless he called her, and she spent an agonising five days after she turned the lines on a pregnancy test bright pink before she could tell him. In that time, she had bitten all her nails down to the quick until they were red and bleeding and failed to get any sleep. Eventually, Ray did call, and they arranged to meet in a pub, but not the local where everyone went. There was another, rather grotty place on the road out of town, which very few people ever drank in and where they could talk privately.

She arrived first by bus and sat herself at a table in the corner, where she sat nibbling at the remaining skin around her fingers and twisting her fine, blonde hair into knots. She gave him a wan half-smile as he approached.

'Hey, Angie baby. You don't look very well. Have you been ill?'

She looked up at his broad, crooked smile lighting up his face and burst into tears.

Ray glanced around. 'Hey, come on now. Whatever it is, it can't be all that bad. Let's not make a scene, eh?'

He sat down, blocking the view of her from anyone who might be looking over. He held her hand.

'Come on, why don't you tell me what's bothering you?'

Angie rummaged up the sleeve of her jumper and produced a soggy tissue. She blew her nose loudly.

Ray put his hand in his pocket and produced a pristine, white handkerchief. She took it gratefully and shortly it was stained with snot and mascara.

'Now, what is it?'

'I'm pregnant,' she whispered, her words almost inaudible. 'I'm not sure how it happened.'

His ruddy face drained to white.

'I thought I'd been careful, you know. And I thought you were going to go on the pill?' he whispered back.

She could not remember having discussed the pill with Ray.

'No, not yet. I have an appointment with the GP to discuss it next week, but I didn't want my mum to know, so it's been difficult to arrange, especially as she works there.'

Her mother was a part-time receptionist at the local practice; a job she thoroughly detested and felt was far below her significant capabilities, as she was happy to tell any patient who would listen and even those who would not.

'Ah, I see,' Ray muttered. 'Well, don't worry,' he replied, his smile if not his colour returning. 'This is easy to fix.'

Angie stared at him with her dark-rimmed panda eyes caused by lack of sleep. 'You want me to get rid of it?'

'No, quite the opposite. I propose that we get married and make that baby legitimate. I've always wanted a son of my own.'

'But what if it's a girl?'

'Well, it's a possibility, I suppose, but fingers crossed. What do you say, to marrying me, I mean?'

Angie replied with a torrent of weeping.

'Shush, Angie. Calm down now. Everyone is looking at us.'

There were only two other punters in the pub - both of whom looked as if they could barely balance on their bar stools – plus the publican himself, who merely raised his eyebrows at Ray when he glanced over as if to express his solidarity over a crying girl.

'So, shall we get married then? Or do you want me to go down on one knee and ask you properly? I mean it's not the most romantic location I would have chosen for such a momentous occasion admittedly, but.'

'Yes, Ray, yes please,' she nodded through her tears.

'Terrific. Let's do it. Shall I go and buy us a drink to celebrate?'

She shook her head. 'Mum will never allow it, you know. She thinks you're a pervert as it is because of our age gap, and she'll go totally berserk when I tell her I'm pregnant. I think she'll make me have an abortion.'

'In which case we must remove her from the equation. Let's elope and tell her afterwards. I'll win her over when we've tied the knot, and there will be nothing she can do about it by then anyway.' He scooted his chair closer to hers and put his arm around her shoulders. 'Trust me, Angie. I'll never let you down.'

So, the following week when Ray was due to come back again, instead of him coming to her, she caught a bus to Stanstead airport and flew to Newcastle on a ticket emailed to her by Ray. They met at the train station and travelled from Newcastle Central to Gretna Green where they were married by teatime - Angie having hastily changed into a faded, pink, cotton dress that she had bought the previous year at Topshop, while Ray wore his usual suit and tie. They spent their honeymoon night in a stuffy, top-floor room at a local pub and then returned to Newcastle by train.

'I'll see you next week and we can talk to your mum then. In the meantime, don't say anything to anyone.' He took her hand, where a thin, gold band nestled on her finger. 'Here, give me that. I'll hang onto it until we've got this whole thing sorted out.'

He pecked her on the cheek and ran off to catch his train to Kings Cross in London, leaving her to negotiate her own way back to Newcastle airport, where she flew in reverse to Stanstead and then caught a National Express coach back to Ely.

She did not hear from Ray for three weeks after that. Every day she expected him to call, but there was nothing, until one day when he appeared at her home unannounced with an ostentatious bunch of flowers and a large box of Ferrero Rocher.

'Ray!' she screamed excitedly, delighted that her mother was still at work terrifying patients instead of her.

'Sorry it's been a while, Angie baby. I got called away on an urgent case and had to take a small trip.'

'Don't worry, Ray. I mean, I was worried, but I know that your work is very important - and secret, obviously. It's just so great to see you. I was beginning to think I'd imagined the wedding. And look what you've bought me. But I don't think I can eat the chocolates. I've been feeling pretty sick, to be honest.'

Ray smiled and kissed the top of her head. 'They're not for you. They are for your darling mother. Is she in?' He scanned the lounge with a frown on his face, as if she might be hiding behind an armchair and be about to leap out at any moment like a ghoul in a horror film.

'No, she's at work for another two hours.'

'Excellent. Well, I am sure we can find something to do to entertain ourselves in the meantime, can't we?'

Angie giggled and led him silently by the hand up the staircase to her bedroom.

'It's a bit messy, I'm afraid.'

The walls were plastered with posters of Brandon Flowers.

'I see that you like The Killers?'

'Well, I like Brandon. He's super sexy, don't you think?'

'Well, he's not my type exactly.'

He eased her gently onto the bed and began to stroke her thigh.

'I think you look a bit like him actually.'

'Oh, so that's the appeal, is it? And I thought I was special.'

'You are.' She looked down at her pink, fluffy slippers.

'Let me show you exactly how special,' he countered, removing her T-shirt, delighted to find as suspected that she was braless underneath it.

A couple of hours later, they heard a car pull up outside. By now, they had showered and dressed and were drinking tea in the lounge. Angie's mother turned the key in the door and entered the hallway mid-sentence.

'Believe what I had to deal with today, Angie. I swear that half of the people in this town are rude, and the other half are stupid. They all moaned on and on about the amount of time they have to wait at the surgery, and then when it came to it, three people had turned up on the wrong day and we had five or six no-shows. There's no consideration whatsoever given to people like me who -' She stopped short as she bulldozed into the lounge, silenced instantly when she spotted Ray sitting in her late husband's armchair. No one sat in that chair.

Ray leapt to his feet and held out his hand to shake hers.

'Mrs Frost, Ray Reynolds. It's a pleasure to meet you.'

Mrs Frost pursed her lips together and then turned towards Angie, who was perched on the arm of the sofa. 'Get off the arm, Angie, I've told you a thousand times that you'll break it.' She gripped her handbag more tightly to her chest. 'What's he doing here?'

'Ray just popped in,' Angie stammered.

'I'll bet he did.' Mrs Frost turned to Ray, who greeted her with a wide, open smile, his arm now dropped to his side.

'Mrs Frost, I understand that you have your reservations about my relationship with your daughter, and I completely understand, I really do, but I want to reassure you that I have only the best intentions at heart.'

Mrs Frost harrumphed like a small pony.

'If I may, I'd like to explain. Is that alright with you?'

Mrs Frost remained static and unspeaking.

'I know that you are concerned about the age gap between Angie and myself. Angie is so special, and I know that you act purely out of love and your desire to protect her. It's only natural. I also recognise how hard it must have been for you since your husband passed away, raising her by yourself and working as hard as you do in such a demanding, responsible position.'

Mrs Frost grimaced, but loosened her grip on her handbag, just slightly.

Ray took a step forward and touched her lightly on the shoulder. 'The thing is, Mrs Frost, I love Angie with all my heart. She has such great intelligence, kindness, and real maturity, which I know must come from you. And she is so respectful and well-mannered. You've done quite an amazing job.'

Mrs Frost sunk down gingerly onto the edge of the sofa, still silent; her fingers on the straps of her bag, which she then placed by her side.

'The moment I met Angie, I just knew she was my soulmate. I may be older, but I think that's a good thing, because I have learnt what I want in a partner and until now I have never been able to find the right person, someone who completes my jigsaw, if you know what I mean.'

'My husband was passionate about jigsaws,' Mrs Frost whispered, pointing at the boxes stacked on the bookcase on the far wall.

'Really, I had no idea, Mrs Frost. Or may I call you -?'

'Sheila,' she whispered, addressing her handbag.

'Sheila.' He smiled again and Mrs Frost sank a little further into the cushions on the sofa. 'Angie, why don't you go and make your mother a nice cup of tea. She must be parched after her exhausting day at work,' Ray suggested, turning to Angie, who nodded and wandered off slowly into the kitchen.

By the time she returned, her mother was laughing, Ray sitting right beside her chattering away animatedly. Angie could not remember the last time she saw her mother smile, let alone laugh.

'Well, that's all settled then. I'll call the registry office in the morning, and we'll set a date for next week.'

Angie muttered something under her breath, spilling the tea onto the carpet as she did so.

'Angie!' shouted her mother. 'Watch what you're doing! See, Ray, this is what you'll have to put up with from now on.'

'Angie, I've just asked your mother for permission to marry you and she has agreed. Isn't that marvellous?' Ray stood up and rescued the mug from Angie, handing it to her mother.

"Yes, but -' Angie remonstrated.

'Yes, I know. There's no time to buy a proper dress etc. etc., but your mum has kindly agreed to help you sort it all out. The wedding has to be next week because I'm off on another extended trip after that.'

'Don't worry, Angie. We'll get everything organised in time for you to marry this lovely young man of yours.' Her mother beamed.

Angie felt a sudden wave of nausea break over her and she rushed out of the room.

Ray followed her into the downstairs toilet and closed the door behind them. It was a very tight squeeze.

'We're *already* married,' Angie hissed.

'Yes, but she doesn't need to know that, does she? And neither does the registrar. It's easier than telling her we've already done it, which she'll never forgive. Run with me on this, Angie baby. It'll be fine.'

He pecked her on the nose and sidled out of the loo.

Just under a month later, they married once again in the registry office in Cambridge, with Mrs Frost - resplendent in her navy suit and matching feathered hat purchased especially for the occasion from Country Casuals - and a random person from the street as witness. Mrs Frost, while now accepting of the union, was still reluctant to make it common knowledge, hence the stranger. Afterwards, they had a celebratory afternoon tea at a small cafe on Magdalen Bridge and then Ray drove everyone back to Ely.

'Well, I must be going back to London now,' Ray announced as they arrived home.

'Tonight?' the women chorused.

'It's our honeymoon night, Ray,' Angie moaned, grabbing him by the arm.

He raised his bushy eyebrows at her. 'Yes, I know. It's hugely disappointing for me too, darling, but my boss is a complete bastard and refused me any more time off. I'm so sorry.'

And with that, Ray kissed her deeply, jumped into the car and revved the engine, speeding off into the early evening dusk, and not returning for almost another month.

It was just as well that he did show up eventually. Angie was growing increasingly fretful that her mother might begin to do the maths regarding the pregnancy - that was when she eventually got to hear about it. She needed Ray to return supposedly to perform the honeymoon act sooner rather than later, even if it was all a pretence. She felt frightened and alone with Ray uncontactable, tortured by the fact that she was lying to her mother. Her mother might be irritating, but she was her mother after all, and Angie was not used to lying to her. She tended to tell the truth, even when it got her into trouble. And she had resisted the temptation to talk to her friends, who would have been shocked and probably spread the news all over town within hours.

She had not even had a chance to think about what having a baby actually meant. It had been an accident, and before she got pregnant, nothing could have been further from her mind. She had a place at Leeds to read English and she had been excited about it, even if it was not the professional qualification desired by her mother. She had been looking forward to getting away from home and becoming independent. Of course, that would all have to be abandoned now. She had not counted on becoming a wife and mother at the age of eighteen, and she certainly did not want to rely on her own mother. Of course, Ray had reassured her that this would not be the case, but he travelled most of the time and had suggested that for now at least, she continued to live at home.

She was effectively trapped, waiting day to day for Ray to contact her or to arrive to see her. She could not call him, as he said his work phone was restricted. When he called her, it was always from a call box or from a different mobile number. 'Burners,' Ray called them. She had heard the term before, but only in crime shows on television, rather than as part of someone's work.

She lay in bed at night, nauseous and scared, trying to imagine this thing multiplying inside her, and wondering how this had happened. Sometimes, when she was particularly anxious or annoyed because Ray had not been in touch, she questioned whether she should have an abortion and simply tell Ray that she wanted a break or even an annulment, so that she could go to university and lead a teenaged, normal life. She could ask Ray to wait. After all, he was so busy that he might not mind. But when she thought about Ray, her body and brain melted. She loved him and she wanted to be the most important thing in his life. She knew he would be unlikely to wait for her and he seemed to really want to have this child. Maybe she was lucky because she did not have to wait years to find true love. Maybe this was another way to get out from under her mother's rule, which would truly be a blessing.

Never religious, she lay there, talking to her bedroom ceiling, hoping for some guidance. Mostly, she spoke to her father, whom she had lost eight years before. He had developed liver cancer and was dead within four months of the diagnosis. She had watched him wither away to skin and bone - this huge, powerful man who had been able to take her on adventurous bike rides and toss her high in the air and who now did not even have the strength to hold a spoon to his own mouth. Angie thought she would never again be able to picture him as the person he had been, but only as the skeleton he had become, and sometimes the vision of him as he was at the end still reared up before her in her dreams like a horrifying ghoul. But most of the time, she could regress to a time when he was fit, healthy, and smiling. Her mother had smiled often then as well, but her father's death had soured and hardened her.

Sadly, her father had offered her no real solutions as she lay in her bed in those first solitary weeks as a married woman, but one morning when she woke up, her favourite Brandon Flowers poster had fallen off the wall and Angie thought to herself that maybe it was a sign that her childhood fantasies were over, and that she needed a real man like Ray to replace Brandon and her father. Ray would protect her.

And protect her he had to, because several weeks later, her life was overturned once again. Ray had come back on a Monday, and they were enjoying a passable lamb stew that her mother had made for dinner. Sheila tended to batch cook at the weekend, so that she did not have to worry about making food from scratch after work. She was a stickler when it came to feeding Angie homemade food, refusing to buy ready meals. She believed that they were invented for the idle, and abhorred pizza and the like, which she pronounced tasteless and always cold and soggy. She had become even more fastidious now that her grandchild was on the way, feeding Angie the best food she could afford to buy. Angie, just overcoming nausea, was grateful to her, while at the same time wishing that her mother would stop fussing over her. She felt cooped up and bored, just waiting for this baby to arrive and yet dreading it all at the same time.

'So, Ray, when are you coming to live in the village permanently? I know you've got a swanky place in London, or so

Angie tells me, but you can't keep leaving her behind like this for much longer, you know. You really need to sort out a place of your own soon. After all, you don't want to be moving in after she's given birth with a squealing infant. Are you thinking of staying in London or moving out a little? A one bed will be quite awkward with a new-born. More broccoli?' She paused for breath, spooning a huge heap onto Ray's plate before he had time to answer.

'I've got everything in hand, Sheila. Don't you worry. Angie and I will be out of your hair very soon.' Ray gulped his red wine and reached over to the bottle of Tesco Bordeaux that he had plucked off Sheila's wine rack in the kitchen to refill his glass.

'Oh, I don't mean to suggest anyone is in the way,' Sheila protested, shaking her glass towards Ray so he could top her up as well. 'I just know that you'll need some privacy and time to get to know each other properly that's all. And I just want you to be comfortable before the little one destroys all your peace.' She downed her wine and burped. 'Oh, I'm so sorry. I don't know where that came from. Apple pie anyone?' she asked, her face vermillion as she rose from the table.

Angie and Ray burst out laughing the moment she left the room.

'I think she's a little tipsy.'

'I wish I was,' Angie moaned, sipping her water.

'Oh, I know. Just a few more months to go, hey, and then you can get pissed.'

'With a baby to look after? I doubt it. I'll just have to get Mum to babysit when I feel the urge!'

Ray reached across and squeezed her hand.

Three days later, Ray left before it was light outside, and Angie was only vaguely aware of him slipping out of the bedroom. She heard his car engine fire, and he was off again, while she snuggled back into her duvet and went back to sleep. She did not hear her mother leave for work either. She was just so tired; the baby seemingly devouring all her energy, leaving her hollow.

She was woken much later by an insistent ringing on the doorbell. She groaned and slipped one arm out of bed to retrieve her dressing gown which she had dropped by the bed when she got in the night before. Ray liked to sleep naked and insisted that she do the same.

'I like to feel your skin when I roll over in the night. It connects us,' he had told her.

She stood up and pulled the robe around her, the person at the door now ringing and knocking at the same time. 'Bloody delivery guys. No patience,' she muttered to herself as she headed down the stairs.

'Where's the fire?' she demanded, throwing open the front door.

'Angela, may I come in?'

It was Dr Collins from the surgery. 'Did my Mum ask you to come? It's totally unnecessary. I've been very sick in the mornings, but otherwise I'm fine and I'm not due a check-up for a few weeks yet.'

Dr Collins had walked through the door and closed it again while Angie was remonstrating with him. 'Can we sit down?'

'Of course. Can I get you a cup of tea or coffee?' Angie wondered if the doctor was unwell.

'No, I'm fine, thank you.'

Angie showed the doctor into the lounge.

'Sit down, Angela. I need to tell you something.'

She sat down on the sofa and the doctor sat next to her. 'I'm sorry to have to tell you that there was an accident this morning on the lane running up to the main road.'

He paused and considered the faded paisley pattern on the Axminster carpet. Angie spotted a Kit-Kat wrapper stuck under the table and thought how cross her mother would have been if she had had a visitor and it had been lying there, dropped by Angie and not picked up.

'It's your mother, Angela. She was late for work, which as you know is unheard of. I've never known anyone with better timekeeping. It's why she's the most efficient person I've ever employed.' He looked down at his shoes, which were slightly dusty from the gravel drive outside.

'Anyway, around nine-thirty, a patient arrived, who told me there had been an accident down the road and that it looked bad. Someone appeared to have driven into a tree. You know the big oak on the bend before you reach the T-junction?'

Angie stared at him blankly.

'Anyway, I jumped into my car and drove down there to see if there was anything I could do to help and also because I had a bad feeling on account of your mother not arriving on time and all that.'

He coughed into his hand.

'Look, I'm sorry, but when I got there my premonition was right. It was your mum, and she had crashed into the tree. I can only assume that she was running late and maybe took the bend a little too quickly and – '

'Is she alright?' Angie felt her heartbeat begin to quicken.

'No. I'm afraid not, Angie. I'm afraid to tell you that she has passed away. The ambulance crew thought it was probably instantaneous, as she hit the tree head-on. Maybe a deer ran across the path or something. There were no witnesses apparently. I'm so very sorry.'

'But she never drives too fast. She always drives much too slowly. There's usually a huge line of cars behind her hooting.' Her mother's driving drove her mad. 'Are you sure it's her?'

Angie dug her nails into her palms, thinking that perhaps she was still asleep, and this was one of her many nightmares where she woke up with a start, whimpering and sometimes screaming.

'Yes, sadly I'm absolutely certain. The ambulance was already there by the time I arrived. I identified her car.' He focused on the carpet again, or perhaps it was the still-visible Kit-Kat wrapper that bothered him.

'Where is she now?' Angie whispered.

'At the hospital, but I would not advise going to see her. She's not, well, she isn't very recognisable.'

Angie stared at the doctor.

He paused. 'Is there anyone you'd like me to call?'

Angie hesitated. Ray was still a secret; at least, she did not think that her mother had told anyone yet that she was married. The doctor knew about the pregnancy, but he had not asked any questions about the father and no information had been offered.

'No, no, thank you. I think I'll go back to bed. I'm exhausted.' Angie rose and staggered zombie-like past the doctor, up the stairs, diving under the duvet and covering her head.

'I'll pop back in later to check on you!' she heard a muffled voice shout up the stairs.

When she heard the front door slam, she began to shriek, and she did not stop until her lungs could shriek no longer.

Ray arrived back at the house that evening, unexpectedly - as he was usually away for several days, yet fortuitously, he explained, his next trip had been postponed. He scooped Angie up in his arms and held her tight.

'Don't worry, I'm here now. I'll sort everything out.'

True to his word, Ray was a total marvel. He organised the funeral just as her mother would have wanted, with perfect flowers and the right kind of canapés. It was very well-attended by everyone who had known and liked her mother and many, many people who had not particularly, but who enjoyed a decent wake and a nose about. While Angie could barely think or function, Ray located the will and organised probate very swiftly, only bothering Angie when she had to sign something as next of kin and sole beneficiary. She was eternally grateful to him.

'I think it would be best if we put the house in joint names, given that we are officially married, and it will be much better legally for the baby,' he suggested. 'Just sign here. I've checked it all thoroughly. I'm using my London solicitors, who are very good. I've used them for years.'

On the days when Ray was around, life was exhausting, as he took her through papers and reorganised the house. Her mother had been a fastidious saver, it turned out, leaving Angie with a decent nest egg, which allowed them to kit out the nursery and buy new lounge furniture. They had decided to stay at the house rather than move now that they had it to themselves. Ray reasoned that they would never be able to afford anything as big in London.

'I don't know how I would have got through this without you,' Angie whispered to Ray as they lay in bed one evening. 'I've been so thrown by Mum's accident, and I can't get used to her not being around. I always dreamed of getting away and of having a new life with you, and now I feel as if I might have willed this to happen.'

'Angie, baby, don't be ridiculous. None of this is your fault. If anything, it's mine. I wasn't careful enough and now we're having a baby. And it's dreadful that your mum won't be here to see him, but I will always look after you and my son. I will never abandon you.'

'Or daughter,' she sobbed into his chest as he stroked her hair.

Angie felt so blessed and grateful for Ray's thoughtfulness and attention, especially now that her mother was gone, who she missed every day, far more than she could have ever thought possible.

And she missed Ray when he was away, particularly as they were so rarely able to speak when he was working and she had to wait patiently for him to call her. But eventually, after the initial shock and grief of losing her mother subsided, or at least became less all-consuming and the baby growing inside her became more so, she got used to having her freedom. This was her house now. If she left the dirty dishes in the sink for hours or did not empty the bin bag every day, no one castigated her. She made up her own rules.

The last month of Angie's pregnancy was brutal. It was only May, but it was unusually hot. Her ankles swelled and just became an extension of her calves, so that she could only wear slippers. She could not sleep, because her stomach was quite simply in the way. She suffered from dreadful heartburn and every day, time seemed to move slower than the last. She just could not wait until the baby arrived and she could deal with it from the outside instead of in. But she was also frightened. She did not want her waters to break and to go into labour all alone.

'What will I do if you're not here when it happens!' she bleated down the phone to Ray one evening when he did manage to call her. 'What should I do?'

'The week you're due, I'll try to ring every day,' he soothed.

'But can't you just take some time off and be here?'

'That's totally impractical. I can't be away for weeks on end, and you could be a month late.'

'Don't say that! And anyway, they induce you after two weeks. I bloody hope it's not late. I can't do this for much longer.'

The baby gave her an extra-hard kick, probably instructed to do so by her mother, who had forbidden all swearing of even the mildest kind.

'Look, you know what you've got do. Doctor Collins is on standby. You will call him as soon as anything happens, and he will sort it all out. He told me it was the least he could do for your poor mum.'

'But I want you to be there!' she moaned.

'Now, come on. Be my big girl. You've got this. Women give birth every day.'

'Easy for you to say.'

'I did my bit. It was tough but I got through it.'

'Very funny. Just make sure you're here, alright?'

But inevitably he missed it all. Angie was woken in the middle of the night by painful cramps and when she stood up, she soaked the carpet by her bed as her waters broke. She wobbled there for a moment, surprised and uncertain, before remembering Doctor Collins. She called his mobile and he picked her up within the hour and took her to hospital. Hours of painful labour followed, with gas and air the only pain relief on offer as the hospital was short staffed and by the time the obstetrician came, it was too late for an epidural. Eventually, almost twenty-four hours later, at around one the following morning, the baby arrived, howling like a banshee from the moment he hit fresh air, as if disturbed from his pleasant slumber far too early. The nurses checked him over and then placed him on her chest, where he stopped crying instantly and stared up at his young mother with huge, mauve eyes.

'Hello,' she whispered. 'So, it's you who's been kicking me for months, is it?'

They went home the following day, Ray still oblivious to the fact that he was now a father. Doctor Collins dropped her home and made her a cup of tea, while the baby, tiny in a white sleep suit and matching hat, slept swaddled in his Moses basket.

'Let me make you something to eat,' the doctor offered.

Angie shook her head, but he ignored her and when he returned with a steaming mug and a plate of tuna sandwiches, she gobbled them all down gratefully, realising that she had barely eaten for the past forty-eight hours.

And then she was all alone with this minute, alien creature, who she had been desperate to emit yet was now terrified to manage. She stared at the baby and her gaze woke him up. He started to chirrup, which turned almost instantly into a wail. She unbuttoned her blouse, and he began to feed easily and greedily. He had growing to do and so did she.

Ray did not call until the following day, when she told him the news.

'You clever girl! And a boy as well, just as we hoped. Excellent news.'

'Are you coming? I can't wait for you to see him.'

'I'll be there on Monday.'

'But it's only Friday. Surely, you're not waiting three days until you see your son?' She gulped back tears that had risen unbidden into her throat, throttling her.

'I'm abroad, Angie baby. I don't fly back until Monday, but I'll come straight from Heathrow. It's completely out of my control. I'm sorry.'

Angie's face was wet from the fat tears, which seemed to have fallen unbidden down her cheeks with regularity since giving birth. She struggled to reply, instead emitting a huge sob down the phone.

'Don't cry. It won't be long until we are all together.'

'Where are you?'

'I'm away, I told you. You know better than to question me on an open line, Angie. Think, will you?' He paused and whispered something inaudible. 'Look, I have to go. I love you. Kisses to the baby.'

And the line went dead.

Ray arrived the following Monday laden with an enormous bouquet of flowers and a blue helium balloon with 'Welcome to my beautiful baby boy' scrawled across it. He kissed Angie on the head and then cradled the baby along his forearm, cooing to him. 'Hello, little man. Welcome to the world.'

'So, I wondered if we could call him Ben?' Angie asked, clinging onto his waist, completing their family unit.

'After your dad?'

'Yes.'

'OK. I have no objections or indeed any other suggestions.'

And so, the baby became Ben and the next seventeen years followed the same pattern. Ray was there for a few days a week, or most weeks at least, and away working the rest and she got on with bringing Ben up as a hybrid single/married woman. She floundered quite badly at the beginning, constantly anxious about whether or not she was doing things the right way. Angie was permanently exhausted until the Doctor Collins' wife took pity on her. She arranged to come over a couple of times a week so that Angie could at least shower and have a short nap in peace without worrying that the baby might do something fatal if she left him for one moment.

Once Ben was a year old, Angie had managed to establish a reasonable routine. He was a good baby, sleeping through the night and constantly gurgling and smiling, lighting up whenever he saw his mother's face. She started to take him to the local mother and baby group in the village, which is where she had first met Julia. Julia was ten years older than she was, but they hit it off straight away and Angie was relieved to have someone else to share her concerns with when it came to motherhood. Julia was there with her younger son, Tim, so she had done it all once before. She was also instrumental in helping Angie think about what she might like to make of her future beyond motherhood.

'I know you missed out on university initially, Angie, but you are so young and even if you can't actually go to one physically, you should at least do an online degree. You're so bright and I think you'd really enjoy it,' Julia encouraged her. 'I'll send you a few links.'

So, with Julia's stalwart encouragement, once Ben started nursery, Angie had mooted the idea of signing up to an English Literature degree by distance learning with the Open University.

However, Ray had objected, as he was reluctant to spend money on her fees. He controlled all their finances, so she had to get his agreement.

'But I can use some of the money Mum left me, can't I?'

'You could, yes, but raising Ben is not going to be cheap and I don't earn a fortune, you know. And English? Really? What are you going to do with it afterwards?'

'But you went to university, Ray. Surely you can appreciate the benefits and hopefully, I can get a decent job on the back of it.'

Ray had secured a top first from Oxford in PPE and he told her that he had been begged to stay on as an academic by Trinity College, but by then he had been approached by MI5 or 6, she could never remember which, and had decided that espionage would be a far more interesting proposition.

'I must agree with your late mother on this one. Even accountancy would be preferable, because at least you can get a good career from that.'

'But I hate maths, Ray, and I'm no good at it.'

'I don't think that matters too much.'

They compromised, and instead, Angie took some much cheaper writing courses online and eventually took on some copywriting jobs working with a couple of local advertising agencies, which she could manage from home. She found that she was good at it, with clients happy that she delivered quality work on time.

'You should set up on your own and cut out the middleman,' Julia suggested. She was self-employed, running a small company selling wooden toys sourced from Poland. She had given Ben a number of wooden, hand-crafted cars and trains over the years, which he loved to play with, and which were virtually indestructible. 'I'll help you to set up the website and I have a good online accounting platform I use to send my invoices.'

'I might not need anything that complicated,' Angie replied. 'I'm only selling copy, not hundreds of items a year.'

'Still useful, though, to keep a check on things,' Julia insisted.

The next time Ray was home, Angie discussed this idea with him and he was very supportive of her setting up her business, reassuring her that he could manage her bookkeeping when he was at home, so that she could concentrate on the copywriting. He set up an account for her and clients paid directly into it. Angie received a monthly salary from the profits and Ray invested the rest for Ben.

'It'll pay for his university fees and if you're really successful, it'll help to set him up with a deposit for a house for the future - if I chip in as well of course.'

'Yes, I think that's a great idea. Mum was clearly saving for me.' Angie bit her lip. 'I wish she could have lived to see Ben. I think she would have adored him.'

'Yes, it's a real tragedy,' he agreed, picking up a copy of The Times and beginning to flick through it.

Angie and Ben padded along very happily together for most of his school years. But now, at seventeen, Ben did not need her as much anymore. Angie was often restless and lonely, spending most of her evenings alone, flicking through Netflix and finding very little of interest to watch. Work interested her less because she had more time to do it. She saw Julia once a week, but Julia was busy with her own kids, her husband, and her thriving business, which had now expanded to include a store in Cambridge. With this extra time to dwell on things, her doubts, about Ray and his elusiveness, sewn by Julia, multiplied in her head. She knew that it was strange to begin to question him after so long, but they were entering a new phase of their lives when they could have more time together as a couple. She wanted to spend this time with him, as in a way, they had never had it at the start, because Ben had arrived so quickly.

The filing cabinet might be a good place to start unlocking any secrets if indeed there were any. But she had absolutely no clue where to find the damned key.

Chapter Sixteen

———

The funeral was a quiet affair. Diana and Patrick had never socialised very much, so the congregation consisted primarily of two colleagues from Patrick's office (the head office was based in Manchester, so there were never going to be many attendees from work), two or three of the neighbours and a few of Diana's regular customers who wanted to pay their respects. Diana's mother did not come because she had a nasty cold and Diana worried about her getting worse if she left the house. If Diana was being honest, it was also a bit of a relief. She did not feel strong enough to bury her husband and to prop up her mother all at the same time.

The service was held in the West Herts Crematorium just off the North Orbital St Albans Road. The dead were lulled to rest by the continuous thrum of traffic in the background, as if to signal that you may have stopped, but the rest of the world intends to carry on regardless. Patrick would have been mortified that this was to be his final resting place, but Diana had decided that this was the right course given the priest's attitude. He had been less than sympathetic when discussing the manner of Patrick's death and, even though the church would conduct services for those who took their own lives, he was clearly disapproving. Diana had wanted to scream at him for his hypocrisy - for ignoring Patrick's true devotion to his faith over all these years, not to mention the many notes and coins he had placed in the collection plate and work he had done for church fundraising overall. It appeared to count for nothing now.

Diana was chauffeured there by her neighbours, Fred and Janet. She could have hired a funeral car to follow the hearse, but frankly, she felt it was both a ridiculous expense and that it might be rather lonely to travel less than twenty miles from Harpenden to Watford in a limousine all by herself. It was certainly a level of extravagance that Patrick would never have approved of, or at least while he had been alive. The bizarre pre-suicide shopping spree he had embarked upon was quite out of character, but then so was his suicide - the two issues as baffling as each other.

Fred drove at a respectful distance behind the hearse, while Diana sat in the back by herself. They had offered for her to sit up front, but she preferred to be alone with her own thoughts in the back of their ancient Honda Civic. Janet tried to twist around to chat to her, but it hurt her neck, so she had to stop and instead she just whispered quietly to Fred in the front, who was so hard of hearing that he could not catch a word she said. They were a couple in their late seventies. Janet commented that they seemed to be going to more and more funerals these days, but Patrick had been a good decade or so younger than them - so who would have thought that it would be him next? It was a real tragedy, as she and Fred had both agreed.

'You never know what goes on behind closed doors though, do you, Fred?' Janet had commented as she fiddled around with her black, felt hat with its wilting feather before trudging across the road to collect Diana. 'He was such a quiet chap and seemed to be very successful at what he did.'

Fred nodded, his arthritic hands hampering his ability to knot his tie.

'Here, let me do that for you.' She turned to him and managed his tie in seconds. 'There you go. You look lovely.'

'Do think they were unhappy?' Fred asked, sitting down on the chair in the corner of their hallway to pull on his shoes, which he had polished to a high shine earlier that morning.

'I never saw any sign of it myself, but as I say, you just don't always know, do you? I always thought they were a lovely couple. It's very sad.'

Fred finished tying his shoelaces and stood up with difficulty, like a car jack being opened up very slowly. He had patted Janet on the arm. 'Come on, love, or we'll be late.'

As they now pulled into the crematorium, Diana wondered to herself why such places all looked the same, with their bare concrete construction, utterly lacking in soul. Perhaps they had been built that way so as not to heighten the raw emotion that most of the visitors felt when they found themselves arriving at a splendid church, or maybe it had merely been cheaper to build them all to a similar formula. Diana shook herself out of her reverie, wondering why she was thinking about crematoria architecture and economies of scale when she was about to commit her husband to the eternal flames. The mind, her mind, seemed to work in utterly bizarre ways at the moment, diving off into random corners at times of greatest stress.

The hearse drew to a slow stop outside the entrance and the little Honda halted neatly behind it. Fred got out and walked around the car to open the rear door for Diana. She thanked him and slid her legs out, feeling unusually light-headed as she stood up. Fred held out his hand for support and she took it gratefully, attempting a grim smile. She watched as if from a long distance away as the undertakers opened the back of the hearse and gently slid the coffin out of the back and onto their shoulders. She found it incomprehensible that Patrick was inside this simple, mahogany box, fully paid up by his Co-op plan. How could anyone ever be sure that their loved one was actually inside? He could have been muddled up at the mortuary, or disposed of elsewhere and replaced by a few bricks for all she knew. She supposed that you could only be certain if you insisted on an open casket, but Diana found that whole concept abhorrent.

She floated behind the coffin, lightly supported by Fred and Janet, who deposited her on the front pew before moving to a few rows further back. She was aware of other people filing in, but she could not turn around to see who they were. What would she have done if she had caught their eye anyway? It was not exactly a smile and wave occasion.

Suddenly, Diana felt a light tap on her shoulder and looked up to see a lady of indeterminate age standing there.

'Diana? Hello, I'm Lucy Watkins, your celebrant. We've spoken over email.'

Celebrant, Diana thought. *A perfect description for someone officiating at a wedding or a christening - but a funeral?* What was she celebrating exactly? A life cut short by her husband's own hand and a future loaded with regrets, sadness, and deep uncertainty? It all seemed very wrong somehow. She glanced down at Lucy's shoes, noticing that they were scuffed and speckled with mud. Suddenly, all the anger she had been bottling up for the last few weeks welled up in her throat, almost choking her. How could this woman, who was here to lead the service for her dead husband, have the nerve to turn up looking like she had hiked across the fields to get here? To add insult to injury, the sleeves of her jacket were frayed, and her skirt was badly creased. How could she take so little pride in her own appearance and have so little respect for the dead?

'Did you walk here?' Diana croaked, scanning her up and down.

'Well, no. I came by car. Why do you ask?'

'No reason.' She fiddled with the order of service that lay on the seat beside her.

'I think we are ready to begin in a few moments. My sincerest condolences to you and your family.'

She shuffled off to the podium, and as she did so Diana noticed a large ladder running up the back of Lucy's tights. She would speak to the undertakers who had hired this celebrant about it later.

Diana had taken a great deal of trouble to hone the service so that it ran in a way that she felt Patrick would have liked. She minimised any religious readings (though included the Lord's Prayer as a nod to her husband and his beloved church) adding instead a couple of poems which she felt Patrick might have liked, although as far as she knew, he had never actually read or enjoyed any poetry during his lifetime. She had penned a brief summary of his life and achievements, and the celebrant had said that it was sufficient for her to create a short eulogy. Diana had declined to speak, as she could not be sure that she would be able to stop herself from crying and she did not want to crumble in front of this audience. Patrick would have wanted her to hold it together.

She also chose the music. Barber's *Adagio for Strings* had played as Patrick had been carried in, watched solemnly by the mourners. For the committal, *Adagietto* from Mahler's Fifth was piped through the intercom. And for the filing out, she had chosen Albinoni's *Adagio in G minor*. Neither she nor Patrick had been classical music aficionados, but she felt such music was appropriate for a funeral. She had chosen the pieces by googling the best classical music for funerals and choosing some of Classic FM's top ten recommendations. She had liked all of them when she listened to them on YouTube, and recognised the tunes, but could not have told you what they were called or who played them before she copied them down. She hoped that Patrick would have approved, but she knew that in truth he probably would either not have offered much of an opinion or would have suggested some amusing songs to fit with such an occasion, like *Return to Sender* by Elvis or even *Ring of Fire* by Johnny Cash. That had been exactly his sort of gentle humour.

The celebrant began the service in a flat monotone, which never wavered for the duration. Diana sat marooned on the front pew, digging her nails into her hands to help her control her emotions, and taking deep, mediative breaths to assuage her annoyance at the shambolic woman who was holding forth. Patrick would have been utterly appalled not only by the relatively secular service, but mostly at her lack of professionalism - and Diana was equally disappointed at her total lack of empathy. All the personal touches that she had worked so hard to include in the service were ruined, Lucy delivering them to the congregation as if she were reading the list for her weekly shop at Sainsburys.

Mahler began to trickle through the speakers as Patrick slid backwards and the curtains began to close. Diana let out an involuntary cry, or perhaps more of a noisy gulp, as she attempted to hold back the enormous lump that squatted in her throat, dabbing at her eyes with her sodden handkerchief. 'Goodbye,

Patrick,' she whispered to herself as he disappeared. 'I think I can forgive you, but I wish I could understand.'

The celebrant concluded by inviting everyone back to Diana's house for refreshments. Diana knew this was protocol, but she vehemently wished that she did not have to do it. All she actually wished for was to dive under the duvet with a hot water bottle and go to sleep - if sleep would ever come. And having people back to her place also meant that she had to move the armchair; which in its own way, had meant moving the last thing that Patrick had touched, effectively de-sanctifying the place where he had died. Part of her wanted to keep that grotty old chair in the hall forever. Instead, she had asked the local junk collector to take it away, who had duly obliged for the price of twenty pounds. Since, or obviously just prior to his untimely death, Patrick had purchased a new chair anyway - one of the many, many items that kept on arriving over the last few weeks - it was the only thing that she had actually kept.

Most of the returns had been extremely time-consuming, but ultimately possible. It was the embarrassing ones that had been far more challenging. She had had to return boxes of sex toys, including an advent calendar filled with all sorts of items that both fascinated and revolted her in equal measure. She could not even begin to comprehend why Patrick had purchased any of these items, but the sex stuff was particularly weird. Patrick was very conventional in the bedroom, to the point of being fundamentally disinterested most of the time - which if she was being brutally honest, had been a disappointment to her for the first few years of their marriage, yet one that she had learnt to live with. It was alright most of the time if there was a decent series on the television to distract her.

In truth, Patrick had been rather a prude: tutting at any sexual scenes on television and noisily chomping his popcorn if anything too raunchy came on the screen at the cinema. She wondered if somehow all of this was some form of elaborate puzzle that Patrick had set for her to solve, or whether her husband was really a very different man from the one she had known and lived with for the past thirty years. But surely that was impossible? No one could dissemble for that long and their partner never suspect a thing. He was probably simply having a late mid-life crisis and it went too far; a male menopause of sorts perhaps, which according to the press, did actually exist.

The service ended, Albinoni striking up right on cue. Diana was aware that she was expected to move first, but her legs refused to work, so she remained in her seat, immobile, incapable, until one of the undertakers strode over and held out his hand. Gently, he assisted her to stand, and she clung to his arm as she wobbled out into the remembrance garden at the rear of the building. It was a gloomy day, with huge, threatening rain clouds thumping into each other as they fought their way across the sky. Diana pulled her scarf a little tighter around her neck as she began to greet the mourners, each of whom offered their condolences; either kissing her cheek, squeezing her arm, or shaking her hand depending on their level of acquaintance. The line was not long, which was a relief, yet she felt a deep sadness at the same time that Patrick had so few people to mourn his passing.

Diana barely registered the people that she did speak to, her mind as numb as her freezing hands. She had stupidly forgotten her gloves, which was a mistake. She suffered badly from Raynaud's Syndrome and frequently lost all feeling in her fingers and toes, even when she went near the freezer aisle in the supermarket.

The line was ending and at the back came Ian, his eyes red and raw.

'Ian,' she stuttered. 'Thank you for coming. I didn't expect it.'

'Diana, I am so sorry for your loss.' He sniffed, then blew his nose nosily into his handkerchief. 'I felt I had to come.'

'Did you know my husband?' she asked, looking up and staring straight into his eyes.

'No, not at all. I came for you, to pay my respects, and well because I really do understand. I don't share this with people very often, but my own father killed himself when I was very young. I don't think that I ever got over it really. So, when I heard what had happened, I wanted to be here. Because I get it.'

Diana felt her heart lurch.

'Ian, you poor boy. How dreadful for you.' She held out her hand and squeezed his. 'Please. Do come back to the house for a drink.'

'Thank you, I'd like that very much.'

Fred drove her home at a similarly hearse-like pace to the journey there, but Diana did not mind, as she was in no hurry to face everyone and be forced to make coffees and small talk. When they arrived at her house, several of the mourners were already there, presumably incapable of driving quite as slowly as Fred. Diana fumbled with her key in the front door and eventually managed to turn it. She removed her coat and scarf and hung it on the coat rack by the front door. Fred and Janet did the same and then Fred instructed the others to pile their clothing on top, so that eventually the rack tottered precariously from the weight and Diana had to remove some of the items to avoid an accident.

She had prepared everything in advance the night before. Coffee and teacups were lined up with military precision on the countertop and she had arranged sandwiches and small cakes on platters placed on the kitchen table. Now, she removed the clingfilm and moved to put the kettle on.

'Why don't you let me do that for you, Diana? You must be exhausted.' Janet took the kettle from her. 'Go and sit down in the living room and I'll make you a nice coffee. Milk and sugar?'

'Just black please.' She hesitated. 'Thanks, Janet. I really do appreciate it. I am feeling rather tired.'

Diana wandered in a daze through to the living room, where a couple of Patrick's work colleagues were standing by the fireplace taking in low voices.

'Shall I switch the gas fire on? Are you cold?' Diana asked them.

'No, not at all, but if you are, I can do it for you,' replied one of the two, a tall willow of a man. Diana knew his name, but could not recall it at this instant.

'I'm fine, thank you.' Diana sank into the new armchair, which still smelt of the plastic in which it had arrived, despite the copious amounts of Febreze she sprayed onto it. She rested her head back and closed her eyes for a moment.

'Here you go, love,' Fred called softly, handing her a strong, black coffee, 'and there's a couple of sandwiches for you, in case you're hungry.'

Diana nodded her thanks, too fatigued to speak.

The wake milled about around her, and Diana sat there motionless, as if she were watching a foreign film without subtitles. She could follow the action, but not what was being said. Occasionally she nodded thanks to someone as they offered their sympathy, but was otherwise mute. Afterwards, she could not have recounted how many people were there or indeed who exactly was there, and after an hour or so, they mercifully all melted away. She had still not left her chair. She must have appeared quite inhospitable, but then it was her husband's funeral and hopefully everyone would have understood.

Suddenly, the house was eerily quiet, and Diana sat there in the gathering darkness of the late afternoon, unmoving, unseeing, unthinking.

'Diana, can I get you another coffee?'

She screamed herself out of her slumber.

'Jesus, Ian! I didn't know you were still here. You nearly gave me a heart attack.'

'I'm so sorry. I was in the kitchen clearing up for you. I suggested that Janet and Fred go home and offered to finish up. It's too much for them at their age and I didn't want to leave it all for you after you've had such a traumatic day.'

'Oh, that's very sweet of you, Ian. Really, there was no need. I could have done it later.'

'Nonsense. You shouldn't have to do anything today. It's been hard enough.' He ran his fingers through his thick hair, creating a tuft which stuck up at the front. 'So, can I get you anything before I go?'

'You know what I'd really like? A small brandy. I shouldn't, I know, but well, it's an unusual day and I feel like breaking my rule of only having a drink at the weekend. I think it's merited, don't you?'

'Absolutely.'

'Will you join me?'

'Only if you're totally sure. I mean, if you're too tired, I can get one for you and just go.'

'No, please, stay for a bit. The brandy is in the cabinet behind you.' She gesticulated at the old, wooden Welsh dresser that she and Patrick had bought in an antique shop in the Cotswolds a thousand years ago. 'That's it, in the cupboard on the right.'

Ian retrieved a bottle of Rémy Martin, rolling it in his palm. 'Glasses?'

'In the kitchen above the toaster.'

He returned with a couple of tumblers and poured two generous drinks, handing one to Diana before settling himself on the sofa opposite.

Diana took a sip of the brandy, the strong liquid warming her throat. 'Thank you, that's just what I needed.' She sighed heavily. 'Now, why don't you tell me all about your father?'

Chapter Seventeen

'You know, Tom has been an absolute marvel, Diana,' Marjorie gushed as she wiped the cream from her chocolate eclair from her lips with her serviette. 'I can't begin to tell you how helpful he's been, especially while you've been otherwise engaged.' She lifted the teacup to her lips as if to drink, but then put it down again, sloshing tea into the saucer as she did so. 'It's good to have all that unpleasant business out of the way, isn't it?'

Diana ignored her jibe.

'Tom?'

For a moment, she could not think who her mother was wittering on about. Her brain appeared to have gone on strike since Patrick's death, lacking all ability to remember names, people, places, or even what day of the week it was.

'You know, Tom. The young man from the council. He has helped me to organise all my paperwork. You should see my filing now. When I pop my clogs, you'll be able to find everything you need straight away.'

'I don't think you're going anywhere for the moment, Mum.' She raised her eyebrows skyward and drained her cup. 'But you shouldn't let this guy look at your private papers. You've absolutely no idea who he is. I really don't think you should let him in anymore.'

She had brought her mother out for afternoon tea at Sopwell House, a rather smart hotel in St Albans. She wanted to spoil her because she was aware that she had been rather neglecting her of late and she felt extremely guilty about it. And she also appreciated the fact that her mother had avoided having any unnecessary accidents or crises over the past few weeks. In truth, if she had, Diana would have been unable to cope with them.

'More tea, Mum?'

'Yes, please. These cakes are delicious. You should try one. You're looking very skinny, Diana. Are you eating anything?'

Diana smiled at the irony of her mother nagging her to eat, when she subsisted mostly on biscuits and Carte d'Or vanilla.

'Since Patrick died, I haven't had much of an appetite. And when I do eat, everything seems to taste like cardboard.'

Diana picked up a slice of Victoria sponge cake and laid it on her plate to appease her mother, even though she had no desire to eat it.

'Going back to Tom, Mum. You've no idea who this guy is. He could be anyone. At least let me try to find out who he is before you let him in again.'

She waved to the waitress to see if she could ask for more hot water for the teapot, but the girl walked straight past her as if Diana was invisible. She sighed.

'Your problem has always been that you're too suspicious of people, Diana. I've told you before. He works at the council. I've seen his badge. He's very polite, handsome in an ordinary sort of way, and I enjoy his visits. Don't take away the only pleasure I have at the moment.' She frowned. 'I thought we were getting some more tea.'

An hour later, Diana dropped her mother back at her bungalow. She said her goodbyes and promised to call her in the morning. The light was fading when Diana got back into her car. Even though it was only four in the afternoon, winter was closing in around her. She ran her hands over her face and took a deep breath, attempting to summon up the energy to start the car and drive home. She wanted to have an early night, because the following day she had vowed to return to the shop, which had been closed for around a month now. Christmas was almost here, and she was keen to try to make some sales, even if she had missed most of the festive window. She shook herself out of her reverie and started the engine, glancing over at the bungalow. Her mother was standing by the kitchen window, giving her a little wave. Diana waved back, but she did not think that her mother could see her from the car in the dark. She smiled to herself, pleased that she had made the effort to take her mother out for tea. She promised herself that she would do it more often now that she had laid Patrick to rest and had to force herself to move forwards.

She pulled away and pressed the button on the car steering wheel. 'Call St Albans Council' she commanded. The circle on the screen in the middle of the dashboard whirred around for a moment before the automated voice announced that he was indeed doing her bidding and calling the council. The phone rang out for fifteen minutes before the operator answered it at the other end.

'St Albans Council, how may I direct your call?'

'Please could you put me through to Thomas Maloney?'

'Please hold.' *Dancing Queen* by ABBA began to play for a couple of minutes.

'Can you tell me which department he works in? I can't seem to find him.'

'Adult social care.'

'Please hold again.' *Dancing Queen* gave way to *Gimme! Gimme! Gimme! A Man After Midnight.* Diana laughed. Whoever was choosing the music was either stuck in the 1970s, or had recently been to see *ABBA Voyage.* She had desperately wanted to go herself, but Patrick had flatly refused, and she had no one else to ask.

'I'm sorry, but there doesn't appear to be anyone of that name working here. Can I help you with anything else?'

'Are you sure?' Diana gripped the steering wheel tightly, her knuckles white.

'Yes, I've checked the whole database. Are you certain that you've got the right name?'

'Yes, definitely. He's been calling round to see my mother claiming to be working at your council.'

'Sorry, I can't help you. Maybe check the name again with your mum? She might have got it wrong.'

'OK, thank you.'

Diana pressed the red button on the car screen to stop the call as she drew up outside the rear entrance to the shop. She knew the name was right, because she had seen it on the business card that he had left with her mother. So, who the hell was he and what was he up to? Her head span and she felt suddenly extremely dizzy. She sat in the car for a while with her eyes closed. She had driven to the shop on autopilot, but now that she had arrived, there seemed to be no point in going in. She would come again tomorrow morning to open up, right after she had been back to see her mother to talk about this strange man again. It was too late to go back to talk to her about it now.

That night, her dreams tormented her. She was in a coffin, alive and wide awake, vaguely aware of the celebrant's voice droning on somewhere outside her sarcophagus. She strained to hear the words that were being said about her, but she could not make them out. And then suddenly, she felt herself sliding backwards, hitting such intense heat that she was unable to breathe. Diana awoke violently, coughing; her body cold with sweat, the sheets sodden. Glancing at the clock, it was only five-thirty in the morning, but she was too scared to stay in bed or to close her eyes again. She stood up too quickly, the room spinning as she did so. She waited for a moment until it stopped, before flicking on the light beside her bed and moving across to the chest of drawers. She pulled the top drawer open and pulled out a clean pair of pyjamas, before going into the bathroom to empty her bladder and to find her dressing gown.

She walked downstairs slowly, glancing left into the empty hall where Patrick's chair had stood sentinel, before entering the kitchen. She made herself a strong, black coffee and slumped onto one of the chairs. She hated her current state of malaise, having always prided herself on being someone who just got on with things. But recent events had completely floored her, and she was struggling to get going again. She hugged the mug more tightly, feeling the heat through her fingers, wishing she could work out how to move on.

Suddenly, her mobile trilled, making her jump and spill her coffee.

'Bloody hell,' she muttered, rummaging in her dressing gown pocket for her phone.

She always carried her phone around wherever she was, just in case.

'Hello?'

'Hello, Diana?' It was her mother, shaky and barely audible.

'Yes, Mum, it's me. Are you alright? It's very early.'

'I haven't slept a wink all night, Diana. I think something's wrong.'

'What do you mean?' She paused. 'Have you had a bad dream?'

'No, no, it's not a dream. Or I don't think it is. Can you come over? I think I've done something stupid.'

Diana raised her eyes to the ceiling, wondering what on earth her mother could have done this time. It must be bad if she was admitting to it.

'Give me half an hour to shower and get dressed and I'll come over.'

'Come soon, Diana,' Marjorie implored, and she began to cry.

'I'll be as quick as I can.'

Diana raced upstairs and, forgoing a shower, threw on the sweat top and leggings she had worn the previous evening to watch television. Suddenly feeling a tremendous sense of panic, despite having dealt with so many emergencies relating to her mother in the past, she screeched out of the front door to the car, pulling on a pair of trainers as she went. She drove quickly - much faster than she should have - but traffic was light. There were just the very early commuters on their way to park at the station before heading into London, as well as the occasional delivery van. She parked haphazardly on her mother's drive and ran to the door, fumbling with her keys. Oddly, the bungalow was well lit. In fact, every single light was on, even though it was only six-fifteen in the morning.

'Mum?' she shouted, barging through her mother's bedroom door. 'Are you OK?'

The bed was empty, the sheets rumpled. Diana checked the tiny ensuite bathroom, but she was not in there either. She stormed into the lounge and saw her mother sitting with her back to her in her chair, a cup of coffee beside her; clearly cold, a congealed skin floating on the top of it.

'Oh, you're in here. Thank goodness!' Marjorie exclaimed, her face swollen from crying and her eyes red and sore.

Diana knelt down and held her mother's hands. 'You're freezing cold, Mum. Let me get you a rug.'

She stood and fetched a tartan rug which was lying strewn across the sofa. She wrapped it around her mother's shoulders. 'Now, shall I get you a hot cup of tea?'

'No!' Marjorie shrieked. 'No, listen Diana, that man I told you about.'

Diana's skin prickled.

'Yes, the Tom man?'

'Yes, Tom.'

'What about him?'

'He came round again last night, Diana, after you left and I, well, he, I.'

Diana knelt down again and stroked her mother's arm. 'Calm down, Mum. Take some deep breaths. Four breaths in, six breaths out. That's it. That's better. Now, what happened? Did he hurt you?'

Marjorie shook her head.

'OK, so what did happen?'

'Well, I let him in, and he made a cup of tea and we ate some custard creams, which are his favourite.'

'Right,' Diana muttered through gritted teeth. 'And then?'

'And then he said he would help me sort out my banking, because apparently there had been a problem with my council tax payment and he said he could sort it out for me if I could give him my bank details. He was on his way home, you see, so he said it was no trouble at all.'

'And did you? Did you give him your details?' Diana's heart was beginning to race, her palms sweaty against her mother's dressing gown.

'Well, I did, yes.'

'Did you write it down for him?'

'No, I showed him my chequebook and then he got his computer thing out so he could check a few things on the council website. He had to ask me a few more questions while he did it.' She squeezed her eyes, and another tear ran down her leathery cheek. Diana reached over and took a tissue from the cube on the coffee table and wiped it away.

'What other things did he ask you, Mum?'

'My date of birth and my mother's maiden name. That sort of thing.'

'Oh my God! You didn't, did you?'

'I've been silly, haven't I? You must think I'm a total fool.' Huge sobs wracked her small, wilted frame.

'Why didn't you call me last night when he was here or after he left?'

'I didn't think about it then. I went to bed because I was tired. I'm not used to visitors so late on. It was only when I woke up in the night that I wondered if I'd made a mistake. Oh, I don't know, Diana. I feel all muddled up.'

'It's OK, it'll be OK, don't worry. But just hang on a minute.' Diana stood up, her left knee creaking as she did so, and she grabbed her mobile from her handbag. 'I'm just going to check something. OK?'

'He told me it was all sorted out. He said that he'd fixed the problem. But it was odd, because he left immediately and he didn't take the tea things through to the kitchen or offer to wash up - which isn't like him, as he's always very helpful like that. He just stood up and left.'

Diana was tapping away on her phone, logging into her mother's bank account. She had power of attorney and managed all her mother's finances for her.

'Jesus,' she whispered, struggling to breathe as though she had just been kicked hard in the chest. 'I don't fucking believe it.'

'What is it?'

'He's wiped you out, Mum. This Thomas guy, whoever he is, has taken you all your money. He's robbed you of everything you've got!'

She glanced up from her phone. Marjorie's face had taken on an odd blue tinge.

'Mum, Mum! Are you OK? Can you hear me?'

Marjorie made a gurgling sound, and her face was oddly contorted like that of a gargoyle.

Diana dialled 999.

'Ambulance. It's my mother. I think she's having a stroke.'

She knelt down beside her mother again and held her hand.

127

'Hang on, Mum. The ambulance is on its way. Don't worry. Everything will be fine,' she reassured her as tears ran riot down her cheeks.

In her head, she begged her mother not to die. She had had enough of death.

Chapter Eighteen

Angie was agitated. Ben was becoming more of a handful by the day, and she was struggling to discipline him. He often stayed over at friends after school - claiming that it was easier than commuting backwards and forwards from Cambridge all the time. When he was home, he was surly, communicating with her rarely. Angie did not know many of Ben's friends very well, as most of them lived much closer to town. When he had been at junior school, she knew all of them, as they lived locally. She often had a house full of children, which she loved, but now it felt desolate. Sometimes, when he reappeared, she wondered if he was slightly hungover, but when she asked him if he had been drinking, he barked at her that it was none of her business.

'I'm not a baby,' he wheedled.

'As you keep reminding me. But as I must remind you, you're still underage and still very much my responsibility. When you're out, I have no idea who you're with or what you're up to and it worries me. And you're not old enough to go out drinking.' They were sitting at the kitchen table, and she reached out to touch his hair.

'Mum, I'll be eighteen soon. Be reasonable. When's Dad coming back anyway?'

'Do you miss him?'

Ben shrugged. 'I guess so.'

'Truthfully, I don't know. Soon, I hope. You know it's difficult for him to keep in touch when he's in the field.' She fiddled with the sleeve of her jumper.

'Will he be around at Christmas?'

'I don't know, darling. I hope so. He's normally here, there, or thereabouts, isn't he?'

'Everyone else's dad is always home for Christmas. What can he be doing over that time of year?'

'Well, I suppose government business doesn't stop for the festive season.' She began to clear up the plates.

'I'm going to take a shower,' Ben announced, scraping his chair back from the table.

Angie was relieved to hear it, the stench of pungent teenage boy being hard to bear in their small kitchen. She heard the shower pump beginning to whirr and moved upstairs to pick up Ben's dirty clothes, which inevitably lay strewn partly on the landing and mostly across his bedroom floor. She bundled up his sports kit, underwear, and school shirt and threw them into the laundry basket in the corner of the landing outside the bathroom door. She returned to his room and picked up his trousers, folding them neatly to place on a hanger for the morning. As she did so, a small plastic bag fell out of the pocket. She retrieved it from the floor and put it in the palm of her hand. It contained a few tablets. She removed one from the bag, but there was no identifying stamp on it.

The cold hand of fear grabbed the back of her neck. The idea of Ben taking drugs terrified her and she did not know how to begin to handle it. What she did realise only too well was that if she accused him outright, he would deny it, even if she had the evidence in her hand, and any iota of trust that did currently exist between them would be destroyed. On the other hand, if she did not tackle this issue head on and swiftly, Ben might continue to use - if indeed these pills were his and were dodgy - and who knew where that could lead.

For the moment, she decided to replace the pills back into the pocket of his trousers. She needed thinking time. Actually, what she really needed was to speak to Ray. He would know precisely what to do and how to handle this situation. He had always been able to reason sensibly with Ben and the boy listened to him. But of course, she had no idea where Ray was. Julia crossed her mind as another option, but she did not want to confide in her, even though she was a very good friend. Ray would consider it to be a case of washing their dirty linen in public and would definitely not approve of anyone outside the family knowing their business. But if she could not get hold of him, what was she supposed to do?

She slunk into her bedroom and closed the door softly behind her. Pulling her mobile from the back pocket of her jeans, she performed the forbidden sin and dialled Ray's number.

Inevitably, it went straight to voicemail.

'Ray, hi it's me. I'm sorry to ring, but I've got a very awkward problem with Ben, and I don't know what to do. I really need your help. If you can call me back as soon as you can, I'd appreciate it.' She hesitated. 'It's urgent, Ray. You know I wouldn't try to contact you if it wasn't.' After a further pause, she added, 'I love you and I really miss you.'

One week later, Ray had still not returned her call. On that particular evening, when Ben was out once again and she was at home alone, pacing up and down the kitchen with a mug of cold coffee in her hand, Angie felt suddenly broken. All week, she had suffered from nausea, as if something terrible was about to happen. She couldn't shake this feeling of dread which stuck in her throat like a stubborn lump of catarrh. All these years, she might have simply been lying to herself, persuading herself that she and Ray had a normal, happy marriage, when in fact, it could not have been more abnormal. Of course, she had known little else, but she was no longer so naive. She looked around and saw her friends and their partners; interacting, sharing, arguing, supporting. She had none of that. It was as if she and Ray had been conducting an illicit, long-distance affair for the past eighteen years.

She banged her mug down onto the kitchen table and stormed upstairs. Ray kept the few clothes that he had at the house in the tiny wardrobe in the spare room. She threw open the doors and surveyed his half a dozen shirts hanging together in companionable silence. Women's wardrobes were never uniform like this, because female clothing was always of differing lengths and shapes, but men's shirts lined up like soldiers. To assuage her sudden rush of anger, she yanked open the shallow drawers inside the wardrobe, pulling out Ray's boxers and socks, which she threw behind her onto the floor. Now the drawers were empty, underwear carpeting her feet. She pulled the shirts off their hangers and shook them, followed by the trousers. She flumped down on the floor, creasing the shirts that she had taken such care to iron and thinking instantly that she would have to press them again. Ray was extremely fussy about his shirts.

Resting back on her hands for a moment, her rage dissipated by this quick burst of temper, she glanced upwards, and that was when she spotted it. On the side of the wardrobe, at the very top, was a small square where the wood had been cut. It was miniscule and the wardrobe was dark, so it was invisible when the clothes were hanging there, but now she could see it, along with the piece of ribbon or string protruding from one side. Slowly, Angie stood up. Standing on her tiptoes, she tried to reach the ribbon, but she was not tall enough. She raced into her bedroom and picked up her dressing table stool, which she placed in front of the wardrobe and stood on it. Reaching up again, she just got her fingertips to the ribbon. She tugged on it and as the tiny door gave way, envelopes fluttered down around her head like confetti. Carefully, she climbed down from the stool.

She picked up the first one and stared at it, then at another and then another. None of them were addressed to her, or to Ray, or even to her mother or father who had lived in this house for decades before she and Ray had inherited it. They were all in the names of several different men, none of whom Angie had never heard of before; all at different addresses which she also did not recognise.

She began to open them.

Chapter Nineteen

It took almost forty-five minutes for the ambulance to arrive, during which time Marjorie could neither speak nor move. Diana became increasingly agitated, alternately talking to her mother and pacing up and down to watch for the paramedics. When they did come, they acted with great efficiency and within fifteen minutes she was riding in the back of an ambulance as Marjorie was blue-lighted into hospital.

The ride was slow and tortuous, as much due to the dreadful suspension on the ambulance as to the terrible traffic they encountered. Once they eventually reached A&E, they were admitted reasonably swiftly and seen by a doctor, who confirmed that she had suffered a stroke.

'We will have to do some CT scans later today to establish the level of damage. You're welcome to wait with her until we can find her a place on a ward. I'll be back shortly.'

The doctor scurried away, and Diana was left to watch over her husk of a mother. A few hours later, Marjorie was admitted to a ward and Diana was told to go home and that the doctor would call her when they had the scan results.

'You can come back this evening. Visiting hours are between eight and nine pm,' the sister informed her. 'I'd go home if I were you, and get some rest while you can.'

Diana called an Uber back to her mother's bungalow, where she had left her car earlier that morning. She let herself in and boiled the kettle. While it heated up, she called her mother's bank and explained what had happened.

'So, this man, he is completely unknown to you?'

'Yes, I don't know who he was. He told my mother he was from the council and that she hadn't paid her council tax.'

'And she believed him?'

'Well, evidently, yes, she did. There had been something rather odd going on, which was worrying me. This man had been hanging around her. She told me that he was from the council and that he was helping her with her bins initially. I know I should have got more involved at the time, but I was rather distracted because I have just lost my husband and it's been an extremely difficult time. But then she said that he was assisting with her paperwork as well. That's when I became really suspicious. I mean, why would someone from the council come round to help with paperwork? Or bins for that matter? So, I called the council yesterday, and they told me that they had never heard of him and that he didn't work there. I was going to come back here later this morning to tell Mum not to let him in anymore. But I was too late. He came back last night. I can't believe how these bastards prey on the elderly like this.'

She began to sob, her chest heaving with the strain.

Trying to regain control, she asked, 'But I assume that you can trace the withdrawal and get the money back?'

'Well, it's not as simple as that, I'm afraid. These fraudsters are very clever and sometimes we can't trace the money. We will do our best, obviously, but there is a possibility that we will not be able to retrieve it for you.'

The operator spoke as if reading from a formatted card.

'But you must. He's taken literally everything. And she's had a stroke as a result. I mean, that's criminal. There must be something you can do.'

'As I say, Madam, we will do what we can. In the meantime, you need to report the matter to the police and try to get a description of the man from your mother if you can.'

'She's had a stroke and she can't speak!' Diana shouted louder than she had intended.

'Hopefully when she's recovered, she might be able to tell you more.'

If she recovers, thought Diana. Guilt overwhelmed her. If only she had got on top of this threat earlier. She knew it was odd as soon as her mother mentioned it, but losing Patrick had distracted her. And her mother had paid the price.

Diana slumped onto her mother's sofa and closed her eyes. She felt as if she may never be able to get back up, her body was so drained of energy and spirit. Yet oddly, as she lay there, her mind drifted back to the evening of Patrick's funeral, which was only a week ago, and yet now seemed like a distant memory in light of the latest shock that had blindsided her.

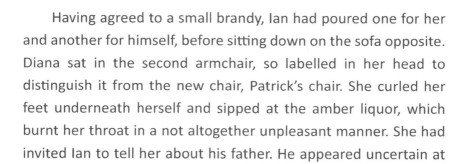

Having agreed to a small brandy, Ian had poured one for her and another for himself, before sitting down on the sofa opposite. Diana sat in the second armchair, so labelled in her head to distinguish it from the new chair, Patrick's chair. She curled her feet underneath herself and sipped at the amber liquor, which burnt her throat in a not altogether unpleasant manner. She had invited Ian to tell her about his father. He appeared uncertain at the beginning, swilling the brandy around in his glass and staring at it intently as if seeking answers from it. But once he started to talk, it was clear that he could not stop.

'My father was, well how can I describe him? Overwhelming, I suppose.' Ian had taken a long draught, wincing as he swallowed. 'I'm not used to drinking the hard stuff anymore.'

'Overwhelming? In what way?' Diana leant her head back on the chair.

'In every way. He was an extremely big personality and always needed to be the most important person in the room. I'm sure you know the type. In restaurants, he always had to have the best table in the place, so that he could be seen by everyone. He held long, pretentious, excruciatingly boring dialogues with the sommelier in an overly loud voice, before choosing a ridiculously expensive bottle of wine, or often two or three. He drank rather a lot, you see.' Ian drained his glass and moved to refill it. 'Can I top you up?'

Diana covered the top of her tumbler with her hand and shook her head. 'No, but you go ahead, please.'

Ian filled his glass halfway again and settled himself back down on the sofa. 'At home, he was domineering, always lecturing me long and hard on the importance of being the best, at school and in life. *You've got to believe in yourself above everything else, Ian, because if you don't, no one else will,* he used to tell me, repeating this mantra again and again like a broken record.'

'And how did you respond? It couldn't have been easy.'

She shifted her legs to avoid the cramp that she could feel creeping into them.

'Badly, is the answer. I could never measure up to his expectations. I was shy around people, excruciatingly so, and I was less than average academically at school. I wasn't particularly good at sport, or even interested in it for that matter, whereas my dad loved rugby and cricket. He used to drag me out to corporate days with clients, where he would drink until he could barely stand and make lewd comments to the waitresses, while I shrank further and further into the corner. I was a total embarrassment to him, I suppose.'

'And he to you by the sound of it. How dreadful for you. What about your mother?'

'She embodied all the traits that my father deplored. He called her his little mouse, because she scurried around in the background, keeping his house, washing his clothes, feeding him, and disappearing conveniently when it suited him.'

'It sounds like an odd match. Did they have anything in common?' Diana put her glass on the side table carefully, the effects of the alcohol pleasantly numbing her senses.

'I suppose initially they must have, but not by the time I came along. They were childhood sweethearts, but while she had always just hoped for an ordinary life, he made quite a bit of money very quickly and wanted to move up into a different social sphere. So, he began to go out alone and had many, many affairs, which she must have known about, but if she did, she never confronted him about them, or at least not to my knowledge. It was only after he died, at the funeral, when a few women showed up to pay their respects, all of whom wept noisily throughout the service, that my mother finally seemed to realise that he had not been exactly faithful. It was then that her docility turned quite quickly to hatred, but I think that truthfully she had really hated him for years. She just managed to keep it all bottled up. When he died, she didn't need to keep it hidden anymore. I think that's what killed her. Living in misery for so long, and once she was free, she was simply a puddle of bile.'

A small tear leaked from Ian's left eye, and he wiped it away quickly, downing his brandy to disguise it.

'What do you mean by that's what killed her?' Diana asked, picking up her glass again and taking another minute sip.

'She died of stomach cancer a year later. I believe it was all the venom she had stored up for years, all the animus she felt against him for making her feel so insignificant for so long, for ignoring her as a person in her own right.'

'I can understand that,' Diana murmured almost to herself. 'It's hard to be dismissed as irrelevant. And your father? You said he committed suicide?'

'Yes, that's right. He made a great deal of money, as I said, but he also had a terrible gambling habit. It appears that he fell in with some rather unsavoury characters, taking loans against his business so that he could keep betting, but he continually lost money on the horses and at the casino and the wolves had their teeth stuck right into him. When he died, we found threatening emails on his computer. I think he took the coward's way out before they did it for him.'

'I thought that sort of thing only really happened in books and on television, but I suppose I've led a rather sheltered, boring life. It's extraordinary and extremely sad how some people get themselves into such a terrible mess.'

'If he had just got himself into trouble and left it at that, it would have been fine, but he left my mother and I with a massive mountain of debt. He had gambled away the house, the car, everything. We had to move into a cheap, rented flat where we relied on foodbanks and local charities for handouts. That's probably what killed her off in the end.' He slammed his glass down on the coffee table with such force that the base chipped. 'Oh! I'm so sorry, Diana!' he cried, jumping up to retrieve the piece that had fallen to the floor.

'Please don't worry about it, Ian. I have other glasses. Sit down, please. Look, I get it, really, I do. You obviously still feel such raw emotion because you were so let down. I completely understand.' She reached across and touched his arm for a fleeting moment. 'How old were you when all this happened?'

'I was sixteen when Dad topped himself and seventeen when Mum died.'

'And what happened after that?'

'I dropped out of school and took odd jobs, dossing on friends' floors. I drank too much and got into a bit of trouble with the police for shoplifting and stuff like that. It was a downward spiral.'

Diana felt a rush of emotion for him, suddenly fighting back her tears. 'And how did you get out of it?'

'I met a girl and fell in love. She cleaned me up and I got a better job. It didn't last for more than a couple of years – with the girl, that is – but it was enough to set me back on the right path.'

'And you've never settled down with anyone?'

'I've never met the right woman, but I'm still looking,' he laughed, draining his glass.

'What about your sister?' Diana asked, suddenly remembering her first encounter with Ian, when he had run into the shop panicking about a gift for her.

He bent down to wipe something off his shoe. 'My sister?'

'Yes, where was she when all of this as going on?'

He hesitated. 'She was, um, well, she was long gone. She's older than me you see, and she didn't really speak to my parents. She and I don't talk regularly either. In fact, we don't even know each other all that well, but we reconnect on birthdays and Christmas. I don't think of her as family if I'm being honest.' He jumped up rather abruptly, and picked up his glass. 'What do you want me to do with this?'

'Nothing, just leave it there. I'll throw it away.'

'OK, well I've got to go. I'm sorry for your loss once again. Don't get up. I'll see myself out.'

And he was gone, slamming the front door a little too violently as he went.

Diana had not seen Ian since the evening of Patrick's funeral, which was a relief in some ways. He was a rather intense, slightly odd man and while she felt great sympathy for him and his suffering, he also made her feel a little wary and on edge, although she could not quite figure out why that was.

Diana jolted awake. She must have dozed off and now her phone was ringing.

'Mrs Whitlock, it's Doctor MacKenzie from the Luton and Dunstable here. We won't get the scans back today, but your mother is comfortable. We have sedated her, and she is sleeping. There's very little point in you coming back to see her tonight. If you call the ward in the morning, they will update you.'

'But what's the prognosis? Do you think she'll recover? Has she spoken at all?' she asked, her words tumbling over themselves as her heart raced.

'We will know more tomorrow. Please call back then.'

'Thank you,' she replied quietly, realising that further questions at this point were futile, as she would receive no answers.

She lay there, knowing that she should tidy up her mother's place and get a bag together to take to the hospital, before going back to her own empty, desolate house, but she could not seem to move.

Part II

Chapter Twenty

The interesting thing about being considered unremarkable is that you mostly pass by unnoticed, and this in turn provides a unique opportunity for you to notice absolutely everything.

Daniel was indeed quite unremarkable. Of average height – five foot ten inches – with a pleasant face and with features arranged in a perfectly acceptable way, neither bordering on ugly nor handsome. He preferred to dress inoffensively; without any particular sense of style, but without being too obviously scruffy. He was sociable when spoken to, but not over-confident, preferring to absorb and learn rather than express any particular opinions of his own. Academically, he was mediocre, neither struggling nor over-achieving. He was simply middling.

Daniel did have an overlooked, special gift, however. As an attentive wallflower and an exceptional listener, he found that he could uncover people's secrets and this, he quickly discovered, was a superpower that he could easily turn to his own advantage. It began to blossom at school, where he worked out who was responsible for stealing money from people's lockers or smoking weed in the toilets. This might have led him to a job in the police force, where there is little doubt that he would have had a highly successful career as a detective, much like his much-admired hero, Hercule Poirot. However, Daniel chose to profit personally rather than professionally from the information that he gleaned and the more he succeeded with each endeavour, the more he enjoyed it.

He began small, blackmailing the dinner money thieves by threatening to reveal their identities to the headmaster. He took a cut of the cash in order to guarantee his silence. Later, he did the same with the cannabis smokers who lurked in the loos. He got paid to remain anonymous and he was extremely talented at being anonymous. It was as if he was never really there.

Chapter Twenty-One

'What are you doing?' Ben demanded as he filled the doorway, his shirt untucked and with a large ink stain down the front of his striped tie.

Angie started.

'Jesus, Ben. I didn't hear you come in. You scared me.'

'You must be going completely deaf.'

He threw his school bag onto the landing behind him with a thump and stepped into the room, still wearing his filthy trainers and spraying mud in various directions onto the oatmeal carpet.

'What is all this?' He pointed at the piles of letters scattered all around Angie on the floor. 'If I'd left my room in such a mess, you'd bloody murder me.'

'I'm, well, I'm just having a tidy up, that's all. I must have lost track of the time. Are you hungry?'

'I'm always hungry.'

'Come on then, I'll make you some pasta,' she replied, standing up with difficulty because her legs had cramped up from kneeling on the floor for so long. She began to usher Ben out of the room, but he dodged past her and picked up one of the bank statements which were strewn right across the floor.

'Who's Neil Edmonton? And how come he's got so much money?'

'I don't know. It's obviously some old correspondence from when your granny lived here. Come on, out of here, Ben.'

'And who's Liam McNeill?' he asked, picking up another. 'And why are none of these addressed to the house?' He turned to her, waving the paper at her.

'I don't know, Ben. Truthfully, I don't. I've only just found them.'

'Well, some of these are not that old, look. Some of these are dated last year and the year before that.' He pulled a letter from its envelope. 'This one's older. Christ, have you seen? It's for £55,000. Who's David Prince?'

'I've told you, I simply don't know, Ben. I don't know what any of this is. It's a mystery.'

'Maybe these are all Dad's work aliases that they set him up with and the bank accounts are part of his cover story? I'll ask him when he finally comes home.'

'No, Ben, I don't want you to do that. Please. Just don't mention it to him.' She spoke more sharply than she meant to.

'Why not?' Ben picked up another envelope and pulled out the contents. 'Ah, I get it. You've been snooping around in his stuff, and he'll go batshit crazy if he finds out.'

'Yes, you're obviously right. He wouldn't like it, would he?'

'Well, it would serve you right, wouldn't it? You shouldn't poke your nose into other people's things.' He paused. 'Is that what you do in my room when I'm at school?'

'Of course not. I only go into your room to hoover, dust, and hang your clothes up. And these days sometimes I don't even bother doing that.' She blushed heavily, thinking about the tablets and the fact that she had snooped, though had not summoned up the courage to confront him as yet.

'I don't believe you. I bet you're in there all the time.'

'Believe me, Ben, I've got better things to do with my time than spend it in your smelly bedroom.'

'Have you really? I doubt that very much.' He shoved past her and picked up his bag, barrelling into his bedroom and slamming the door behind him. Moments later, she was greeted with Post Malone blaring out from Ben's speakers.

'*I'll make dinner now*,' Angie decided. Food always improved his mood. He was dreadful when he was hangry.

Chapter Twenty-Two

Marjorie lay motionless in bed, a barely living corpse: her breath shallow, skin waxy, mouth hanging open, eyes unseeing. She had remained exactly like this ever since her stroke, unable to communicate except by the occasional squeeze of her fingers around Diana's hand, and even then the pressure she could exert barely registered. The doctors had warned Diana that her mother would be unlikely to recover her powers of speech or movement, such was the severity of the damage the stroke had wrought on her ageing brain. They had shown Diana the moving images from the CT scan, but the psychedelic film meant nothing to her, and she struggled to relate them to the person who was now lying catatonic in a hospital ward. She rued all the times that she had cursed her mother's sharp tongue and even her various silly accidents. At least in those moments, however irritating, she had had a life of sorts. Now, she had no reason to go on.

The hospital was intending to transfer Marjorie to a nursing home as soon as they could find a suitable place for her intensive needs, and they had drawn up the discharge plan. This process was clearly going to take some time, not only because they had to find the right home with the right facilities, but also because the system appeared to be in chaos. There were too many departments involved between the NHS and Social Care and it seemed to Diana that they were all run quite separately, despite the fact that they must have to deal with moving older people from hospital to care and vice versa all the time. It was particularly frustrating to be the relative, stuck in the middle feeling at the same time utterly helpless and extraordinarily frustrated. It took all of Diana's willpower to stop herself from shouting at them, but she was sensible enough to realise that raising her voice would probably only slow the process down even further. She knew deep down that they were doing their best and that, sadly, her mother was not the only person in such a terrible predicament.

In the meantime, she dutifully visited her mother every day, wittering on to her endlessly about everything and nothing, and when she faltered with that, she just stared at her mother, wondering for how long she would have to suffer in this vegetative state before finally finding peace. Some people managed to survive for an extremely long time in such a condition and the prospect of this seemed terribly cruel for both of them. Sometimes, she wondered whether smothering her mother with a pillow might be the kindest thing to do, but of course, she would never have actually done it. However, in her darkest moments, Diana wished that someone would do it to her, such was the depth of despair in which she was currently drowning.

She was also grappling with Patrick's probate. The forms she was required to complete were daunting and highly complex, consisting of one main form and then many sub-forms relating to specific sections. She contemplated hiring a lawyer to help her, but she dismissed this as an unnecessary expense, believing that she could do it alone if she could only concentrate properly. Of course, this was easier said than done. She felt more exhausted than she could ever remember, which of course was totally understandable given the trauma of Patrick's death and her mother's illness, not to mention the theft of her mother's money, which she was still no nearer to recovering. Her brain felt like it was out of battery, sluggish and distracted. She would sit down to begin a task and then find herself staring into space, or checking the weather app on her phone for the umpteenth time that day when she could have just looked out of the window.

She had at least managed to get into Patrick's bank account. They had always held a joint account for household bills, which Patrick had paid in the main, but they also held separate accounts; Patrick's for his personal use and she had her own, as well as her business account for the shop. She had never stopped to consider what Patrick might use his account for. In her own case, she used it for clothes, hairdressing, gifts and so on and she assumed that he had done the same. When she finally did access his account online, his payments were rather minimal. His credit card bill was paid off monthly in full and he had a couple of subscriptions to gardening magazines and one to *Private Eye*. There was a monthly donation to the local church and another to the charity Crisis. There were very few personal expenses. Patrick had never been one to shop for himself or others. However, there was one significant monthly payment to an individual, an H. Carpenter, who did not appear to be linked to a particular business and of whom she had never heard. Patrick had been paying him one thousand pounds every month dating back over many years. Diana wiped her face with her clammy hands, her heart pounding. She had no idea who Patrick had been paying, or for that matter, why.

She logged into his credit card statements, which she also now had access to, but they offered no further clue as to the identity of this mysterious man. What was extremely odd, however, was that there were no payments showing for any of the bizarre purchases that Patrick had sent to her after he died. So, if they were not showing on his bank account or on his card statements, how had he paid for them? She had assumed that when she returned the goods, the refunds would show up, but they were not there either. She searched all his papers for signs of an additional bank card, but she found nothing.

Diana snapped her iPad shut, panic gripping her chest like a tight fist. Perhaps she had never known this man with whom she had spent the last forty years. Was it possible that they had shared the same bed, the same food, the same house, and yet he had been so completely unknown to her? Well, she decided, slapping the table where she sat so hard that she hurt her palm, if she never really knew him when she was alive, she was damned sure she was going to find out the truth about him now that he was dead.

Chapter Twenty-Three

Daniel had always felt that he did not quite fit in anywhere.

His sense of unease with the world had begun at home. His parents, or rather his guardians as he preferred to think of them, had made it very clear from an early age that he was adopted.

'But we love you just as much as we would if you were our own child, Daniel. You must always remember that,' his mother had reassured him, hugging him close to her bony chest, pressing the life out of him.

His father was a largely distant figure, out working all day and quite often not returning until the early hours, usually stinking of cigarettes and whisky. He had little patience for Daniel, shushing him whenever he prattled on. When his father was particularly tired, which was usually after one of his benders, he would wallop Daniel across the back of his legs with his hand. The slap would sting his tender skin and tears would begin to fall.

'Stop being such a sissy, Dan,' his father would scold.

At such times, when his father showed him no sympathy, his mother would usher him out of the room and take him into the kitchen for a biscuit and a cuddle.

When Daniel was eight years old, a miracle occurred. His mother, now almost forty, fell pregnant, despite being told by several doctors over many years that she was infertile. His sister, or half-sister, or not really a sister at all in truth, arrived just before Daniel's ninth birthday and everything changed. His father, up until this moment a man who apparently had no truck with children and the interference they wrought upon his life, transformed overnight into a doting parent, but only as far as his new-born was concerned.

'Hey, Jackie, my gorgeous girl,' his father cooed, jiggling his daughter on his knee, and kissing the top of her head. He had never once sat Daniel on his knee, or found the time to play with him.

His mother battled extremely hard to retain her affection for Daniel, but her daughter was her own flesh and blood, and she was a pretty little thing. She dressed her up in frilly clothes and flaunted her in front of his father like an expensive doll, because she knew it pleased him and that made living with him easier for her. Daniel became her helper, or slave as he came to think of it: fetching and carrying nappies and bottles, running errands and being a big, grown-up boy. He was too old for even the uncalled-for cuddles now Jackie had arrived.

Chapter Twenty-Four

———

Sleep was extremely elusive these days, so Angie had begun to bake in the small hours of the morning. At 2 a.m. on this particular day, she had endeavoured to make a chocolate sponge cake, and she was gratified that it had turned out rather well, overflowing in the centre with thick whipped cream.

That afternoon, she set it down in front of Julia with a flourish.

'My goodness, it's as if the Mary Berry fairy has visited your kitchen in the middle of the night!' Julia exclaimed, unwittingly licking her lips.

'Would you like some?' Angie asked, knowing that it was a stupid question.

'Absolutely! I'm bloody starving. I've been on the go all day, so this is such a treat.'

Julia took one of the plates that Angie had placed on the table earlier and held it out in anticipation. Angie cut a generous slice and carefully manoeuvred it onto the plate.

Julia took an enormous bite without setting the plate down first. 'Jesus, Ange, this is fucking fabulous,' she declared, her words muffled by her mouthful.

'I'm glad you like it. I was watching *Bake Off* the other night and suddenly felt inspired. I actually find it very relaxing, especially when I can't sleep.'

'I bloody hate baking. It's one of the most stressful things anyone can do. I get all the measurements wrong, or I forget an ingredient - or often both - and then I can't remember when I put it in the oven, or I wander off to do something else and an hour later the house smells like it's on fire and then I have to chuck the whole thing in the bin.' She smiled and took another bite. 'The bit I do like is the cake mix though. Sometimes, there's nothing left to go in the tin!'

Angie laughed as she handed Julia a mug of tea and sat down at the table opposite her.

'Are you alright, Ange? If you don't mind me saying so, you do look a bit peaky.'

'I'm OK, I suppose. I'm just struggling a bit with Ben.' She cut herself a sliver of cake and ate it off the knife.

'Bloody teenagers. We should have both got dogs instead. Mind you, I've got two of those as well, and they are completely crazy, so I'm not one to give advice.' Julia paused. 'Is it something in particular with Ben, or just the usual surly adolescent crap?'

'I don't know. I'm finding it difficult to adjust from mothering the boy who told me everything to the one who tells me nothing, or worse, just grunts at me. It really doesn't help that Ray has been missing in action for so long. Ben really misses him when he's away for longer than usual, and I need him to come home to play bad cop.'

'Still no word?' Julia cut herself another slice of cake and more for Angie while she was at it. 'Eat some sugar. It calms the nerves!'

Angie pushed the plate away from her and began to fiddle with the cuff of her sweater, which had begun to fray.

'I just don't know where Ray is, and on top of that -' She hesitated.

'On top of that what?'

'I don't know if I should say or not. It's quite personal.'

Angie felt her face glow red.

'Don't tell me you're having an affair! Is it that new teacher who's just started at the primary school? He's hot, and I spotted you chatting to him in the SPAR the other day.'

'Don't be ridiculous! He's also not much older than our boys, Julia.'

'No, but a toy boy might be just what you need to cheer you up a little!' She slapped Angie on the arm playfully. 'Let's face it, your sex life is effectively non-existent. I'm not surprised you can't sleep.'

'Julia, stop it. I am *not* having an affair, and I'm not interested in toy boys or anyone else for that matter. It's just that I found something, and I don't know what to do.'

'Jesus, Ange. If you've found a lump, you must go to the GP straight away. It's no good pretending it's not there. My aunt did that, and she died within the year from stage four breast cancer. No, that's it! We are calling the doctor right now to make an appointment and -'

'Julia, no, I have not found a lump. There is nothing physically wrong with me at all. At least, nothing that I am aware of. That's not it at all.' She rocked back on her wooden chair and almost overbalanced, grabbing onto the kitchen table to right herself again.

'So, what *is* going on?' Julia leaned towards her and held her hand. 'You can tell me, Ange. I won't tell a soul. You know that.'

Angie closed her eyes for a moment. 'If I do tell you, you can't say anything to anyone. Promise me.'

'I just told you that I wouldn't. What is it? Just tell me. I can't bear this.'

'Well, it's very odd. The thing is, I found a load of papers, none of which make any sense. There are letters and bank accounts all addressed to all sorts of different men at different addresses.'

'Where did you find them?'

'In Ray's wardrobe. I was in there, cleaning, you know, and I looked up and saw a ribbon sticking out of a flap in the wall. I'd never seen it before.' She paused. 'Clearly, I'm not the best cleaner!'

'I make it a rule never to look up or to delve into corners. If I don't look, no one else in my house will.'

'True. But the fact is that I did look up and I pulled at the ribbon and all these papers fell out. And I don't know what they are, and I don't know who they belong to, but I can guess that Ray must have something to do with them. And I simply don't know what to do next. I can't contact him, and he hasn't contacted me, I don't know if he's alive or dead. But worse than that, I'm not even sure who he is anymore. And that's what really frightens me.' A tiny tear drizzled from the corner of her eye, and she rushed to wipe it away with her hand.

'Angie, oh you poor thing. Look, I'm sure we can get to the bottom of this. If you'd like me to have a look at them and see if I can help, I'm very happy to, but only if that's what you want.'

Julia drained her mug.

Angie nodded. 'Yes, I think I would like to show them to you, if you don't mind.'

'Not at all. Lead on, Macduff,' she announced, rising from her chair. Angie stayed sitting.

'Come on, Ange. There's no time like the present, two heads are better than one etc. etc. I guarantee that I will keep on spouting cliches until you get up and show me these sodding papers.'

Angie smiled weakly and stood up. 'Follow me.'

An hour later, they had polished off the rest of the cake and had papers strewn all across the kitchen table. Angie had been worried about bringing them all downstairs - in case it was even more obvious that she had looked that them when Ray did eventually return - but Julia had been right when she suggested that sorting them out on the large, wooden table in the kitchen would be much easier than attempting to look at such a wealth of information on a small patch of carpet.

'Well, I really can't seem to spot any kind of obvious pattern here. Clearly, some of the accounts show regular payments coming in and others are one-off sums. Amounts vary considerably. There are three letters where the money appears to come from being named as a beneficiary in a will. But all of them are in different names, as you said. It's so weird.'

Julia glanced up at Angie, who appeared ashen under the harsh halogen lights. 'You OK?'

Angie gulped and passed a document over to Julia without speaking.

'So, this one is in Ray's name, is it?'

'Yes, it appears to be the only one. But look what it is.'

'The deeds for your house.'

'Yes, that's right.' She took the paper back and pointed to the top of the page. 'But look, Jules. It's dated two months after my mother died. She left the house to me. Ray and I agreed to transfer ownership into joint names, but this states that it belongs solely to him.' She leant back on her chair and closed her eyes. 'I feel sick.'

'But how did he manage to do that without you signing it away? Unless -' she hesitated.

Angie opened her eyes. 'Unless he forged my signature somehow. But I just can't believe he'd do that. I trust him implicitly. I always have.'

Julia emitted a strange noise, the meaning of which was suggestive of a lower level of confidence.

'Or unless you didn't read the paperwork properly when he put it in front of you. I mean, your mother had just died and you were pregnant. Just one of those events is enough to mess up your head, but together, it could have scrambled your brain completely.'

'What the hell do I do now? I feel like I can't be sure of anything anymore,' Angie whispered in a voice strangled by emotion.

'I think you have two options. Either you confront Ray with all of this.' She waved a sheaf of papers in the air. 'But I think that might prove unsatisfactory, or possibly dangerous.'

'Dangerous? I really don't think so. Ray's never touched a hair on my head, or been aggressive towards me ever. I just can't see it.'

'But he's always been in charge, hasn't he? You don't know how he'll behave if he's challenged.'

Angie jumped up from her chair. 'Look, I know you've never liked Ray, but he's my husband and I love him, and I do challenge him from time to time, but it's difficult because of his work and ...'

'Calm down. I've never said I don't like him. I don't know him well enough to have an in-depth opinion of the man, but you must admit that this is all very odd. I'm merely proposing that you need to handle the situation carefully, just in case.'

'So, what do you suggest?' Angie flumped back onto her chair, her body suddenly weary with exhaustion.

'Option two.'

'Which is?'

'Which is we work through all the names and addresses on these documents and try to trace who has made these payments and who they made them to.'

'I wouldn't know where to start,' Angie struggled to hold back tears.

'I'll help you, OK? Together, I'm sure we can figure it out. And once we know more, it will be easier for you to have the necessary conversations with Ray. There may be a perfectly innocent explanation.'

Julia fought the urge to roll her eyes.

'Ben thinks these are all work aliases.'

'And maybe they are. But if they are, why would they be here and not in his office? And can I ask, why would he need aliases if he works as a diplomat in the Foreign Office?'

'Because he doesn't,' Angie replied in a small voice. 'He works for MI5, but you must never tell anyone that I told you that.'

'So, he's a spook?'

'Effectively, yes.'

'Hmm, OK, well that might make this more plausible, I suppose. But I still think we should do some sleuthing of our own, just to see what we can find out.'

'But what if Ray discovers that we are prying into his work. He'll go bloody berserk.'

'Look, some of these papers are not as recent, with payments stopping ages ago. They are dead cases, I suspect, so why don't we start there.'

Angie stared at Julia, wordless.

'Let me think about it and I'll come up with a plan. Leave it with me and in the meantime, try not to stress. I'm sure it'll turn out to be nothing to worry about.'

'But you don't think so really, do you?'

'No, I'm afraid I don't.'

Chapter Twenty-Five

———

Ian had turned out to be an absolute godsend. While Diana had been utterly distracted with Patrick's death and then by her mother's stroke, and the financial fraud, she had been forced to shut the shop. She knew that she might have to decide to close it if she could not go back to running it fulltime as before. The rent and rates alone were crippling her without the sales to pay for them. But she was also aware that once she got through this horrific period in her life - if indeed she did get through it - the shop would be more important than ever to give her days meaning.

She had not seen or heard from Ian since he had opened up to her after the funeral, but he got back in touch a week or so after Marjorie's stroke and asked if Diana would like to meet him for a coffee to catch up. Diana was unsure at first, preferring her own company to that of anyone else's at the moment. The thought of making conversation with anyone was simply too exhausting, on top of which she looked dreadful. Her skin was dry and flaking, her hair lank, and she sported deep, dark circles under her eyes. Even worse, she did not seem to have the energy or the desire to try to cover them up, which was unusual for her, as she had always taken great pride in her appearance. But Ian had been so solicitous and kind on the phone when she told him about

Marjorie's stroke that she capitulated and agreed to meet him in Costa in Harpenden on a drizzly, cold Wednesday afternoon.

He was already there when she arrived and had seated himself discreetly on a fraying red velour sofa at the back of the cafe.

'I took the liberty of ordering you a latte and a piece of lemon cake.'

'That's very kind of you, thank you. I'm not sure that I'll manage the cake, to be honest. My appetite seems to have completely disappeared.'

She laid her dripping umbrella onto the floor and sat down.

'Thanks for the coffee. I think it's the only thing keeping me going at the moment. Caffeine, I mean.' She lifted the cup to her lips and took a sip.

'You have lost quite a bit of weight, Diana. You must look after yourself.' He passed her the plate with the cake sitting on it. 'Here, at least try to have a small bite.' He held out the cake.

'Listen to you, Ian! You're what? Twenty years younger than me and – '

'Sixteen,' he interrupted.

She looked at him in surprise. 'OK, if you say so, sixteen, but either way, you're talking to me as if you're my parent.' She paused. 'Don't take that the wrong way. It's very sweet, I just don't know why you'd want to hang out with an old lady like me.'

'What's age got to do with it? I'm friends with people of all ages. I believe that age doesn't matter, because it should be about what a person is like, not what age band you place them in.'

'No, you're right, of course. But it's a refreshing viewpoint that many people don't hold necessarily.' She took the proffered plate from him and nibbled a tiny piece of the cake. 'That's actually very nice,' she commented, taking a bigger bite before leaning forward and placing the plate back onto the low coffee table in front of them.

'So, how's your mum doing?'

'Oh, she's exactly the same sadly. No progress whatsoever.'

'And the prognosis?'

'Not good. They don't expect her to recover either her speech or her mobility. It's a question of keeping her comfortable until she eventually passes away. But of course, that may not be for many years. Having googled it - which I know you should never do, but everyone still does - it appears that people can live in a vegetative state for years.' She sipped at her coffee again.

'So can she recognise anyone at all?'

'I don't know. It's impossible to tell.'

'And will she stay in hospital?'

'No, she'll have to move to a home. I'm waiting on confirmation of where she will go. It's a genuine nightmare finding the right home that can provide the appropriate level of care, and which is local. I also have no idea what it will cost, because as I say, it may be long-term, and she doesn't have any money apart from the bungalow.' Diana took another bite of cake. 'Do you know, I think this is just what I needed.'

'So, she hasn't any savings?'

'Well, she did have quite a bit of money saved, but it appears that she has been scammed out of it by some awful guy who befriended her by pretending to be from the council, and then got her to sign over all her money to him. It's just terrible.'

'Oh, Diana. I'm so sorry. How dreadful for you.' Ian patted her arm and Diana flinched involuntarily. 'There really are some wicked people out there.'

'I know. I'm at my wits' end. It's been one thing after another and -' she bit her lip to try to stop her tears from forming, but a couple slid down her cheeks before she could wipe them away. '- and, well, I feel so guilty about it, because I've been so distracted with Patrick dying that I didn't even attempt to find out about this man when Mum first mentioned him and if I had she might not have had a stroke or lost all her money.' She took another sip of coffee in an attempt to calm herself. 'And on top of all this, I've had to keep the shop closed, as I am spending so much time with Mum, or on the phone with the bank, or the police, or sorting Patrick's probate. Even if I was there, I'd be effectively useless, as I can't even think straight at the moment and the very last thing I want to do is to talk to bloody customers. I'm coming to the sad reality that I think I might have to close it permanently. If I can't stay open, I'll have to sell, as I just can't afford to keep it going.' She drained her coffee and looked at Ian. 'I am so sorry to offload all of that on you. You're the first person I've spoken to properly since everything has happened and I'm afraid you are bearing the brunt of it.'

'Don't be silly. That's what friends are for, isn't it?'

She placed her cup back onto the table and stood up, picking up her handbag which was beside her on the couch. 'My round, I think,' she declared.

'Thanks, Diana. I'll have another hot chocolate please.'

'Cream?'

'Definitely.'

'You do have a sweet tooth, don't you? OK, I'll be back in a minute.'

When she returned, balancing two cups and another slice of cake, Ian stood and helped her to put them on the table.

'I reciprocated and got you some chocolate fudge cake.'

'Thanks so much.' Ian took an enormous bite. 'That's delicious,' he declared. 'Now I could eat that all day!' He chomped on the cake again and then set it aside. 'Look, Diana, I've got a proposition for you, which might just help you out. You can say no, obviously, but at least hear me out. I've just resigned from my job. It's a long and very tedious story, which I won't bore you with right now, but as I'm free for a while, why don't I run the shop for you? If you can spare a few hours to take me through everything - the till, the stock control, how to work the till and what not - I'm sure I can do a decent job of it and then when you're feeling more in control, you can take over again. What do you think?'

Diana almost spilt her coffee onto her lap.

'Well, I don't quite know what to say. I mean, it would obviously be an enormous help and a huge weight off my mind, and I suppose that it would mean I can stay afloat until I get all the other stuff in my life sorted out. But, I mean, are you absolutely sure?'

'I've never felt so certain of anything in my life,' he declared slurping his hot chocolate and then licking the cream off his lips. 'You're a lovely lady and you're going through a horrendous time at the moment. It would be a great pleasure to help you out.'

She placed her coffee cup back onto the table and slumped back on the sofa.

'Well, I suppose it would be a great temporary measure. Wow, Ian, I can't quite believe it. It seems like you're a small ray of sunshine in my otherwise dark existence. Wasn't it lucky that I met you that day when you came into my shop?'

Chapter Twenty-Six

Daniel's parents had always been somewhat vague when it came to filling him in on his origins. When he was younger, his mother fed him a variety of different stories about how they came to adopt him. In one story, he had been left on the church steps and the vicar had asked the congregation the following Sunday if anyone wanted to adopt a new baby. Another version ran that he had been left by an unknown passer-by on their doorstep. Alternatively, the doctor had found him at his surgery one day and given him to his current parents as he knew they could not have a baby of their own.

'But Mummy, which story is actually true?' Daniel demanded, tapping her on the leg with his remarkably strong eight-year-old arm.

'They are all sort of are, darling,' she soothed, drawing him in for a cuddle, but he wriggled free.

'That's silly, Mummy. They can't all be right. It doesn't make any sense.'

'Well, Mummy is a bit silly, isn't she?' she smiled. 'Now, I need to go and make your father's tea. Do you want to help me?'

And she would wander off into the kitchen leaving Daniel feeling increasingly frustrated and distrustful.

Once his infamous little sister arrived, no one would answer him on the subject at all - his mother and father claiming they were far too busy to have the conversation at that particular moment in time - and so they never had the conversation at all.

'And anyway, Daniel, what does it matter now anyway? We are your family,' his mother soothed.

'But why didn't my real parents want me?!'

'Because they knew how annoying you were going to be, that's why,' his father retorted. 'Now go and find me my slippers.'

'And be quiet about it, Daniel. Your sister is sleeping,' his mother urged him.

When Daniel was fifteen, he marched up to the desk of his local library. He spent a great deal of time rooting around its shelves each week, as he loved reading all kinds of books, although his favourite were adventure stories.

'Hello, Daniel. How are you this afternoon?' whispered Mrs McCavity, an ageing Scotswoman, who always dressed from head to foot in brown, including her ageing Hush Puppies.

Daniel believed she wore them because their brand name implied silence.

She was extremely short, her head only just appearing above the edge of the giant desk. Daniel already towered over her, yet she exerted a distinct authority which he did not dare to test too far.

Daniel heaved a pile of books onto the desk.

'Fine, thank you.'

'Have you read all of those already, young man?' she hissed in her soft, Highland twang. 'We'll be running out of books in no time at the rate you're reading them.'

Daniel did not smile. 'Can I ask you where you keep the records of births, deaths, and marriages please?'

'Well, we don't keep them here. They are all kept centrally at the National Archives. Why? Are you doing a project at school?'

'Something like that. It's like a personal history.'

'So, why don't you ask your parents to show you your birth certificate? That would be the best place to begin.'

'It's complicated. My parents don't seem to keep any paperwork, and I don't want to bother them when they are so busy.'

Mrs McCavity frowned at Daniel. 'Well, I still suggest that you ask them. They will definitely have your birth certificate somewhere. It's a very important document and everyone keeps it at home.'

Daniel hopped from one foot to the other. 'But supposing they can't find it, how would I get hold of a copy from the National Archives?'

'The simple answer is that you can't without their permission, or at least not until you're eighteen. Until you reach the age of majority, you need to have their consent.'

'But that's ridiculous!' Daniel exclaimed, raising his voice.

'Shush, Daniel, this is a library,' she reminded him.

Daniel clenched his fists by his sides and grimaced.

'Why do children in this country have no rights?' he muttered.

'You do have rights, but there are laws in place to protect you.'

'But why do I need a law to stop me from seeing my own birth certificate?'

'In your case, Daniel, I can't necessarily see a problem and I'm sure if you ask your parents again, they can help you to find it so you can complete your project. But in other instances, children need shielding from certain pieces of information until they are old enough to know how to process it.' She picked up the stack of books that Daniel had returned and placed her glasses on the end of her nose, which otherwise hung on a lengthy metal chain bouncing over her ample chest. She opened the first of the books to begin stamping the date, signalling the end of their conversation.

'What sort of information?'

She peered over her spectacles at him and tutted. 'Say for example that you were adopted. There may be several reasons why adoptive parents might be concerned about telling a child who their real parents are until they are old enough to understand.'

'What sort of reasons?' Daniel asked, rising up on his tiptoes to lean over the desk in a vain attempt to increase his stature.

'Could be anything, Daniel. Now, are you here to choose a book, or are you leaving? Your mother must be expecting you home for tea and I have better things to do than stand around discussing hypotheticals with you.'

'I'm leaving, don't worry,' he harrumphed, turning away, and slouching towards the door. On his way out, he kicked the plastic guide dog full of coins destined for charity. It had been a wasted exercise except for one key piece of information that he had picked up. He now knew that his birth certificate must be somewhere at home. All he needed to do now was to find it.

Chapter Twenty-Seven

Angie's mobile alerted her to a new WhatsApp message.

'Found our first possible lead. Pick you up this afternoon at 2.'

'Got to finish leaflet by 3.'

'Finish it by 2.'

Angie sent a thumbs up. There was no way she could finish the copy by two, but she had learnt some years ago that Julia could not be argued with when she was determined to do something, so she decided to go with the flow. She felt queasy for the rest of the morning, unsure about pursuing any of this. In a way, she wished she had never mentioned it to Julia, but she had had to tell someone. Worry and suspicion were eating her up from the inside and she knew that she had to make it stop.

Julia honked her car horn at five minutes to two, but Angie was already waiting by the front door looking out for her, wrapped up in last year's pale pink Uniqlo puffer and her new boots, that she had treated herself to recently in an Asos sale. The weather was filthy, and they got soaked just rushing from the front door to the kerb.

'Jesus, this fucking rain!' she exclaimed as she jumped into the passenger seat, slamming the door behind her. 'Is it ever going to stop?'

'I don't know why you're moaning, Ange. I had to walk the sodding dogs in it this morning and by the time we got back, we all needed another bath.'

Julia laughed as she indicated to pull away.

'Where are we going exactly?' Angie enquired, turning the blower on the dashboard towards her to try to direct a small semblance of heat at her trembling body.

'Just outside Cambridge. I found a guy there whose name matched one of the payments.'

'How did you do that?' Angie enquired.

'Well,' Julia began, turning down Ed Sheeran who was warbling about shivers on the radio. 'I searched on Google for some of the names and most of them either drew a blank or there were a thousand people with the same name. But this guy's name appeared as part of a newspaper story. And he was local, so I called the paper and asked if they had his contact details. I said I was a lawyer following up on the story, as I had been dealing with similar cases myself and it would be helpful to speak to this chap. Miraculously, they gave it to me, which frankly scared the hell out of me, as clearly data protection is not high on their list of priorities, but anyway.'

'Hang on, go back. Which paper? What similar cases?'

Julia unwrapped a toffee from one of the many that overflowed in the cup holders below the dashboard. 'Want one?' she offered Angie.

'No thanks,' Angie replied, wishing that Julia would keep her eyes on the road ahead. She was a terrifying driver, always too close to the car in front.

'So,' Julia chomped, 'this guy is called Jim Grant and he paid £25,000 to a man called Brandon Bell.'

'Yes, I remember that name from the statements. It's very alliterative,' commented Angie as she gripped the inside of the door as if this would protect her in the event of a crash.

'Correct. Look, all I know is that Jim was the victim of fraud. It was a three-line article in the paper, which said the man who defrauded him was never caught. So, I thought we should ask Jim directly and see if he can tell us anything about this character who scammed him. Look, we're here now.'

They turned off a narrow lane and down a long drive, just avoiding a deer that ran across their path.

'That was close,' Julia chortled.

Angie was thankful to arrive. 'What is this place? A stately home?'

'He wishes, I'm sure. No, it's a care home.'

'Oh, I see.' Angie paused. 'So, what are we going to say to him? We can't just walk in and start asking him questions.'

'Don't worry, Ange. Just follow my lead,' Julia reassured her, parking haphazardly across two spaces in the car park. 'You ready?'

Angie nodded and ran across the drive to the front of the care home, the rain as intense as before. They pressed the buzzer, huddling under the small cloth awning that offered scant protection from the storm. The door released and they entered into the brightly lit hallway.

'I think it's this way,' Angie indicated, pointing at the sign to the reception.

They made their way along a narrow corridor towards a desk at the bottom.

'Can I help you?' the woman behind the desk asked, turning her head away from her computer screen and looking up as they approached.

'My name is Julia. I called earlier to arrange a visit with Mr Grant.'

'Ah yes, sign here please.'

She passed a visitors' book across the desk, which they both duly signed.

'Jim is in the TV room just along the hall. I told him you were coming.'

'Thank you.'

They could hear the television blaring away from the reception, so the room was not difficult to locate. There were several armchairs arranged in a row all facing the screen. David Dickinson was screaming out quiz questions, but no one in the room appeared to be listening. Two ladies were snoozing, one of whom was snoring almost as loudly as the television was shouting, and there was an older man sitting quietly in a chair at the end, his eyes also closed. He was smartly dressed in khaki cotton chinos and a blue shirt.

The women approached him. Julia reached out and gently touched his arm. He opened his eyes, which were cloudy blue and unseeing.

'Mr Grant, I'm sorry to disturb you. My name is Julia, and this is my colleague, Angela. We are investigating old cases of fraud and wondered if we might ask you a couple of questions.'

Jim inclined his head towards them. 'Hello. Yes, they told me you were coming.'

'Hello,' Angie replied.

'Are you police?' he whispered.

'No, Mr Grant, we are journalists trying to get more information on fraud in Cambridgeshire as part of a wider story. If we are successful, we hope that the police might be able to use some of the information, but we don't know yet,' Angie reassured him.

'So, Mr Grant, or may I call you Jim?' Julia asked, pulling over a chair to sit next to him. Angie grabbed another chair and seated herself on his other side.

'Call me Jim.' He reached out and fumbled for Julia's hand, which once found, he held onto tightly.

'So, Jim, we understand that a number of years ago you knew a man called Brandon Bell?' Julia began.

Jim twitched involuntarily.

Angie reached forward and held his other hand. Jim squeezed hers in reply.

'Do you remember him at all?' Angie stroked his hand.

'Who?'

'Brandon.'

He twitched again. 'I do, unfortunately.'

'Can you tell us anything about him?' Julia asked.

'He seemed like a nice fellow. I met him playing bridge — before I lost my sight, obviously. He used to run the local centre where we played and if we were short, he would make up a four. Charming chap. Very chatty. He used to bring in biscuits from M&S. You know, the really good chocolatey ones.'

'And can you tell us what happened with your money?' Angie asked gently.

'He, Brandon that is, said that he'd help me out, you see. My bank was going to go under, he told me. He said that he had inside information from a good friend of his and he wanted to tip me off before I lost all my money. He offered to transfer it to a safer bank for me. He said it would save me trouble if he did it and I was never very good with that sort of thing.' He began to shake slightly, and his eyes grew watery.

'So, you transferred money to him and then what happened?'

'I never saw him or my money again.' Jim began to cry silently.

Angie rummaged in her handbag and found a packet of pocket tissues. She handed one to him and he wiped his face.

'Sorry,' he muttered. 'It's just that I feel so ashamed, you know, to have been taken for a total mug.'

'Don't be silly, Jim. We are sorry that we have upset you.' Angie squeezed his hand, glancing at Julia. 'These things can happen to anyone.'

'What did Brandon look like, Jim?' Julia asked.

'He was average-looking, I suppose, not especially handsome or ugly. Non-descript, really. He was quite quiet, and he liked to listen to our stories. I thought he was a friend, even though he was much younger than me. I did wonder why he liked hanging around with older people so much, but some people just do, don't they?'

'They do. I have a lot of older friends myself,' Julia reassured him.

'Can you get my money back?' Jim's eyes grew red and sore.

'I don't think so, as this was quite a few years ago now, but if we can, we will. I promise we will do our best.' Angie rubbed his arm.

'It was my life savings, you know. It was all I had. I was such an idiot.'

'Not at all, Jim. You weren't to know.'

'It was the bank, you see. It was going bust. I was going to lose everything.'

Julia and Angie drove home in silence. When Julia dropped Angie home, Angie asked if she would like to come in for a cup of tea.

'I would like to come in for a brandy, actually, but I need to get home. That poor man! How could that guy do that to him?'

'But we learned nothing about who he was or even what he looked like. We've just distressed a lovely old man for no reason.'

'Shame he couldn't have looked at the photo I took with me.'

'Of who?'

'Of Ray. In case he recognised him. You know, in case he's somehow involved.'

Angie felt panic rising in her chest.

'I don't feel comfortable with that, Julia. We could blow Ray's cover going around showing his photo. We still have no idea what we are dealing with here.'

Julia opened her mouth as if to say something, but thought better of it.

A moment later, she said, 'But we did establish that one of the documents in your house is linked to fraud, so we need to try to find out about some of the others to see if there is some sort of pattern.'

'I'm exhausted after today and I'm not sure I've got the stomach for any more of this. What are we even going to do with any of this information if we do find more people?'

'I don't know, but we simply can't stop now.'

Chapter Twenty-Eight

Diana was no closer to discovering the identity of Mr H. Carpenter. She had contacted the bank where he held his account, but they were unable to give her any details at all, so she was still at a complete loss as to who he was. Diana sat at home one evening, sipping mint tea and nibbling on a square of dark chocolate, which was all she fancied eating these days. She could not even concentrate on reading, which she normally loved, often losing herself for hours between the pages of a book. These days she spent a great deal of time simply staring into space, wondering how it was possible for everything to have collapsed around her in such spectacular fashion.

She glanced up at the bookcase and spotted the photograph albums on the top shelf which she had lovingly collated over the years. She jumped up in a burst of unusual energy and dragged one of the chairs from the dining room table over to the edge of the bookcase. She perched on the chair, wobbling precariously as she lifted the albums down one by one. Snapshots of a lifetime together.

She opened the first volume and smiled. Patrick looked so young smiling out from beneath the plastic sleeve, sporting a thick head of dark hair, his fringe flopping over his forehead, his body lithe and athletic. He had been a keen footballer when they first met, although a hamstring injury a year later put paid to his playing career, such as it was, on the local team who he had lined up with on a Saturday afternoon. After that, he had not maintained his fitness, although Diana thought that it had been harder for everyone to do in the eighties. There were no gyms on every corner as there were these days, or as many physiotherapists to rehab you.

She first met Patrick at a party. She did not enjoy parties. She never knew what to wear and would spend hours before she had to leave trying on different permutations of the few outfits she owned. The truth was, she never liked herself in any of them. Her chest was too flat, and her waist was too straight; running parallel with her hips, denying any discernible curve. She looked more like a young boy than young woman, especially because she kept her hair short. Diana was not someone who felt particularly at ease with her own sexuality. In fact, she felt a strong urge to disguise it rather than flaunt it, because male attention frightened her. In fact, any kind of attention was not something she sought, which was why she hated walking into a room full of people that she did not know. But sometimes, it was unavoidable, such as on the night she met Patrick, because the party was being thrown at her own flat which she shared with three other girls. Not only did she have to be there, but she could not even leave early.

She made herself useful in the kitchen, ladling punch for anyone who wanted it from a huge plastic bucket that they cleaned out as best they could before using it for this alternative purpose. As the evening wore on, it became impossible to know what the punch recipe was, because as new people arrived, they poured whatever bottle they had bought with them into the bucket. When asked what was in it, she muttered, 'I don't know, but I call it a Recipe for Disaster.'

Eventually, as always happens at parties, the kitchen became unbearably crowded, so she fought her way out and into the living room, murmuring apologies as she unavoidably bumped into people, although nobody seemed to care. She had intended to try to get to her room, which was on the next floor, but the stairs were littered with arms and legs meshed inextricably together. So, she headed downstairs instead and out into the cold air of the street, which rushed at her like a blessed relief after the heat of the press of bodies inside. However, after a couple of minutes, she began to regret her flimsy blouse. She shivered, wrapping her arms around herself.

'Would you like my jacket?'

She jumped, startled. Turning, she saw a guy removing his anorak and offering it to her.

'That's very kind of you, but I'll be fine,' she spluttered.

'Please, don't be silly. You're obviously freezing. Here.'

He held the coat towards her, and she took it, draping it around her shoulders.

'Put it on properly,' he cajoled. 'It's clean, or reasonably clean anyway.'

'Thank you.' She threaded her arms into the sleeves and hugged it round herself.

'Better?'

She nodded.

'I'm Patrick by the way, but you can call me Patrick. If you like, that is.' He laughed, revealing his snaggle tooth.

'Hi Patrick, I'm Diana.'

'Well, we have something in common at least.'

'How do you mean?'

'Well, we both have rather old-fashioned names. I've always hated mine.'

'Me too,' she admitted.

'I like Diana. It's a nice name.'

She smiled and studied her feet.

'So, are you fed up with the party too?'

'I never wanted to be here in the first place, but unfortunately I live here, so I didn't have any choice in the matter. It sounds miserable, I know, but I've never enjoyed parties.'

'Me neither,' he admitted. 'Gum?' he asked, offering her a stick of Juicy Fruit.

'Thanks.'

They chewed for a moment in companionable silence.

'So, why did you come?' she asked, studying him slyly under the illumination of the streetlight.

'Some friends of mine dragged me here under sufferance. We met at the pub earlier and they insisted I join them, but I've no idea where they are now, so I was about to head home.'

'Oh, I'm sorry. Do you want your coat back?'

'No, you're alright.' He hesitated. 'Look, if you're not going to be able to get back to your room for a while, do you want to go for a walk?'

Diana studied him, knowing that it was possibly not a great idea to wander the streets of London with a guy that she had only just met, but there was something so unthreatening about him that she felt at ease, comfortable. 'Alright.'

Diana's flat was off Caledonian Road, just a street away from Pentonville Prison, where she was sure the inmates would have been delighted to be invited to the party. Instead of walking that way they moved off in the other direction towards Kings Cross, which was on the verge of changing from a busy daytime station to its nocturnal purpose as the red-light district. They hurried past and on down the congested Euston Road, until they reached the leafier squares of Bloomsbury. Past Russell Square, they carried onto Holborn and into Covent Garden, where the restaurants were closing for the night, the staff lugging bulging black bin bags onto the pavements for collection. Having walked past the brightly lit shops in the central arcade, all full of luxury items that neither of them could possibly afford, they found themselves wandering down the Strand to Trafalgar Square, where they paused briefly before the lions guarding Nelson on his column.

'Do you remember seeing John Noakes off *Blue Peter* climbing to the top of that without even a rope when we were kids?' Patrick asked, craning his neck to get a look at Nelson on his lofty perch.

'I do. I remember that it gave me vertigo just watching it!'

Having rested their feet for a while, they continued along the Mall, reaching Buckingham Palace at its end. The flag was flying at half-mast, so the Queen was clearly away. They made the usual joke about how disappointing that was, because otherwise she might have invited them in for tea, although it was currently five in the morning and the Queen would most probably have still been fast asleep in bed. So, they strolled on, finishing their epic walk at a greasy spoon in Victoria by the coach station, where they each ate a bacon sandwich and drank a large mug of extremely strong tea.

What did we talk about for all that time? Diana wondered as she sat back in her armchair with the album on her lap. She wished that they had had a camera with them that first night to capture their journey, or at least the beginning of what their journey would be. It had been a magical night, the moon high, lighting their way and showcasing London in all its glory. She sighed and closed her eyes, trying to recapture her memories.

'So, why did you move to London?' he had asked her.

'For work, I guess. And I needed to get away from home. I kind of fell out with my parents.'

'Why was that?'

She stopped walking and stared at him.

'Oh, I'm so sorry. That was rude of me, asking you something so personal when I've only just met you. It's none of my business.'

'It's OK, but it's a long story for another time. I moved here at seventeen with very little idea of what I wanted to do. I missed out on my O-levels so my choices were limited. I decided to train at secretarial college. Boring, I know, but it's worked out alright, as I've had a couple of decent jobs so far.'

'What would you really like to do if you could do anything?'

'Oh, I don't know.' She blushed. 'Maybe run my own shop. I think I'd like that.' She pulled his jacket a little tighter around herself. 'What about you?'

'Well, I have been toying with entering the priesthood.' He looked away from her as he said this.

'Oh, right. I, I didn't realise that you were religious. What I mean is, you don't come across as religious, I mean, oh I'm sorry. Now I'm the one being rude.'

'Not at all. My family is staunchly Catholic, and my mother has always dreamed of me being a priest, and whilst I feel a deep sense of faith myself, I don't think I can please her, or indeed Jesus himself, by doing so. For a number of reasons, I don't think that I'd be any good at it.'

'Well, it's a huge decision, I guess. I mean, giving up the prospect of having a wife and a family. To me, it seems unnatural, but. Sorry, have I offended you?' She was relieved that it was dark and that he could not see her blushing furiously.

'No, not at all. I suppose I agree with you. I just need to find a way to tell my mother that I am not going to go to the seminary. And then if I don't go, I need to decide what I am actually going to do.'

'Why does your mother want it so much?'

They walked side by side, not catching each other's eye.

'Well, she has six sons and she's always wanted one of us to be a priest. The others have shown no interest in it whatsoever. They are all very boisterous. I think she sees me as the last hope, and I'm quieter, I suppose. I don't fit in so well with the others.'

She was silent for a while. 'How old are you?'

'Twenty-four. I studied Theology at Kings College here in London and have just completed my Masters. I think that everyone just assumed I would carry on with it.'

She stopped and touched his arm. 'Patrick, you must do what's best for you in life. If you feel that this is the wrong thing, then you must follow your gut instincts. It's your life and you mustn't feel guilty about your choices.'

'Thank you. That means a lot. You are a very wise woman for someone so young.'

'I'm nineteen,' she countered.

'Positively ancient!'

'Look, I haven't always been given a choice, but now, here in London, I feel that I can live my own life, and I can decide what I want to do without anyone judging me or blaming me and that makes me feel a little bit better about myself.'

'So, what choice would you like to make now?' he asked as they walked along the rear of the Palace.

'Truthfully, I'd like to choose somewhere to have some breakfast. I'm bloody starving.' She stopped.

'What's the matter?'

'I swore, in front of a potential priest!'

'I forgive you, my child.'

He linked his arm through hers and marched towards Victoria. 'Come on, let's eat.'

Chapter Twenty-Nine

For the next year, Daniel kept watch. It was remarkable how much paperwork there was. Letters arrived daily and were propped up on the mantelpiece in the sitting room beside the ugly wooden clock that ticked too loudly, waiting for his father to return from work to open them. When his mother and sister were out of the room, he noted the stamps and the postmarks, as well as return addresses when given. Most were bills waiting to be paid, but sometimes there was other mail, which was harder to identify. Occasionally, there was a handwritten postcard from a relative. Daniel could never see the point in postcards. There was no space to write anything other than the shortest of pleasantries; or worse, banalities about the weather and the hotel - all of which would be repeated in person or by phone when the sender came home anyway. It seemed to him to be a complete waste of a stamp.

If his mother went out, Daniel had greater opportunities to pry. He became adept at steaming letters open and then resealing them, although admittedly he did make a hash of one or two at the beginning, and in one case he had to dispose of the letter completely, as he tore the envelope and part of the letter when he opened it. However, soon he was a master at it, yet despite this new skill, disappointingly, he learnt very little.

His father kept his papers in a locked filing cabinet in the box room and the key was in an old fountain pen box in the top drawer of his bedside cabinet. He had seen his father removing and replacing it by looking through the crack in the door. Daniel had opened the cabinet several times, always careful to replace everything he touched back exactly as it was. It contained insurance documents, the deeds to the house, receipts for jewellery, none of which were for jewellery his mother possessed. There were I.O.U.s scribbled out and scattered gambling chips. Both his parents' and his sister's birth certificates, alongside his parents' marriage certificate and his grandparents' death certificates and grants of probate, were there. But his own birth certificate was missing, conspicuous by its absence, as if he did not actually exist.

He had examined every possibility: checking empty suitcases and searching under all the beds and mattresses, as well as scouring the insides and behinds of all the wardrobes, where he found far too many spiders, some disgusting cobwebs, and some wads of cash his father had hidden away from his mother, but no birth certificate. He knew it must be somewhere, he felt it in his bones. He just had to be constantly vigilant.

His father was always complaining about money, or rather the lack of it. He fell into arrears on their household bills and his mother complained constantly that he never gave her enough money for groceries to get the family through the week. And yet, his father was often out until the small hours of the morning, gambling, drinking, and - Daniel suspected - sleeping with other women, so clearly he had enough cash for those activities. But regardless of whether he arrived home drunk or sober, his pockets secretively stuffed with bankrolls or broke, he always returned silently like a cat burglar breaking into his own home. On these evenings, Daniel forced himself to stay awake, certain that one night his father would reveal something which might provide the answer to the question he so desperately sought.

Some nights, Daniel failed, falling asleep despite his best efforts, but he became increasing adept at becoming nocturnal. He knew from his extensive reading that many successful people such as Winston Churchill and Thomas Edison had got by on as little as four hours sleep a night. Nikola Tesla was purported only to sleep for two. Daniel tried Leonardo da Vinci's polyphasic sleep schedule for a while, napping for just fifteen minutes every four hours. It had allowed da Vinci to pursue his thirst for knowledge across art, anatomy, engineering, and botany, but it only served to make Daniel anxious and tetchy.

But one particular night, his valiant attempts at sleeplessness paid off. Daniel was lying in bed, his head propped up by his hands to ensure that the pillow did not muffle any sounds. He heard the soft turn of his father's key in the lock, followed by the rustle of his coat being removed. He did not hear him remove his shoes, but did hear him tiptoe upstairs in his socks. There was one stair that creaked regardless of how lightly you trod on it, but otherwise his father made no sound as he approached the landing.

Daniel opened his bedroom door a crack and peered out into the darkness. His father had slunk into the box room, emerging moments later wearing just his underpants. He was clutching something in his left hand. He headed to the bathroom opposite Daniel's bedroom, where he pulled the cord which clicked sharply as he switched on the light. Daniel shrank backwards slightly so that he could not be seen. He assumed that his father would pee and possibly clean his teeth, although there was no guarantee of this, given that his father's breath reeked of cigarettes and his teeth were almost as yellow as his beloved Colman's Mustard which he consumed with everything. But instead, he picked up the small plastic stool, which was kept in the bathroom so that his mother could reach the highest shelf in the bathroom cabinet, she being extremely short at just under five foot tall. His father certainly did not it need to reach the cabinet. Instead, he placed it on the tray in the shower. Daniel could not see what happened from his vantage point, but he heard his father step onto the stool and then fumble around with something for a few minutes. When he finished, Daniel heard something like a snap and then his father re-emerged, dry as a bone, placing the stool back where it usually sat. He pulled the cord to turn off the light and walked to the end of landing to his bedroom, closing the door behind him.

Daniel could not sleep for the rest of the night, even though he knew he was now free to do so, given that his father was home and in bed, therefore unlikely to reveal anything else. But he dared not risk rooting around in the shower with his father so close by, realising that he would have to wait until ideally everyone was out of the house.

As it happened, he did not have to wait too much longer. The following Saturday, his parents decided to take his sister shopping for some new shoes followed by a visit to the ice cream shop. A new one had opened recently in the local shopping centre in Milton Keynes offering over twenty flavours and it had proved to be a great draw for the local community. Luckily, Daniel was excluded from this excursion on the basis that he would be in the way. While he would have dearly loved to sample the exotic ice creams, he was certain that staying behind would prove to be far more rewarding, so he acquiesced quite willingly, much to his parents' surprise.

'We'll bring you a tub back, shall we, Dan?' his mother suggested, struggling to shovel his sister into her coat.

'That'd be nice, thanks.'

He smiled and his mother tried to hide her shock at his courteous reply.

'Any particular flavour?'

'You choose for me.'

She looked him up and down with concern, as if he was ill. 'OK then. See you later. Be good.'

And they headed out, slamming car doors before his father sped off the drive revving his souped-up Escort as he went.

Daniel watched them go and then spent an agonising fifteen minutes waiting, perched on the sofa in the sitting room, staring out of the window just in case they came back again having forgotten something. Once he was fairly sure that he was in the clear, he took the stairs two at a time, his heart banging like a hammer against his ribs. He switched on the bathroom light and pulled open the shower door. He looked around, but could only see the usual bottles of shampoo and body wash. He felt the walls, but there were no loose tiles. He knelt down and examined the shower tray, but it was secure. Then he looked up and that was when he saw it. There was a small trapdoor in the ceiling, barely perceptible because it was cut out of the tile, blending in with the rest of the décor. Daniel turned and grabbed the stool. It wobbled as he stood on it, and he had to steady himself for a moment against the shower wall. He could not instantly see how to open the trapdoor, feeling around its edges for a gap, but then he pushed upwards on it very slightly and it moved. He slid the tile away and placed it carefully outside the shower before climbing back onto the stool. He could not see what was up there, but he could feel around with his hand.

The first thing he got hold of was an enormous wad of banknotes, presumably recent winnings from his father's frequent bets on the horses, soon to be squandered no doubt on less successful bets. The next package he brought down was a pack of handwritten letters, held together with a brown elastic band. They were all addressed to Frank, his father, written in a variety of handwritings and coloured inks, which appeared to be from a variety of women who professed their undying love. Daniel would need to read these properly at another time, but right now, they were not what he was looking for. He placed them on the bathroom floor and stepped back onto the stool. He reached up again, straining to feel if there was anything else left in the space. He felt something heavy wrapped in a hessian bag. He dragged it towards him, carefully brought it down from the ceiling, and unwrapped it, dropping it as soon as realised what it was. The gun thudded onto the bathroom tile, a couple of loose bullets landing next to it. Daniel stared at it for a moment, before hurriedly wrapping it back up.

Before he replaced everything, he double-checked that the space was empty and as he did so, his fingers caught the edge of something. He fumbled around - trying to grip it, while growing increasingly sweaty with the effort - until eventually he got hold of it and pulled it through. It was a small, brown C5 envelope with nothing written on the front. He stepped down and took the envelope to the toilet, where he sat down on the closed lid. He opened the letter, which was easy because it was not sealed. And there it was, the birth certificate that he had been searching for.

He scanned it quickly and almost fainted when he read the details. Now, finally, he knew the names of both his parents. And the really shocking thing was that he was already well acquainted with one of them.

Chapter Thirty

After their trip to the care home, Angie and Julia ceased their investigation. If she was honest, Angie was unsure about how much they would learn by pursuing these people even they could find them. So far, they had only succeeded in distressing an old man by forcing him to relieve his crippling embarrassment and at the end of it, they were no closer to knowing who had defrauded him anyway.

Anyway, she was far more distracted by Ben. When she tried to clean his room that week, she could not get into it. It appeared to be locked. The doors in the house did have keyholes, but there was only one key that fitted all of them and it was never used. It now appeared that now Ben had taken the key out of the lounge door, where it had resided for as long as Angie could remember, and used it on his bedroom. The key itself was nowhere to be found. It was another reason why she wished she had never found those papers. It had made Ben suspicious of her and even more difficult to deal with.

Her train of thought switched suddenly, cold fingers of fear tracing her spine as she suddenly wondered again if Ray might be dead. It would be one way she might be able to forgive him for this long spell of being completely out of contact. The uncertainty of the whole situation was killing her. She needed someone to help her to anchor Ben. She had no idea any more about how to do it alone.

I was never a difficult teenager, she thought to herself, but then she burst out laughing in her empty kitchen. She had momentarily forgotten that she had fallen pregnant and then been married when she was merely a year older than Ben was now, all against her mother's wishes. Suddenly, she stopped laughing, gripped by sudden panic. What if Ben got himself into a similar situation? He was not in a position to have a baby. At least Ray had been older and able to help her. She had no clue who Ben saw most days or what he was up to. Had he had sex yet? Girls were never mentioned, and friends never visited because of where they lived. Their remote home was isolating for both of them. She resolved to talk to him when he got back that evening after school, assuming he actually arrived home on the bus and did not ring her from a friend's house saying he was staying over, which had of late become standard procedure.

Ben did not return on the bus, nor did he call. He had done this before, but eventually, usually by mid-evening, she would receive a text in reply to the thousands she rifled off to him asking where he was. But not this time. Angie was frantic with worry, pacing the hall and the kitchen feeling nauseous, not knowing who to call. When it got to eleven, she broke down and rang Julia.

'Hello?' a voice groggy with sleep greeted her.

'Julia, it's me, Angie. Look, I'm so sorry to wake you up, but I didn't know who else to call.' She tried to speak normally, but her terror had taken over and she began to cry.

'What's the matter?'

'It's Ben. He hasn't come home, and I can't get hold of him anywhere. Normally when he doesn't get the bus, he calls me eventually, but today I've heard nothing. I don't know what to do.'

'OK, Ange, deep breaths. Come on. I'm sure he's fine. Have you called any of his friends?'

'That's just it,' she heaved between sobs, 'I don't have their numbers and what's even weirder is that Ben has locked his bedroom door. He just never does that, but I think the thing with him seeing all the letters has spooked him and, oh I don't know. I'm just petrified that something terrible has happened to him.'

'I'm sure it hasn't. Try not to catastrophise. Look, hang on a minute. I'll call you straight back.'

Julia hung up and Angie was left alone in her silent house once again. She sat down on one of the kitchen chairs, her legs shaking. The phone warbled.

'Hello?'

'Hi, it's me. Listen, I've spoken to my boys, and they know a couple of Ben's friends. They are messaging them now to see if anyone has seen him.'

'Oh. Amazing, thank you.'

'Give me a few minutes and we will see if we get anywhere.'

Someone shouted 'Mum' in the background.

'Hold on a sec.'

Angie could hear muffled conversation, but not what was being said.

'Tim, tell Angie what you've just told me.' She paused. 'Angie, I'm putting Tim on.'

'Hello,' greeted a shaky teenaged voice.

'Hi, Tim, how are you?'

'I'm fine, thanks, Mrs Reynolds, how are you?'

'Well, thanks. Just a bit worried about Ben, that's all. Have you managed to find out where he is?'

'So, I've just texted Gavin, who is a good mate of Ben's, and he messaged back to say that Ben was going gaming after school with some guy.'

Angie felt a cold hand grip her tightly around the neck. She gulped. 'Do you know who this guy is, or where they went?'

'Gavin thinks the guy lives close to school. Ben said he was walking there.'

'OK, thanks so much, Tim. And please thank Gavin. But we still don't know where he is.'

'Gavin's texting Ben now, so he said he'll let me know if he replies.'

'Amazing, thank you. Please let me know as soon as he messages you, I mean straight away. Although, I know it's a school night, so you probably need to go to bed.'

'I'll leave my phone off silent just in case.'

'Thank you.'

Julia jumped back on her phone.

'I'm sure it'll be OK. Ben is probably just gamed all evening and fallen asleep. You know how they never even consider how worried we get when they don't get in contact. It's hell.'

'Yes, you're probably right, but I have such a bad feeling. You know one of those that you just can't shift.'

'I do, but your mind is running riot. I'm sure Ben will be back at school in the morning and if I were you, I'd call the school and then go there to meet him at the end of the day. Then you can lamp the little bastard and ground him, or whatever you need to do to get him back in line.'

'Yes, good idea. But the morning seems very far off right now.'

'I know, but try to get some rest and I'll let you know if Tom hears anything further.'

'Thanks, Jules. I can't tell you how much I appreciate it.'

Angie made herself a hot chocolate and went into the sitting room where she flicked through Netflix but found nothing to keep her attention. She must have dozed off eventually, because she was woken by her phone, which she had turned to maximum volume. It was Julia.

'Angie, listen. Gavin got a message from Ben.'

'Where is he? What did it say?' she gasped, gripping her mobile tightly to her ear.

He just said, "Tell Mum not to worry. I'm OK."

Chapter Thirty-One

Diana and Patrick began to see each other several times a week. They often met up after work for a drink in the pub, or for occasional trips to the cinema. After much encouragement from Diana, he had plucked up the courage to admit to his mother that the priesthood was not his calling. Instead, a few months later, he secured a totally secular job as a junior salesman for Pioneer, who sold HiFi systems, requiring him to travel all across the South East selling their wares to retail stores.

'It's not glamourous and it's not exciting, but it's work and there is no praying involved,' he told Diana.

'There's that Catholic guilt,' she teased. 'It's OK to forgive yourself for choosing a different path, you know.'

They sat somewhat glumly over a pint in the Marquess of Anglesey in Covent Garden. It was not their usual haunt, but they had decided to come into the centre of London to see *Ghostbusters* at the Odeon in Leicester Square. Diana adored Sigourney Weaver and Bill Murray, secretly wishing to be swept off her feet in some grand romantic gesture one day, as long as it was in a less a spooky manner than Sigourney experienced in the film. Yet she was realistic enough with herself to admit that such grand love would never happen to her. Patrick offered good, solid friendship, or maybe even a little more than that, but she could not be sure. He always kissed her on the cheek at the end of the night, but so far, he had made no move beyond that.

Sipping her rum and coke, she shifted in her seat before suddenly blurting out, 'Do you believe in sex before marriage?'

Patrick spluttered into his beer, splattering his chinos. 'What?'

'I mean, given your background and the possible priest thing and all that, I just wondered if you thought it was important to wait?'

Patrick put his glass onto the table and looked down at the spots of beer on his trousers. 'No, not at all.'

'Right.'

'Right?'

'It's just that we've been seeing each other for a while now and I like you, Patrick, I really do, but you've never tried it on, which is odd as most blokes I know do, and maybe it's because you don't find me attractive, and it's absolutely fine if you don't, but if you do, then I just wondered why you hadn't and -'

'Stop it, Diana. You're a lovely girl and of course I find you attractive and I really enjoy being with you, obviously, as otherwise I wouldn't see you so often, would I?'

She took another sip of her drink. 'I suppose not, no.'

'So, we're good then?'

She nodded, then shook her head.

'Come on, we'll be late for the film,' he said, downing his beer and standing up to pull on his coat.

Diana followed him outside into the cold night, buttoning up her coat before threading her arm through Patrick's. Together, they walked briskly down to Leicester Square.

'I'll get the tickets,' Diana offered.

'You sure? Alright, I'll grab the popcorn.'

Diana returned from the ticket kiosk a few minutes later. 'Blimey, they're slow at the counter!'

'Come on. We'll miss the start,' he urged, steering her by the elbow towards the screen.

They found their seats and as the screen went dark, Diana reached out to hold Patrick's hand, which he took. She leant her head on his shoulder and began to watch the film. It transported her into her favourite fantasy world, where it is possible to overcome grief and find love again. Tears of laughter streamed down her cheeks as Sigourney and Bill finally defeated Zool. In her joy, she turned to Patrick, who was just finishing the dregs of the popcorn, reaching up and turning his face towards her. She kissed him, pushing her tongue between his lips, but he did not kiss her back and she pulled away, her face hot with embarrassment.

They stood up to leave, marching in silence towards the tube.

'Sorry,' she muttered.

'What for?'

'For kissing you. I was carried away by the film.'

'It's fine. I had a mouthful of popcorn at the time, that's all. You kind of surprised me.'

'So, you didn't mind?'

'Of course not.'

She smiled broadly, lacing her arms around his shoulders. 'Kiss me back now.'

'What, here?' He glanced around as people rushed past, jostling them. 'It's packed. We'll get knocked over. Come on, let's keep moving. Anyway, I thought you wanted an early night, because your boss has got that big presentation for you to type out tomorrow.'

'True.' She hesitated. 'It's just that I hoped we might, that you might like to come back tonight?'

'No, not tonight, Diana. I'm really tired,' he yawned.

They walked into the underground station and threaded their tickets through the machine.

'Right, well I'll see you later in the week then,' Patrick said, turning towards the Piccadilly line. He bent down and kissed her on the head.

'Sure, see you then,' she replied, before moving off to the Northern line escalator to trudge back to her flat alone.

Chapter Thirty-Two

Daniel bided his time. He needed to catch his father at exactly the right moment, in the sweet spot between when he was sober enough and when his mother and sister were out of the house. Such opportunities were rare, but one did present itself about ten days later. It was early evening, and his mother had taken his sister out to Brownies. They would be away for at least a couple of hours. His father had been home from work for a while and had eaten his tea. He was now sitting in his favourite armchair, sipping a whisky while scanning the *Racing Post*.

Daniel tiptoed in, envelope in hand, and seated himself on the sofa opposite his father. He took a moment to glance around the over-crowded room, stuffed full of useless ornaments and ugly bric-a-brac that his mother could not help collecting. He smiled to himself, knowing that he finally had an escape route.

His father had not looked up when he entered.

'Dad, can I have a quick word?'

'What is it?' his father snapped, flicking over a page of his sports paper and starting to scan it.

'I think you might want to concentrate on what I have to say. I'm only going to say it once and I think you might want to listen.' He stroked his envelope.

His father slammed the paper onto his knee.

'I found my birth certificate,' Daniel announced, leaning back in his chair, smiling.

His father's face drained of its familiar ruddiness before Daniel's eyes. 'How the bloody hell did you find that?' he hissed.

'To be honest, the how is irrelevant. It's the who that's far more interesting.'

His father said nothing.

Daniel persevered, sweat trickling down the inside of his shirt. 'Now, you've always told me that I was adopted. Why is that?'

'You *were* adopted by me and your mother.' His father gripped the sides of the armchair, his knuckles white.

'But that's not strictly true, is it?'

'Well, your mother adopted you.'

'Yes, but she thinks you did too. She thinks that we are all completely unrelated. What happened? You suddenly announced to her that a baby had been left on a doorstep and needed a home or some shit like that? How do you think she'll react when she finds out the real truth? What will she do when she understands that you are actually my father and that my real mother was a fifteen-year-old girl?' The words gushed from him at speed before he drew breath for a moment. 'You should be in jail. You're a bloody paedo.'

'Now, you listen to me, you little bastard. If you ever breathe a word of this to your mother, or to anyone else for that matter, I will quite literally tear you apart.'

Daniel shot up off the sofa. He was already taller and broader than his father. 'Try it,' he mocked, waving the envelope.

His father darted up from his chair and made a grab for the envelope. He snatched it off Daniel and ripped the top off shoving a meaty hand inside. 'It's empty,' he gasped.

'You don't think I'm stupid enough to bring the actual certificate into the room with you, do you?' He laughed. 'I've got it hidden in an even more secret place than the one you use to stash all your stuff above the shower!'

His father lunged at him, shoving him backwards, but Daniel was so much stronger. He pushed his father, knocking him onto the sofa. He sat on top of him and held his hands until he stopped struggling.

'So, what do you want?' asked his father, panting.

'I simply want money, quite a lot of money actually. The deal I propose is this. If you agree to pay me fifty thousand pounds, I'll leave this house and I'll never come back. And into the bargain, I won't tell Mum that you're a filthy paedophile, or a rapist, or possibly both,' he spat.

'I don't have that kind of money to give to you.'

'Ah, but you do, don't you? You've got at least half of that stashed away in cash in your oh so secret overhead cubbyhole, so I know you must have more snaffled away somewhere else. Give it all to me and I'll be gone. It'll be as if you've never known me, which is of course what you have always wished for most.' He tightened his grip on his father's shoulders, before climbing off him. 'There's a deadline. You've got today to decide, and I want the cash by tomorrow, or I swear that I tell Mum everything.'

His father remained squashed like a small child in the cushions of the greying Ikea sofa, for once silenced.

Daniel stalked out of the room.

Behind him, he heard his father roaring and tearing his beloved *Post* into shreds.

Chapter Thirty-Three

Angie had rung 999 immediately the following morning to report Ben missing, as she had still heard nothing from him directly. She perched on the sofa, shivering with fear, as they asked her all the routine questions you might expect about his physical features, what he would have been wearing (she assumed he was still in school uniform), and any medical conditions he might have. However, they appeared far less concerned than Angie about his disappearance when she told them Ben's age.

'Many boys of your son's age stay out. He will probably be back later on today.' The policeman sounded jaded, as if she was wasting his time.

'But he's never stayed out overnight without calling or messaging me before. That's why I'm frantic with worry. This is completely out of character.' She felt her anger rising. 'And then there's the text message we got.'

'I thought you just told me that he hadn't messaged you?' the policeman at the end of the line queried wearily.

'He didn't. I asked my friend's son who knows someone who knows Ben to text him, and he replied to him.'

'Right. I think I'm following. And did your son say where he was? If he did - and you know, but he won't come back - that's really not something we can help you with.'

'No, of course not, or I wouldn't be calling you,' Angie responded, her voice high with frustration. 'He just said to tell me he was OK. Look, please, I'm not a timewaster. I've never even called the police before. But you have to take this seriously.'

'Did this friend of a friend have any other information?'

'Only that Ben had apparently been gaming with someone and that they had agreed to meet after school. He said that he thought they were meeting somewhere close to their school in Cambridge, The Perse, but that's all he knew.'

Angie's hands were shaking so uncontrollably that she could barely hold her mobile.

'I see. And he hadn't mentioned this gaming friend to you at all?'

'No.'

'And have you noticed anything else unusual in Ben's behaviour recently?'

She paused, unsure about what she should say, unwilling to incriminate her son, while realising that it was important to be utterly truthful if she was to help Ben. 'I found some pills in his room recently. I don't know what they were. And today, when I tried to clean his room, his door was locked, and we never lock the doors in our house, well not internal ones anyway.'

'And did you ask him about the pills? What they were or where he got them?'

'No, I, no, I was waiting for the right time. He's difficult at the moment. A teenager, you know. They're not easy to talk to about anything.'

'Don't I know it! I have two of my own.'

They laughed together for a millisecond.

'And his father? Is he around?'

'Well, yes and no. He works away for most of the week and unfortunately, he's been away for months recently. He is unable to keep in contact with us when he's working. Government business if you know what I mean. I've tried to reach him, but he hasn't replied. I think Ben misses him and that hasn't helped anything.'

Her words gushed out as the tears leaked from her eyes. She brushed them off with the back of her hand. Bloody Ray. So much of this was his fault. He had not replied to her multiple messages since Ben disappeared. What kind of a father was he?

'Do you think that Ben could be with his dad, or have gone in search of him?'

'No, not at all. I know that Ben's tried to call and text him, but he hasn't heard anything either. No, it's definitely not that. We need to find who this guy is that he's been gaming with.'

'Do you have access to his computer?'

'Not his laptop, because he'll have that with him, but he has a PC in his room. But as I told you, the door is locked, so I can't get in there.'

'Right, look, I think the best things for us to do is to pop over to you and see if we can get into his room and take a look at his computer, as well as having a general look around. In addition, we will see what we can spot on CCTV in and around the school. We might be able to see in which direction he was headed when he left the grounds. Don't worry, I'm sure we'll have him back to you. There is usually a perfectly straightforward explanation in most of these cases.'

Angie took a deep breath. 'I hope so. Thank you.'

'We'll be over to see you soon.'

She replaced the receiver, and the doorbell rang simultaneously. She raced to the front door, hoping that it would be Ben, but it was only Julia. Julia held out her arms and enfolded Angie, who dissolved into her as she did so. Closing the front door behind her, Julia led Angie back into the sitting room and they sat down together on the sofa holding hands.

'Thanks so much for coming. I don't know what I'd do without you.'

'Don't be silly,' Julia replied, passing the Kleenex tissue box from the side table over to her.

Angie blew her nose loudly. 'The police are coming over to see if they can get into Ben's room and access his computer. I hope they can, as then we might find out where he is and get him back. But what if it's too late by then? What if someone has groomed him and if he's been attacked or worse? What if he's taken an overdose and is lying somewhere dying? I just can't bear to think about it. I love him so much and if anyone has hurt him in any way at all, I'll, well, I'll kill them and then I'll kill myself.'

'Ange, calm down. Look, I totally get it. I'd be a basket case as well, but the police are on to it now, and I'm sure Ben will be back safe and sound very soon. They usually are.'

'That's what the police said.'

'Well then.' She stood up. 'Now, let me get you a cup of tea and something stronger to wash it down with to calm you down.'

'If it was one of your boys and he had sent a message like that, you'd feel just the same. So, stop fucking telling me to calm down and that it'll all be OK when you have no way of knowing that. None of us do! My fucking husband pisses off and won't even reply to such a dire emergency, and now Ben is in who knows what kind of trouble and I'm supposed to act as if everything will be alright in the end. And I just know it's not going to be. I just do.'

She was shaking with rage and fear.

Julia moved back over to the sofa. She sat down again and held her. 'I'm sorry if I sounded so glib. I know I'd be a mess too. But we must have hope, Angie, because as someone once said - I have no idea who - hopelessness is hell.'

Chapter Thirty-Four

Patrick and Diana sat on the top deck of the bus eating a family size packet of Walker's cheese and onion crisps on their way back from Richmond Park. It was a bright autumn day, and the pavements were blanketed with fallen leaves, their red and gold hues slowly mulching beneath the feet of Londoners as they made their way to and from wherever they were going. They sat in silence for a while, staring at the people who kept rising from their seats in front of them, wending their way unsteadily towards the stairs as the bus stopped along its route.

'Do you want to come back to mine for supper? I've got some pasta and a tin of tomatoes. Not exactly gourmet, but if you're hungry it'll fill a small space.' She threaded her arm through his and squeezed his hand.

'OK, that sounds great. I think my fridge is completely bare, so it works for me and I'm starving after that walk.' He pulled his thin anorak across his chest. 'It was much colder today than I expected.'

By the time they reached Diana's flat, it was growing dark, and the streetlights were beginning to flick on one by one, elongating their shadows as they walked along.

The flat was quiet when they got in.

'I think the others must be out tonight. I must admit that do like it when I come in and it's silent. Sometimes, I'm not in the mood for noise or other people,' she commented.

She poured some hot water into a pan and set it on the hob to boil before retrieving a tin of tomatoes from the cupboard and the can opener from the kitchen drawer. She turned and Patrick was right behind her. He took her in his arms with an urgency that took her slightly by surprise. She quickly abandoned the tin of tomatoes in favour of leading him through to her bedroom, forgetting the water which was simmering away.

'Sorry, it's a bit of a mess,' she apologised, chucking discarded underwear and clothing off the bed and onto the floor while firmly keeping hold of Patrick with one hand. They lay down together on top of her crumpled duvet and kissed some more. His hand travelled down to her small breasts.

'Have you got a condom?' she whispered.

'Yes,' he admitted.

'I don't know. I really want to do it, but I'm scared in case something happens.'

He looked at her seriously, his brow crinkling. 'I would do right by you if anything did, Diana. I wouldn't abandon you. I'm not like that. And anyway, condoms are ninety-nine point something safe.'

She smiled, unsure, but also not wanting him to put him off. She pulled his head down towards her mouth and kissed him again.

It was over swiftly and afterwards, Patrick fell asleep almost immediately - as if exhausted by the excitement of it - while Diana lay there dissatisfied and disappointed, staring at the ceiling. Making love to him had been nice, perfunctory, neither earth-shattering, nor unpleasant. She consoled herself. This was their first time, and the first time was not always the best time. She shuddered as a memory skimmed across her mind. In her experience, her first time had most definitely not been the best time. But Patrick was different and even if he was not the most passionate guy, he was kind, and she knew that he would never hurt her. She glanced over at him. Yes, they would be good at supporting each other and she felt it was what they both needed, some stability. Did it really matter if they were not madly in love with each other? Diana reflected that she had never been in love, so she was no judge on the matter. She had not made many friends in life either, but she knew that she would take friendship over love any time. Lust could be dangerous. She knew that better than anyone.

'Shit!' she exclaimed, suddenly jumping up and racing into the kitchen to turn off the hob.

Chapter Thirty-Five

Daniel found himself free. His father had folded like the towers Daniel had enjoyed building from playing cards when he was younger. A huff, a puff and he fell down, and Daniel had walked away with a rucksack stuffed full of cash. It had been so much easier than he expected.

He did not look back as he slammed their flimsy gate shut, smiling to himself as he imagined how his father would explain his sudden disappearance to his mother and sister. The story he would weave would almost certainly be that he had run away with his father's money - an ungrateful thief plotting in their own home.

'I always told you that boy was trouble. We should never have taken him on,' his father might have shouted at his mother.

'Should we report it to the police? He's just a child, after all.'

'Report what exactly? His running off or his stealing?' his father would bluster.

His mother might be snivelling by now. 'I think we should tell them. Anything could happen to him.'

'He's old enough to make his own decisions and if he thinks he will be better off out there on his own, what I say is good riddance to bad rubbish. What I can tell you is that he'd better not turn up begging on our door ever again. He's got a bloody nerve, throwing everything we've done for him in our faces.'

'But what if something terrible has happened to him? He might be in trouble.'

'I've no doubt he's in trouble of some sort, but it's nothing he can't handle. That boy's got a fucking loose screw, and we are better off without him.'

'He might not be the one who stole your money. What if someone else broke into the house, stole the cash and abducted poor Daniel? What then?'

'You're letting your imagination get the better of you. Nothing was disturbed. There's no sign of forced entry. Just forget about him. I already have.' He probably began to stalk out of the room before adding, 'I'm going out now and I won't be back until late. Don't wait up.'

Then Daniel imagined that his sister would have walked in and asked her mother to redo her ponytail or plait her hair and he would be forgotten by teatime. He asked himself years later if he regretted hurting his mother, but he always came to the same conclusion. She was a weak, pathetic woman, who allowed herself to be trampled all over by an ignorant bully. Frankly, she got what was coming to her. They got what was coming to them, all the people he met. He couldn't help it if they were so gullible and vulnerable.

Daniel was certain about only one thing only. You made your own luck in life, and there was absolutely no point in relying on anyone else to make it for you.

Chapter Thirty-Six

Angie felt as though she had descended into hell. Every moment without Ben was more painful than she could explain, as if her heart was being gnawed away piece by piece by small, malicious rodents. She was so alone and so lost. Ray and Ben were both missing and she was rattling around in her empty house, which despite having lived there her whole life, now seemed to overwhelm her completely. She confined herself to the living room, dozing fitfully on the couch covered by her duvet, the television flickering away in the background even though she paid it no attention. For the last three days, she had only moved to urinate or to get a drink, but she had not eaten since Ben had disappeared.

The police had forced the lock on Ben's bedroom. They searched it thoroughly but found nothing of any real relevance. They removed his computer and took it to the station, where they promised that one of their technical wizards would hack into it. In the meantime, all she could do was wait and text and call Ben a thousand times a day, but he never answered or replied. He had asked her not to worry, but worry was all she had.

'What if I never see him again and never find out what had happened to him?' she asked Julia, who popped in every day, opening curtains, and switching on lights, boiling the kettle, and placing cake and biscuits on a plate, which she then proceeded to eat because Angie just stared blankly past her offerings.

'You will see him again, Angie. He's simply gone slightly rogue, that's all. I know he'll be back.'

Angie's phone rang, causing both of them to jump. Angie lurched to answer it and dropped it on the floor in her hurry. Fumbling for it, she swiped to answer.

'Hello,' she breathed.

'Hello, it's Detective Sergeant Atkinson. I wonder if you could come down to the station?'

'Oh, my God, oh no, what's happened?'

'Nothing has happened. Please don't concern yourself. But we have some CCTV footage we would like you have a look at. When would be convenient for you to come down?'

'Right now. I mean, I'll be there in the next half an hour. Just let me grab my coat.' She ended the call and leapt from the sofa, tangling her feet in the duvet as she did so, and narrowly avoided crashing into the coffee table.

'They've got footage they want me to see. Can you drive me, Jules? Now? I don't feel up to driving myself.' She stood there, her blond hair wild and tangled, her face pale as a phantom.

'Of course, but you need to put some clothes on first. You're still in your pyjamas and ideally, you should wash your face and your bits at least. I hate to say it, but you're slightly fragrant.'

Angie looked down at herself. 'No time!' she cried, kicking off her slippers. 'I'll just get dressed. It'll take two minutes. I'll find the deodorant.'

'And I've got some perfume in my handbag. You can use that on the way,' Julia called after her.

Angie bolted up the stairs, falling over the top one in her haste. In the bedroom, she grabbed a pair of knickers and a bra from the pile of dirty washing on the floor, sorting through it again to find a pair of jeans and a jumper. In her previous life, a few short days ago, living in such squalor and dressing in yesterday's underwear would have been unthinkable, but that was then, when her life had been still functioning, before the most important piece of her jigsaw had gone missing.

She galloped down the stairs.

'Let's go!' she called, pulling on her puffer coat and boots as she walked.

Julia moved over to her and sprayed copious amounts of Jo Malone's Lime, Basil, and Mandarin over her, which made Angie cough.

Julia was a fast driver, but the traffic was out to thwart her. Whichever back route she tried, they ended up dragging behind a tractor or another car driving well below the speed limit. Once she finally got onto the A road, it felt as if they had hit warp speed. They turned into the police station car park with a screech, causing a policeman who was just getting in his squad car to raise his hand in a go-slow gesture. He was about to walk over to them, but he stopped when he saw their agitated state and got into his own car instead. He appeared to realise that they might have a genuine emergency.

The two women ran into the station, the door slamming in their wake. Angie rushed up to the desk, but the policeman behind the glass did not look up, as he was filling in some paperwork.

'Excuse me,' she said, rapping on the window.

'One minute please, madam,' he replied without making eye contact.

Angie waited, impatience strangling her. She tapped her foot, glancing behind her at Julia, who had seated herself on one of the uncomfortable plastic chairs.

'Now, how can I help you?'

'I've come to view some CCTV. Detective Sergeant Atkinson asked me to come down here immediately, so here I am.'

'As I can see. Let me call him for you. Please have a seat.'

'Thank you.'

Angie moved to sit next to Julia, shivering. 'Why are these places always so cold?' she whispered.

'They're not, it's you. You're exhausted and you haven't eaten. You look ghostly. If you don't start looking after yourself, you'll be no good to Ben when he does come home.'

Angie scowled and pulled her coat more tightly around herself.

A door clanged behind them and a burly man in an ill-fitting jacket and a tie that was half undone lumbered towards them.

'Hello, I'm D S Atkinson.' He held out a meaty hand, which shook Angie's tiny one.

'Hi, I'm Angie. And this is my friend, Julia. Do you mind if she comes with me?'

D S Atkinson nodded curtly. 'Not at all. Follow me, please.'

They trailed meekly behind as he led them through a heavy door to the back of the station and along a lengthy, grey corridor, adorned only by noticeboards with various posters stuck on them with drawing pins at random angles. They moved too quickly to be able to read their contents. At the end of the corridor, D S Atkinson opened a door on the left.

'After you,' he commanded, ushering them through. He gestured to the wooden table in the middle of the room. 'Have a seat.'

The plastic chairs scraped across the lino as they pulled them out. Angie and Julia sat on one side together and D S Atkinson sat opposite them. There was a computer on the desk, which he began to log into, muttering to himself as he did so.

'Just give me a minute,' he said, not looking up from the screen. 'Our systems are a little slow to respond sometimes.'

Julia squeezed Angie's hand.

'Right, here we go.' He turned the computer so that they could all see the screen together. 'Now, I'm going to show you some CCTV footage which we have picked up. It appears to show Ben meeting another man. We have been able to follow Ben en route from the school to the train station.'

'Where did they go?' Angie whispered, her voice weak.

'We don't know where they went once they reached the station. That's as far as we've got, but we are working on it. In the meantime, I'd like to show you what we have got in case you recognise the man or anyone else in the films for that matter. Alright?'

Angie nodded, unable to reply.

He pressed play. 'Now this first piece shows Ben walking up Hills Road by Homerton College. Can you confirm that this is Ben in the footage?' He paused the film.

Angie nodded.

'So that's a yes?'

'Yes,' Julia replied.

'Yes,' Angie whispered.

'And he appears to be wearing his school uniform as you said he would be. Right, the next piece shows him still on Hills Road, but this time we can see him standing outside the Travelodge, where he appears to be waiting for someone. Then, a few minutes later, a man arrives.' He flicked the button to make the film to play again.

Ben was leaning with one leg bent against the wall of the Travelodge, apparently scrolling on his phone. Occasionally, he glanced around. The road was busy with people walking. Suddenly, a man wearing a heavy anorak and a beanie hat pulled low over his head stopped. He was also wearing sunglasses, even though it was getting dark. He seemed to say something to Ben and then they hugged.

'Do you recognise the man at all?'

Angie peered towards the screen. 'I don't think so. It's too dark and it's hard to see his face because of the hat and glasses.' She looked again. The film was grainy, and the man never looked directly towards wherever the camera was.

'But Ben obviously knows him if they are hugging,' Julia commented.

'Yes, he's clearly not a stranger,' D S Atkinson agreed.

'Do you have any better shots of him?' Julia asked.

'Not of his face, sadly no. Now, the next shot we have of the two of them is entering Cambridge Station.' He pressed play and the film showed Ben and the man walking into the station.

Ben looked up towards the camera and Angie began to cry. 'Oh, Ben, what are you up to?'

Julia passed her a tissue and patted her arm.

'Can you just rewind them walking in please?' Julia asked.

D S Atkinson reran the footage.

Julia gasped. 'I think I know who he is. Look, Ange. Look properly. See how he walks with that slight lollop. I think you recognise who it is as well as I do.'

Angie dabbed at her eyes with the tissue as D S Atkinson played the film one more time.

'You're fucking kidding me,' Angie gasped, just before she vomited on the table.

Chapter Thirty-Seven

It was a quiet wedding, witnessed only by Diana's ex-flatmates. Patrick's mother had declined to attend, still smarting from his rejection of the priesthood and her hatred of the audacity of the woman who had encouraged and provoked it. She instructed the rest of the family to stay away as well, and stay away they did, her matriarchal force proving too strong for them to resist.

'I'm sorry none of your family is coming. It's a great shame,' Diana commented as they sat in their local pub a few days before the registry office service.

'I must admit that I feel so guilty for upsetting my mother,' Patrick moaned into his pint of Guinness. 'And I feel guilty about not getting married in church.'

'You know my feelings on religion. I appreciate that it's upsetting for you and you're going against family expectations, but what has God ever done anyway? I know for a fact that he's has never done anything kind or helpful for me, in fact, quite the contrary, and I doubt he's going to start now.' She paused and sipped her gin and tonic. 'And look at what Catholicism has saddled you with. You're riven with guilt about literally everything. And what for? You're a good person, you work hard, you hurt no one, yet you constantly feel inadequate in the eyes of some deity which is floating about taunting you somewhere in the ether. This whole guilt trip thing is utterly ridiculous. It was only invented by the Church to keep people on a string. Look at those wretched indulgences they made the poor pay for all those centuries, which they coughed up even when they had nothing to give, in return simply for a mythical promise of entry into heaven. And who in their right mind can guarantee a thing like that?'

Patrick looked at her speechless.

'Sorry, Patrick. I've probably gone too far, but it's true. It's not right that your mother won't come to your wedding because she wanted you to marry God instead of me. It's like marrying a blind date before you even buy them a drink. Doesn't she want you to have any fun?' She leant over and kissed his cheek.

'I think it's best if I don't ever take you to church.'

'Yes, it's probably for the best.'

Diana's family were also absent from the wedding.

'We don't speak,' was all she had said to Patrick when he originally asked her about them. This was all she had ever said when questioned about her background. In the past when he had probed gently, she had always changed the subject instantly, and he was understanding enough to stop there. He felt that she would tell him eventually when and if she was ever ready. He knew nothing about her life before she came to London, except for the fact that she had vowed never to return home.

The afternoon before their wedding, Patrick's mother rang. Diana was at his maisonette, having lugged over the final bits and pieces from her own flat to his place before spending her last night as a free woman with her flatmates. She could not hear their muffled conversation as she bustled about. Maybe his mother had had second thoughts and decided to come to the wedding after all. Diana hoped that she would for Patrick's sake, as it might temper some of his guilt. His cauldron of supposed trespasses currently seemed in danger of boiling over.

'Diana, can you come here a sec?' Patrick called from the hallway where the phone was anchored to the wall.

'Sure.'

She dropped a blouse that she had been folding onto the bed and made her way downstairs.

'It's my mother,' Patrick mouthed.

'I know!' Diana mimed.

'Mum, Diana is right here. I'll put her on.'

'What does she want?' Diana whispered, panic rising in her throat.

Patrick shrugged.

She took the receiver. 'Hello?'

'Hello,' rasped a voice hoarse from a lifetime of smoking. 'It's Mary here, Patrick's mother.'

'Hello.'

'Now, listen to me young lady, I just wanted to say this one thing to you before it's too late for the pair of you. You don't quite know what you're getting into with my Patrick. He's not quite like other young men, if you catch my drift. You should let him marry into the church. It'll keep him on the straight and narrow.' She paused and clearly took a strong drag of her cigarette. Diana imagined her pursed, wrinkled lips. 'You can still change your mind, you know. It'll be better for both of you in the long run. I know what's best. I'm his mother after all.'

'I can assure you that I know precisely who he is, and I love him for it,' Diana responded somewhat falteringly.

'Well, it's your life, my dear. But once you make this particular bed, you need to lie in it until one of you dies. Patrick does not believe in divorce.'

'And neither do I. And why are we talking about divorce the day before we are due to get married? Patrick is happy, and I intend to keep him that way,' she pronounced – again, a little too forcefully.

'But what about you?'

The line went dead, leaving Diana listening to the buzzing of the line in her ear.

'What did she want?' Patrick asked when she joined him in the kitchen.

'Oh, she was very sweet and just wanted to wish us well. Shall I make some tea?'

Patrick raised his eyebrows. 'OK, thanks, that would be lovely.' He put down the plate that he had been drying onto the rack. 'Are you sure that's what she said? She was still trying to get me to go to the seminary five minutes ago.'

'Absolutely sure. She was very considerate actually,' she told the kettle firmly. 'I think she'll finally come to terms with the whole idea. She's obviously not one to give in too easily, but I reassured her that your happiness was my number one priority and she appeared to mellow a little.'

'I have never seen my mother mellow.' He picked up another plate and began to dry it slowly.

'Well, there's a first time for everything. Now, here's your tea. I'm going to finish my unpacking.'

'OK then.'

'OK then.'

And with that, Diana ran up the short, narrow staircase to recommence her unpacking, her face burning.

The following day, they made their vows in front of a rather dour registrar and a smattering of Diana's friends, before emerging onto a grey Marylebone Road into a light shower of paltry confetti and a great deal of drizzle. They had a drink at The Prince Regent on Marylebone High Street to celebrate with their witnesses, before saying their farewells and walking down to Marylebone station to take the train to Oxford. They could not afford much of a honeymoon, but they decided to splash out on a night at the Randolph Hotel, Oxford's finest, which was an imposing Victorian structure opposite the Ashmolean Museum. Their room was small and rather cramped, the double bed taking up most of the space. The wallpaper in the bedroom was oppressively floral and the ensuite bathroom was ice cold. It was not exactly the honeymoon suite, but it was their honeymoon and Diana was determined not to find fault with anything.

Dinner was included with their stay and they dined in a rather soulless room on cold tomato soup, rubbery pork chops and a rather plasticky tasting lemon cheesecake.

'I think the cheesecake you make is much better than this one,' Patrick remarked as he cleaned his plate.

'Are you finishing yours or?'

'Here, eat it. I'm full,' Diana lied.

After dinner, they wandered down the road to The White Horse, a miniscule pub made to seem even smaller because it was rammed with raucous students.

'Do you ever wish you'd gone to university?'

'Sometimes, maybe. But it wasn't an option for me, so there's no point in thinking about it.'

'But you're bright enough, Diana. Why didn't you apply?'

She took a large swig of her gin and tonic, her face hot. 'Well, I suppose that other things just got in the way. I left school at sixteen and never took my A-levels, as you know, so it was just secretarial school for me.'

'But it's not too late though, is it? I mean, you could go back and take them now.'

She snorted.

'Yes, sure, if we had loads of money, but we don't, do we? If we are going to save up for a place of our own, we need to work. And anyway, there are loads of people who have been very successful without getting a degree. Look at Richard Branson for example. He's got no qualifications, but still he set up Virgin Records and now he's easily a millionaire. I just need a good idea like that!'

'I'll drink to that,' he replied, raising his pint. 'Come on, let's get out of here.'

They finished their drinks and walked back to the hotel.

'Do you want to go through the bathroom first?' Patrick asked.

'No, you go.' She kicked off her shoes and lay on the bed, aware of the noise of his peeing.

'It's all yours,' he announced, remerging, still fully dressed.

Diana went in, nightwear in hand. She had been shopping at John Lewis the week before and bought a rather sexy babydoll chemise in black satin. She had never spent real money on underwear before, or worn anything that wasn't cotton and extremely sensible, but tonight she wanted to look good enough for Patrick to remember. She brushed her teeth and then changed into her lingerie; surveying herself in the mirror, but it was above the sink, and no matter how high she stood on her tiptoes, she could still only see her face and neck. 'You'll have to do,' she muttered to herself, brushing her hair and spraying herself with the sample of Opium that a girl wearing most of a make-up counter had handed to her on her way out of the store.

When she emerged back into the bedroom, Patrick had already turned off the overhead light and was lying in bed on his side facing towards the curtains. Her bedside light was still on. She got into bed and scooted over to him, spooning him from behind. 'It's bloody freezing in this room,' she shivered.

He did not move.

'Patrick?'

'Hmm,' he murmured.

'Are you asleep?'

'Hmm. Yes, sorry, I'm totally knackered. It's been a very long, exciting day, hasn't it? It's all been far too much for me.' He rolled onto his back and kissed her cheek. 'Sleep well, my lovely wife.'

And with that, he turned away again.

Chapter Thirty-Eight

Daniel left the house without looking back and got straight on a train to London. He had spent his entire existence so far in Milton Keynes, a town with excessive amounts of roundabouts, tarmac, and plastic cows. His parents had never taken him into London. His mother did not like to drive and only did so with great reluctance on local journeys to school or to the shops, but she refused to drive on fast roads. Equally, she had an abhorrence of trains or planes. Subsequently, holidays had been rare and those they had taken were to campsites where it usually rained, and everyone argued. Trips to London had never happened, regardless of how many times Daniel asked if he could go.

'I don't feel comfortable in London,' his mother had moaned. 'It's so crowded and it's really dangerous. There are pickpockets everywhere and the streets are dirty.'

'Well, I'm not taking you,' his father answered when asked. 'It's too bloody expensive. You'll have to save up and go yourself one day when you're older.'

So, in a manner of speaking, Daniel had saved up and now, sixteen and keen to make his mark in the world, he set off to find an even greater fortune.

He arrived at Euston, emerging onto the busy concrete road where cars and lorries sat stationary, bumper to bumper, their exhaust fumes polluting the evening air. It was not the height of glamour that he had been expecting. Daniel had no idea which way to start walking, so he simply hoicked his rucksack high onto his shoulder, crossed the road, looked up and down a few times, and decided to turn right. He kept walking until he reached Great Portland Street tube, where he chose to go left, walking all the way up until he hit Oxford Street. It was a Thursday evening and people were out late-night shopping. The pavements were heaving with people, all of whom appeared to be in an immense hurry and as a result simply barged him out of the way. He stood on the corner of Oxford Circus outside the gigantic Topshop and smiled up at the garish lights from the shop fronts. This was where he wanted to be, a place packed with so many people offering so much opportunity. It was as if he had come home.

He kept walking up Oxford Street towards Marble Arch, dawdling past Selfridges and admiring their extravagant window displays. Well-dressed men and woman rushed past him, and he was suddenly acutely aware of how cheap he looked in his badly fitting jeans and thin anorak. If he was going to blend in, he would need to look the part. He decided to come back the following day and get some proper gear, but right now, he was starving, and he needed somewhere to stay.

He bought a pretzel from a vendor on the side of the road to tide him over and began to stroll down Park Lane. Hyde Park was to his right, but he kept left, past the Porsche car showroom and the Grosvenor House Hotel, noticing the smart apartments blocks that lined the route. Eventually, he reached the Hilton Hotel, which was a name that he recognised at least. He decided that they must have a bar or somewhere he could get a meal and he reasoned that he could afford it given his recent stroke of luck. He strolled past the doorman as if he was staying there, who glanced at him with an air of disapproval, following him into the lobby.

'Can I help you, sir?' he sneered.

'No, thank you. I'm just meeting a friend.'

'And where are you meeting them?'

Daniel glanced around and spotted a sign by the lift.

'I'm meeting them in Trader Vic's,' he announced, moving purposefully towards the lifts, and pressing the button quickly.

When the doors opened into the basement of the building, he was thrust into a strange, Polynesian-themed bar. It was dark and exotic, with groups of people huddled together drinking strange cocktails out of coconuts, or from glasses laden with fruit. He threaded his way towards the bar.

'What can I get you?' the barman asked.

Daniel scanned the cocktail list.

'I'll have a mai tai,' he declared, slapping the menu back onto the counter.

'Do you have ID?' questioned the barman, polishing a tumbler.

He had been carrying fake ID for a couple of years now. They were easy to get hold of. He produced a card from his wallet and handed it over.

'One mai tai coming up,' He held a glass up to the light to check for smears.

The cocktail arrived along with a generous portion of spicy nuts. Daniel downed it quickly and asked for another one.

'I'll get that for you,' a woman drinking at the other end of the bar called over to him.

He glanced in her direction. She was forty or fifty, he could not quite tell, in an expensive, low-cut dress with a tight bodice which buoyed up her impressive chest. As she approached, he noticed that her bright red lipstick had bled a little into the lines around her lips. She carried her martini, the glass clinking against the ostentatious diamond ring on her finger, and with a little difficulty, she shuffled onto the stool next to him.

'Are you waiting for someone?' she asked, her voice husky.

He shook his head.

'So, are you just visiting London, or do you live here?' She leaned towards him, the strength of her perfume just about overpowering the smell of cigarettes that emanated from her.

'I've just moved here, actually.'

His second mai tai arrived and he took a large swig immediately.

'With your family?'

'No, on my own. I don't live at home anymore.' He threw a handful of nuts into his mouth, dropping a couple on the floor.

'So, where are you staying?'

'I'm not sure yet. I've just arrived.'

'Well, if you're at a loose end this evening, I am on my own, and you could keep me company if you like. I was about to go for dinner and I really hate to eat alone. Are you hungry or is that a silly question? Boys your age are always hungry for food, and other things too I guess.' He heard a slight twang of an accent, American maybe, but it was faint.

Daniel felt his face flush despite himself. He finished his drink too quickly and choked.

'Put it all on my tab,' she called to the barman.

'Of course, Mrs Montague,' he replied, nodding to her.

She stood up and Daniel followed suit, picking up his bag from between his feet.

'I'm Valerie, by the way,' she told him, threading her arm through his. 'And you are?'

He hesitated for a moment. 'David,' he stuttered. 'David Prince.'

'Right, David, my little prince, let's get something to eat, shall we? Don't worry, I'll pay for everything,' she added, seeing the look on Daniel's face.

She threaded him through the crowd waiting to enter the bar, which had now filled up to bursting, and pressed the lift button for the sixth floor. 'Actually, why don't we get room service? You look so tired and I'm not in the mood to go out. It's too cold, don't you think?'

He had not thought it was in the least bit chilly as he walked through London, but then he had been carrying a heavy backpack and his body had been shot through with adrenalin resulting from the bright lights and the realisation that he had finally escaped from home. He shrugged.

They exited the lift, and he followed her down the corridor. She stopped at a door at the end and tapped her key card against the handle. 'This is me,' she smiled, opening the door.

He followed her in, his bag banging against the doorframe. His cash was buried deep inside a hidden zipped compartment beneath his underwear and shoes. Nevertheless, he was wary. What did a middle-aged woman want with a young, not especially attractive boy?

It appeared that - sadly for Daniel who was now so hungry that he could have eaten a chair leg - food was not on her mind. She opened a bottle of champagne which was already chilling in a large ice bucket on the table, with practised expertise. Next to it was an enormous basket of fruit. She poured him a glass.

'I just need the bathroom. Help yourself to a banana. The potassium is great for boosting your energy. And don't go away.' She winked as she turned to go into the bathroom.

Daniel took a gulp of the champagne, the bubbles hitting the back of his nose and stopping him from breathing momentarily. He looked around the room quickly. Her handbag was by the table. He opened the desk drawers quietly, but only found underwear and a couple of scarves. There was a jewellery box on the shelf inside the wardrobe, but it was locked.

He heard the bathroom door opening and walked over to the window.

'It's a great view out over the park, isn't it?' she commented.

'Yes, it's amazing,' he replied sincerely. He turned around and gasped. She had emerged wearing a red bra and thong with black stockings and suspenders. She was still wearing her stilettos. He had never seen a live woman in her underwear before, except for his mother, and she did not count.

'What do you think?' giving him a twirl.

He made no reply, tilting his glass in his distraction so that some champagne spilt onto the floor.

'Now, don't be shy, David. I take it you haven't done this before, am I right?'

He gaped at her, unable to speak.

'Well, that's just how I like it. Now, you undress like a good boy. Off you go. Don't worry. I pay well.'

He remained still, unable to move, so she sashayed towards him and rubbed her hand between his legs. 'Well, you seem to appreciate what you see, my little prince. Let's have a proper look, shall we?' She knelt down and unzipped his trousers. By the time she had pulled them down, it was all over for him.

'Don't let that worry, you, my darling. The wonderful thing about young men like you is that you'll be ready to go again in a minute.' She laughed and imprinted his penis with a bright red kiss. 'Come, let's get some more champagne and drink it in bed.'

They spent the next few hours experimenting, or rather, practising the moves that Valerie particularly enjoyed. Daniel found it both exciting and extremely instructive, often reflecting to himself many years later about how much he had learnt in one night and how Valerie had set him on such a lucrative career path.

Eventually, Valerie grew tired. 'I think it's time to sleep now, little one.' She rose from the bed and wrapped the bathrobe around herself. She moved over the wardrobe and opened the door. She removed her jewellery and unlocked a small velour box with a tiny key, placing the jewels inside and locking it again. She left the key in the lock. Daniel had rolled over so that he had a good view of her movements reflected in the mirror opposite.

'I'm going to take a sleeping pill now, my darling. If I'm not awake by ten, you know what to do to get my attention!' she cackled. She popped two pills from a blister pack by the bed and was snoring like a walrus within half an hour.

Daniel lay still, his stomach rumbling, painful with hunger. After a while, he poked her gently a few times. She did not move, but merely snored even louder. He slithered out of bed and went into the bathroom, where he dressed quickly and quietly in the dark. He re-entered the room and swiped Valerie's handbag from the table, before tiptoeing over to the wardrobe. He turned the tiny key and emptied the contents into the top of her bag. Just before leaving, he went back to the fruit basket and grabbed a couple of apples before softly opening the door of the room and closing it behind him.

He scooted down the corridor and pressed the lift button, his heart banging against his ribs as if it might break them. Mercifully, it arrived quickly. On the way down, he removed Valerie's purse and the jewellery from her bag and hid it in his own. Then, he threw her bag onto the floor of the lift as he exited and was back out onto Park Lane and on his way within seconds.

'Thank you for a delightful evening, Valerie,' he muttered under his breath as he marched briskly away. He could already tell that he was going to enjoy London very much indeed.

Chapter Thirty-Nine

———

'So, just to clarify, this gentleman who has picked your son up from school is actually his father?'

D S Atkinson leaned back in his chair.

'Yes, but.' Angie stuttered.

'And you are neither divorced, separated nor estranged from your husband?'

'No, but.'

'So, there is, in fact, no crime to answer here.'

'No, not a crime as such, but it just doesn't make any sense. I've been trying to get hold of Ray for months and he hasn't replied, not even when I told him that I was worried about Ben, you know, that he might be taking drugs. Ray works for the government, you see, and he's often away, but rarely for this length of time and he usually gets in touch even when he's not at home. I can't begin to understand why he could turn up out of the blue without contacting me and take Ben on a trip, or why Ben wouldn't have told me. Do you see?' She was aware that she was ranting, but the words simply spilled from her mouth in her utter panic and confusion as if she had no control over them.

'There's no normal when it comes to relationships, believe you me. When you've been policing for as long as I have, you've seen everything and nothing comes as much as a surprise. But the important point here is that this is clearly a domestic issue between you, your husband, and your son. Being incommunicado with your wife is not breaking the law. Your son is over the age of sixteen and if they have chosen to go off for a boys' weekend or whatever it is, it's really no concern of ours.' He stood up, holding his papers.

'Is there nothing you can do?' Angie insisted. 'This just doesn't smell right to me.'

'I think you both need to go home and have a nice cup of tea. Your son is safe with his father, who, as you have made clear, is an important man in the civil service and presents no danger to him. There appears to be no reason for us to be suspicious of either him or your son at this point. I'm sure they'll be in touch soon.'

'But Ben's got exams coming up. He can't afford to miss school,' Angie squeaked.

'Then I suggest you keep trying to contact the pair of them and remind them of that fact. From what you've told me, Ben appears to have been a conscientious boy up until now and his father the same. I'm sure they both will remember their responsibilities.' He walked towards the door of the interview room and opened it, signalling for them to exit. 'Now ladies, if you'll please follow me, I'll show you both out. I've got a rather busy afternoon ahead of me.'

They both rose from their uncomfortable chairs, their buttocks stiff from sitting too long in a chilly room, and followed D S Atkinson back out the way they had come and into the car park. The moment they hit the fresh air Angie began to shout.

'What the fuck, Julia! What's going on?'

'Get in the car, Ange. Let's not discuss it here.'

Julia unlocked the car doors with a beep, and they slammed the doors shut behind them.

'I just don't get it,' Angie muttered, too tired to cry or shout any more.

'Maybe it really is a lads' weekend, or maybe Ray thought that getting Ben on his own for a day or two might help him to understand what Ben's really up to. I mean, that's what he's good at, isn't it? Negotiation, psychology and all that shit.'

'Do you really think that's what he's doing?'

'It's a possibility,' she answered, shaking her head. 'Look, let me drop you off. You need something to eat and frankly, so do I, and I've got to get home to feed my brood before they devour the furniture. I suggest you keep calling the two of them as the guy said. There's probably a perfectly logical explanation.'

'I hope you're right, but it's extremely confusing, Jules. Everything seems to be up in the air.'

She babbled on, while Julia kept her eyes firmly on the road.

'Oh my god!' Angie suddenly exclaimed.

Julia stood on the brakes. 'Jesus, Ange. What? I thought I was about to hit something.'

'No, but I've just had a terrible thought. What if Ray is having an affair? Maybe that's why he's been away for so long. Do you think he would?' she asked, her voice wobbling.

'If he was having an affair, I doubt that he would tip up, collect his son and take him with him.'

'But what if he is running away with another woman and has persuaded Ben to go and live with them?' She stared at Julia wild-eyed.

'I think you are adding two and two and making seven. Look, we're back.' She parked outside Angie's house. 'Try not to worry so much now. The important thing is that you know Ben is safe. Ray isn't going to hurt him, is he? He loves Ben.'

'You're right, I know you're right. I just wish that they weren't excluding me.'

'I admit, I don't get that bit, but Ben loves you to pieces - even if he is currently a stroppy teenager - and he won't stay away for long. He'll call you soon, I'm sure.'

Angie smiled weakly and squeezed Julia's arm. 'I hope you're right, Jules. I really do. Look, thanks for everything today and over the past week. You probably think I'm being a complete idiot.'

'Not at all. I'd be exactly the same if I was in your shoes, and I'm sorry you're going through all this, but it'll work out.'

Angie could not reply, her throat blocked by an overwhelming urge to howl. She simply nodded, her eyes brimming with tears, as she got out of the car and trudged slowly back into her big, empty, lonely house.

Chapter Forty

Diana and Patrick had fallen into a pattern that was middle-aged long before they hit that part of their lives. Patrick proved to be exceptional at sales and travelled around the country for a few days every week. Diana worked her way through a variety of secretarial positions before deciding that she could not bear to type another letter or take any more dictation. She got a job as a shop assistant in Debenhams in the homewares department. Despite the heavy toll it took on her feet, standing for eight hours a day and rushing to and from the stockroom, she enjoyed the banter with her colleagues, some of whom led far racier lives than she did in their leisure time. She also loved dealing with customers and helping them with their queries and solving their decorative dilemmas. She came to realise that she had a good eye for detail and soon had a small group of loyal customers who would visit regularly to ask her opinion on curtain fabrics, rugs, cushions, and bedding.

By the time she returned home each evening, she was worn out. Within three years of marriage, she and Patrick had moved out to Harpenden, a thriving village in Hertfordshire, where they had bought a pretty three-bedroom house just off the Luton Road. It was a relatively easy commute from the station into London, but if the trains were disrupted, Diana often had a very long day.

Patrick drove to his job. He now worked for a white goods manufacturer based in Manchester and his job required him to visit customers across the UK. He was steadily rising up the ranks and he seemed to enjoy it.

The downside was that they rarely got much time together and when they did, one or the other, or both of them were utterly exhausted. Their sex life was perfunctory at best, Patrick seeming to have little interest and Diana eventually having given up trying to persuade him. People at work keep pestering her about when they were going to have children: a topic Diana found insensitive, as how was anyone else to know if they had been trying and failing? It seemed to be an assumption that once you were married, having children was an inevitable progression, and that a failure to produce offspring was somehow unnatural - a presumption Diana thought was quite offensive.

She and Patrick had discussed having children.

'I had kind of assumed that you'd like to have a large family,' she had ventured one evening soon after they were married.

He laughed. 'Why would you jump to that conclusion?'

'Well, there's the Catholic thing, and coming from a big brood yourself, I thought that it would be your preference.'

'You forget that I was aiming to be a priest and therefore celibate. On that basis, I would have had no kids at all.' He picked up the remote control, aiming it at the television, which flickered into life.

'So, you're not that bothered then?' She fiddled with the sleeve of her jumper.

'Not really. I mean, if it happens, it happens, but if it doesn't, I'm fine with that too.'

They said no more and settled down to watch *A Question of Sport.* Diana sat next to Patrick on the sofa while Bill Beaumont cracked a joke which rose over her head. Patrick giggled and then shouted out an answer at the television screen. Part of her yearned to tell him about her own thoughts on the matter; but he had not enquired and anyway, it would have meant delving into other things she would rather not discuss. It was probably best left alone.

'I'm going to put the kettle on. Would you like a coffee?'

'Thanks, love. That would be nice. Ooh, and is there any of that chocolate cake left? I'll have a slice if there is. Just a small one.' He smiled at her before shouting 'It was Roger Bannister!' in answer to a question posed by David Coleman.

Chapter Forty-One

London was proving to be both interesting and profitable. Daniel spent the majority of his days sleeping on a rather uncomfortable futon in a small bedsit he had rented in Camden Town. It was compact, but had everything he needed: a bed, a shower cubicle, and a small kitchenette. He did not see the point of paying out too much of his hard-earned money on rent. His hanging rail was sparse, but functional. He now owned a couple of smart jackets, half a dozen shirts, three ties, two pairs of wool trousers, and a pair of jeans. A few T- shirts and tracksuit bottoms lay crumpled in a pile by his bed. These were his slobbing around clothes. The rail was for work.

Each evening, around seven, he would shave carefully in the poorly lit mirror over the sink, before dressing, spraying himself liberally with Paco Rabanne and heading out. He was careful not to frequent the same area or the same bars in succession. He mapped out his target area for each night well in advance, swapping between Mayfair, Knightsbridge and the West End, frequenting high-end bars or hotels. He would order a drink and sip it slowly, checking out the clientele as they passed through. At the beginning, he waited to be approached, but as he grew in confidence, he began to make the first move. Sometimes he was rebuffed, but usually people were happy to chat. He was just a young guy of no special attraction having a chat.

The routine was always the same. He would have a couple of casual drinks with them, which they always paid for, and then he would wait to see if they suggested moving on together. If they were slow on the uptake, he would prompt them and usually, once they got the hint, they went back to the customer's hotel or home, never to Daniel's. If they tried to push it, he pleaded puritanical flatmates or claimed that he was still living at home. Hotels were the easiest place to find his prey, and foreign visitors were by far the most preferable. They came and they went with no complications. They paid well and had decent valuables to pilfer. They were usually happy to have sex and then, once they were exhausted, Daniel would rob them and leave, slipping out of their lives like a silent ghoul. If they showed no signs of sleep, he helped them along. He always carried a couple of potions in his pocket that were easy to get hold of from a couple of dodgy contacts he had come to know. He had also acquired a variety of IDs, which he shuffled each night before leaving the flat to decide on his persona that evening.

'Tonight, Matthew, I will be...' he said with a smirk into the mirror, pretending to be a contestant on *Stars in Their Eyes* as he got dressed each evening.

Not all of his victims were women. He was increasingly approached by men as well. He appeared to exude a certain appeal of the little boy lost in the big city. In many cases, he actually preferred men. They were easier to deal with, requiring far less seduction and foreplay, usually simply keen to get down to business. The truth was, Daniel did not care too much who he slept with or what he was required to do. It was merely business as far as he was concerned, and as long as it proved lucrative, he was happy to endure a little degradation or even violence if that is what was necessary - as long as he did not receive any obvious cuts or bruises which might keep him out of the game for too long. He was managing to earn an extremely good income, opening a variety of bank accounts in different names and selling off jewellery and other valuables that fortuitously fell into his lap. He got to know some helpful, if somewhat shadowy, people who would move them on for him, careful to keep his network wide and never to be beholden to any of them. He was determined to work alone.

One night, he was loitering in a bar of a luxury hotel that he had not returned to for several months, sipping a beer and keeping his eye on proceedings. He was eyeing up an older man at a corner booth, but every time Daniel glanced in his direction, the man glanced away, pretending to read the bar menu for the umpteenth time. Eventually, Daniel approached him.

'Hi, I'm Hal. How are you doing?' He held out his hand for the man to shake. Before the man could reply, Daniel sidled into the booth so that their legs were almost touching.

'Hi,' the man replied, shaking his hand. 'Would you like another drink?

'Sure, that's very kind of you. I'll have a beer.'

The man signalled to a passing waiter and gave him their order.

'So, are you visiting London on holiday?'

'No, I work down here a couple of days a week. The head office is in Manchester, but now I'm in charge of the whole of the South-East region. I don't stay at *this* hotel, mind you. My company would never pay to put me up in a place like this, but I often wander up here for a change of scene.'

'And why not.'

'And you? Do you live in London?'

'Yes, I moved here a few months ago. I work in the men's fashion department at Selfridges. It's not a bad job and I get an excellent staff discount on the clothes and even on the food in the food hall. I was supposed to be meeting some friends here this evening, but they appear to have stood me up. I've been texting them, but, oh well. People get busy.'

'That's a shame.' He paused and took a sip of his beer. 'Look, Hal, if you're at a loose end, how about dinner? I'm on my own and I'll only sit here and drink too much otherwise. I mean, only if you want to. But I know I'm older than you and you might find that a bit boring.'

'Not at all. I talk to men of all ages every day at work and to be honest, I prefer people older than me. They tend to have so many more interesting things to say.'

'OK, well, as long as you're sure.'

'Where are you staying?'

'At the Metropole on the Edgware Road. It's not the smartest hotel, but it's clean and close to the A40, so I can get out of London relatively easily.'

'Do they have a restaurant?'

'Yes, but it's not great. They just do burgers and the like. Do you want to go there?'

'Sounds perfect. I could murder a burger and fries.'

The waiter was called, and the bill paid. They left the table and exited the bar to call the lift. The man shuffled from foot to foot, avoiding eye contact.

'So, what do you do?' Daniel asked, once in the lift.

'I'm in sales, white goods. You know, fridges, washing machines, that kind of thing.'

'Do you enjoy it?'

'It's a living, I suppose. It's not all that glamourous. I kind of fell into sales years ago. I'm alright at it and I make a decent enough living. At least it pays the bills.'

'And where's home?'

He hesitated, looking down at his shoes. 'Hertfordshire.'

'Oh, I don't know many places out there. I went on a school trip to Verulamium once, you know the Roman site in St Albans. Christ, it was dull.'

'Do you know, I don't live far from there, but I've never actually been. I must make a point of going there one of these days.'

'My advice is don't bother! It's just piles of stones and a museum full of ancient coins.'

The lift reached the ground floor and as they exited, Daniel touched the small of the man's back. He flinched slightly.

They hailed a black cab, which staggered across the heavy London traffic at Marble Arch before making its way stop-start up the Edgware Road. When they reached the hotel, the man paid the taxi, and they entered the lobby.

'The coffee shop is this way,' he informed Daniel, pointing to the cafe entrance on the left.

'Do they do room service here? It looks rather soulless in there, doesn't it? All that neon lighting.'

'True. Yes, we can get room service if you prefer.' The man blushed. 'Let me just go to collect my key.'

He strode off to reception, returning a couple of minutes later.

'Here we go.'

He marched over to the lifts and pressed the up button, glancing around him as if somehow, he should not be there. The lift arrived and they got in, travelling up to the third floor. Once there, it was short walk up the corridor to the room. He unlocked the door with his key card and switched on the light.

'Let me find the menu. It should be here somewhere.' He moved over the dressing table and opened a drawer. 'Ah, here we are.'

He turned around and Daniel was right behind him.

'I'm not that hungry anymore,' said Daniel. 'Are you?'

'Well, I can always eat, but we can just have another drink if you like. I think there are some crisps in the minibar. I don't tend to take anything from it, as they always charge such exorbitant prices and the company doesn't cover it, but...'

Daniel pulled the man towards him and kissed him.

'Oh, look, I really don't do this kind of thing. I think you've misunderstood.'

'Have I?' He began to unbuckle the man's belt.

'I'm married. I have to be careful. I never do anything like this,' he stuttered.

Reaching down inside his trousers, Daniel whispered, 'Well, you seem to want to do it now.'

'I, look, I don't know. I really don't. Can't we just chat? It's a lonely old life on the road.'

'If you want me to go, I can go.' Daniel backed away from him slightly. 'But if you'd like me to stay, I can do that too. Then we can just talk if you like.'

'How much?'

'£150.'

'Wow, that's a lot of money to sit and have a chat.'

'I can do whatever you like for that. It'll be worth it, I promise.' Daniel moved towards him, unbuckling his trousers.

The man gasped. 'I don't have any cash.'

'I'll take a cheque, or you could give me your watch.'

'My wife gave me this watch for our wedding anniversary.'

'Well, you'll have to tell her that you left it behind in your hotel and when you rang them once you realised, they said they couldn't find it. Things get nicked all the time from hotels, don't they?'

'OK, fine, I'll sort something out. But seriously, I just want your company. I've never slept with a man.'

'But you've thought about it.'

The man looked down at his feet. 'All my life.'

A trickle of sweat ran down his temple and he turned back to the cupboard in the desk, searching out two beers from the minibar and handing one to Daniel.

'Look, I really am hungry and you're a young chap. You guys are always famished. Let me order.' He moved over to the side of the bed and picked up the phone. 'It'll be here in twenty minutes. In the meantime, let's eat some Pringles.'

'So, why have you never acted on your impulse?'

'Catholic guilt would probably sum it up in two words. I come from a devout Irish family, and my mother was desperate for me to enter the seminary and become a priest. I think she understood my natural proclivities and thought that the priesthood would shield me from temptation.'

Daniel roared with laughter.

'I know, I know. The church has hardly covered itself in glory, has it? I mean, celibacy isn't normal, and it's bound to warp people and make them do terrible things. And I didn't want to be one of those and anyway, I wasn't religious enough. I went through the motions, sure, because that's how I was brought up, but I couldn't devote myself entirely to Jesus. It would have been a heinous lie.'

There was a knock on the door. 'Ah, that will be the food. Let me get it,' Daniel offered.

'No, don't worry, I'll wheel it in.'

Daniel heard him thanking the waiter, before he trundled the trolley into the room with some difficulty as it kept banging into the wall on either side.

'These things never have straight wheels,' he complained. 'Let's have a look.'

He removed the silver domes to reveal two plates of rather congealed cheeseburgers and underdone chips.

'Well, it's not The Ritz, but it'll do. Do you want a glass of wine? I ordered a bottle.'

Daniel, nodded, his mouth already stuffed with some of the burger, that he had greedily grabbed off the plate. He gratefully accepted the large glass of red handed to him. 'So,' he said chewing, 'you got married instead?'

'Yes, I guess I did. She's a lovely woman, my wife. Very kind and supportive. We met when I moved to London for my job. She's a few years younger than me. In fact, when we met, she was only seventeen. She ran away from home, but she's never told me why. All I know was that she was very unhappy. And I thought I could look after her. We've been married for years now, so it seems to have worked out alright.' He sipped his wine.

'Any kids?'

'No, no kids. We never quite got round to it.' He paused and stared at Daniel. 'How old are you, Hal?'

'I'm almost twenty-one.'

The man raised his eyebrows.

'I know, I look young for my age. I always have.'

'And where did you grow up?'

'All over the place really. My parents died in a car crash when I was a baby, and I was in and out of foster homes my whole life.' He took a handful of chips and gobbled them down.

'Oh, you poor boy.' The man reached across the trolley table and stroked his arm.

'Ah, your priestly empathy is emerging!'

'No, sorry. It's just that you're so young to be up in London and doing this sort of thing.'

'What sort of thing? Eating chips?'

'You know what I mean.'

Daniel shrugged and finished off his glass of wine.

The man fiddled under the trolley and produced a large slice of cheesecake. 'I thought you might like dessert.'

Daniel beamed, before polishing it off in four bites.

'Are you finished?'

'Yes, thank you.'

'OK, I'll wheel this bloody contraption back outside.'

'What do you want to do now?' Daniel asked after the man had removed the trolley.

The man made no answer, so Daniel held out his hand and led him to the bed.

'Can you just hold me?'

'Of course,' he replied.

They lay together on the bed, Daniel spooning the man, and something happened that had never happened before to Daniel when he was working. He fell asleep.

He woke much later, blinking. The bed side light was still on. They were no longer spooning, but instead, Daniel lay on his back and the man lay beside him with his arm across Daniel's stomach. He began to slide from under his arm, but the man opened his eyes.

'Where are you going?' the man asked. 'It's the middle of the night.'

'I, well, I assumed you were tired, and I thought I should go.'

'But I haven't paid you yet.'

'No, no you haven't. I forgot.'

The man undid his watchstrap and handed it to Daniel, who pocketed it. 'Keep this as collateral.'

Daniel leaned across and kissed the man on the lips, but he remained rigid. He kissed him again and this time, he kissed him back. Daniel moved his hand lower moving onto the man's crotch, but he rolled away.

'No, Hal, I'm not ready. I can't.' He sat up and addressed the side lamp, his back turned away. 'Look, I've got a proposition for you. How about we make this a regular thing? I come to London every week and I could take you out to eat and we can talk and maybe.'

'Yes?'

'Oh, I don't know, but is that something you might like?'

'You'd have to pay me for my time.'

'Yes, yes, of course. I'll pay you, naturally. I'll look after you, don't you worry.'

'I don't really have regulars, I'm afraid. I never know where I'm going to be.'

'I'd pay well. It would mean a lot to me.'

The man paused, staring up at a dark stain on the ceiling and then began speaking all in a rush.

'The thing is, I've spent my whole life wanting to, thinking about it, but I've never had the courage. But somehow, I think you might be able to help me. I know you probably think that's absurd. I mean, I barely know you. But give me a chance. Please.'

Daniel turned to him. 'I'll think about it. When are you here next?'

'Next Monday.'

'Alright, I'll meet you here at eight p.m. next Monday. If I don't show up, I've decided against it. If I do, it'll cost you five hundred pounds. For that, I'll stay with you for both nights if that's what you want.'

'It's a deal, Hal.'

Daniel smiled. 'OK then. There's just one more thing. You haven't told me your name?'

'It's Patrick.'

Chapter Forty-Two

———

Angie rang Ray, and then she called Ben, and then Ray, and then Ben again until she could no longer feel her own fingers. She tried calling from her mobile, from the landline and from another old Nokia phone that she found in her kitchen drawer, and which had a number neither of them would recognise. No one answered.

It began to grow dark outside, dusky shadows wrapping themselves like claws around the empty house. She lay on the top of Ben's bed, not wanting to climb inside in case he suddenly arrived home and wanted to crawl into clean sheets. She did not wash, nor eat. She drifted about, half conscious, the walls of the house bending in and out as she looked at them, as if this whole episode was a terrifying hallucination.

If Julia called, Angie did not pick up. She knew deep down that Julia was trying to help her, but she also knew that she judged her for not recognising Ray for what he was for all this time. But what was he exactly? For the past eighteen years, she had trusted him, falling easily into a pattern set by Ray, a life dictated by his schedule and his rules. But she had been so young, had a baby, and lost her mother all at the same time. She had never known another type of life. This had been her normal and she had been contented with it. But now, everything she had relied upon had exploded and the shards of this optical illusion were scattered all around her, unable to be pieced back together again.

Suddenly, her mobile rang out and shocked her out of her strange reverie.

'Hello? Ray, is that you?' Her heart was banging against her chest.

'Yes, it's me.'

'Fuck. I can't believe you've actually called. How's Ben? Where are you? When are you coming home?' The words raced from her.

'That's completely up to you.'

'What do you mean, it's up to me? I've been trying to reach you in like forever. What the fuck is going on? Why did you take Ben away?'

Her voice was reed-thin, her tears cascading down her cheeks unbidden.

'Too many questions. I mean exactly what I said. It's up to you.' He paused and there was silence. Angie could only hear her own erratic breathing.

'I understand that you took it upon yourself to root through my private papers.'

'I, no, I didn't. I wouldn't. It was an accident.'

'If you lie to me, Ange, this is going to get a whole lot uglier. I know you have. Ben told me.'

'Ben told you? When? You haven't been home?'

'He messaged me. He messages me all the time. He keeps an eye on things for me. He's an excellent little spy. He tells me that you and that nosey, fat friend of yours have been running around playing Cagney and fucking Lacey all over the county. Now, why would you want to start doing that?'

'I, we, well, the papers. They were so odd. All those different names and bank accounts and stuff. And I couldn't get hold of you. And Ben was acting up and I didn't know what to do. And Julia thought that we might be able to find some things out.' She sniffed loudly and wiped her nose on the sleeve of her sweat top.

'So, you suddenly decided not to trust me, after all this time, did you? Have I ever let you down? Have I ever been unpleasant to you in any way? Have you had such a fucking awful life so far that you felt the need investigate me as if I was a criminal or something? I'm the good guy here. You've messed with my work stuff and it's the one thing I've always asked you never to do. And I'm your husband! Clearly, if anyone should be hacked off, it's me. You don't trust me anymore and I've never given you any reason to doubt me. And now I quite simply can't trust you.'

'I'm sorry, Ray, I'm really sorry, but where were you all this time? You've never been out of touch for this long and I really needed you. Ben has been very difficult, and I've been so worried about him. It's not easy managing him by myself. He needs his father around. I need you around. I can't deal anymore with your absences and your lack of communication. I want us to be a normal family.'

Ray guffawed as if she had just told the funniest joke he had ever heard. 'A normal family? Do me a favour. There's no such thing as normal, and believe me, I should know. I'm the world's leading expert on relationships and everyone is fucked up one way or another, like that Larkin bloke said. Every family is filled with envy and cruelty and hatred and lust and violence and greed and if you think there's even one standard loving family unit out there, you've been watching way too much shit television.'

'That's so cynical. Do you think we are weird?'

273

'Of course. We don't conform to a standard view of marriage now, do we? We got married because you got pregnant, we don't live together for part of the week, we don't share our everyday experiences. By anyone's book, that's not a usual set-up. But why does everyone feel they have to conform anyway? It's so boring.'

'So, you think I'm boring?' she squeaked.

'No, of course not. You've never been demanding and that's what I wanted: a bolthole where I could be safe and where no one would ask too many questions. And a son, of course. I always wanted a son. I've always loved what we have, but now you've disappointed me by doubting me and by discussing our personal lives with other people. I suppose I should have realised it would happen. Everyone lets me down in the end. But somehow, I had hoped that you wouldn't.'

Angie made no reply. She felt winded, as though Ray had physically punched her in the stomach.

'Now, you need to listen, Angie baby. You need to do exactly as I say.'

'You wouldn't hurt Ben, would you Ray? He's your son. He's our son.'

'What are you talking about? Of course I wouldn't hurt him. I'm not an animal and I love him. He's my own flesh and blood. But I can bend his ear. I could turn him away from you in a nanosecond if I wanted to. He's very malleable and impressionable. I don't think it would be too difficult to make him hate you. He's already at that stage where he's cutting the strings. I could simply sever them completely. But I don't want to turn the boy against his mother. I just want us to be a family again.'

She gulped away another avalanche of tears. 'So, what do you want me to do?'

'I want you to collect every scrap of paper you have found and anything else that you've left in the cubbyhole at the top of the wardrobe and parcel them up. Then I want you to get on a train and come to London with them. I'll message you full instructions about where to deliver them. If you make copies, or if you tell anyone what you're doing or where you're going, I'll make damned sure that you never see Ben again. Do we understand each other?'

'So, if we meet and I give you all the stuff, can we then go back home with Ben?'

'We'll sort it all out. You're just going to have to trust me on this one. I've got it all worked out. It'll all be fine. Don't you worry. Now, I have to go.'

'Wait! Can you put me on to Ben just for a minute?' she pleaded. 'I really need to speak to him.'

'He's not here right now.'

'Where is he? Is he alright? Is he eating?'

'He's fine and you'll see him for yourself in a couple of days, as long as you do exactly as you're told. I'm hanging up now, but keep an eye on your phone. I'll be in touch.'

The screen clicked back to her home screen with a recent picture of Ben smiling and holding a football cup aloft. Angie kissed his image for the thousandth time that day and collapsed into an exhausted heap on to his duvet.

Chapter Forty-Three

———

Diana was on her way to the shop for the first time in several weeks. Ian had kept in touch sporadically. As far as she could tell sales were going well, and he seemed to be keeping it all under control. She was heading up Harpenden High Street and about to drive around the back of the shops near Sainsburys when her mobile rang. She pressed the button on her car screen to answer it.

'Mrs Whitlock, it's Susan calling from the home. I'm afraid your mother has taken a turn for the worse. I think you should come now if you can.'

Diana gripped the steering wheel, her hands clammy. 'I'm on my way.'

She swung the car around, almost knocking a cyclist off his bicycle who was riding along in her blind spot. She waved a quick sorry as he cursed her in the rear-view mirror.

The home was nearby in St Albans on King Harry's Lane. It was a modern, unelaborate building, but the rooms were clean, the corridors did not stink of wee, and the staff were kind. Diana drove there far too quickly, parking somewhat haphazardly in the carpark and running in.

'Ah, Mrs Whitlock, that was fast,' Susan commented, coming the other way along the corridor to meet her.

'What happened?'

'Well, she had a visitor this morning and just after he left, it appears that she has suffered another stroke, I'm afraid. It's not uncommon for another to follow the first, particularly at her age. Unfortunately, the doctor thinks that it is so severe that she may only last a few more hours. I'm so sorry.'

Diana's heart was twitching, and sweat trickled down her spine: a combined result of the stress of this news and a sudden hot flush. She patted her forehead with her sleeve.

'A visitor?'

'A gentleman, a Mr Maloney.'

'Jesus, no!'

Rushing past the nurse, she scooted up the corridor into her mother's room. Her mother lay immobile, her mouth hanging slack, her face sunken and yellow. Her eyes were open yet unseeing and her breath came in sharp rasps, as if she was choking. Diana took her hand, stroking her skin which was as dry as paper.

'Mum, it's me, Diana. Can you hear me? The man who came, was he the man from the council? Did he scare you? Did he try to hurt you

The continuous wet rattle was her only response.

Diana sat with her mother over the next few hours, weeping silent tears and talking to her intermittently, hoping she could hear her and that it might provide some comfort to her. The care staff flitted in and out and brought Diana the occasional cup of tea, which lay untouched, until there were a number of plastic cups loitering on the side table. None were drunk, turning cold and filmy.

As the evening drew in and the room darkened, Marjorie gasped one final time and then all was still.

Chapter Forty-Four

———

Daniel and Patrick fell into a regular routine of meeting on a Monday evening and parting on a Wednesday morning. During the day on Tuesdays was free time for Daniel, and Patrick would often pay for him to go to the cinema or do a little shopping while he attended to work. Patrick had generous discounts at a variety of stores where he had corporate clients and allowed Daniel to use them. They ate out at different restaurants each time, usually of Daniel's choosing. He had no intention of eating in the coffee shop at the Metropole or indeed relying on their atrocious room service menu. It was bad enough that he had to sleep there, given that it was several notches down from the usual high-class hotels he spent the night in. But financially, it was lucrative and provided him with a steady income. Patrick paid him in cash as soon as they met each Monday. It meant that there was less pressure to work the bars every single night.

Patrick was undemanding, kind, gentle and most importantly, nervous, only allowing Daniel to initiate him slowly. For weeks, they merely kissed and held each other while wearing their pyjamas (Patrick had bought him a couple of pairs), Patrick sighing while Daniel rolled his eyes towards the ceiling in the dark. They paid the hotel subscription to the porn channel and watched it together. Over time, they progressed to being naked together.

They stroked each other but went no further, until finally, Patrick decided it was time to be a little more adventurous.

'Would you, you know,' he stuttered one evening, when they had drunk a couple of bottles of wine and spent a good deal of time fondling each other.

'You want to have sex?'

'No, no, definitely not that, not yet.'

Daniel stifled a yawn. 'So, what? A blowjob?'

Patrick nodded almost imperceptibly, and Daniel could imagine his face flushing beetroot with shame in the darkness.

'OK, but only on one condition,' he teased, kissing Patrick.

'What's that?'

'We do it with the lights on. It's only fun if you can watch what I'm doing to you.'

'No, I really don't think so. I don't want to,' Patrick began to protest, but Daniel had already reached over and switched on the light on the side table.

'Now, my darling, don't be silly. You're going to enjoy this. You need to trust me.' He bent down and opened Patrick's fly, pulling Patrick into a sitting position so that he could see himself in the mirror on the dressing table. 'Now, just relax and enjoy. Watch me.'

And the light was just perfect for Patrick to see exactly what Daniel was doing to him, and it was just about good enough for the camera on Daniel's phone to capture all the action as well. It was recording in the corner of the room, just as it did each and every time he visited Patrick. Daniel believed it was always important to have evidence to fall back on just in case he should ever need a safety net. After all, evidence was everything, which is how he had escaped to London in the first place.

Chapter Forty-Five

Angie arrived at the station in Cambridge way before the first train was due to leave. Sleep was a thing of the past and anyway, she wanted to make sure she got a parking space before the hordes of daily commuters arrived. The earliest train to London left at four forty-eight and she was on it. It would get her into Kings Cross just after six a.m., far too soon for her rendezvous with Ray, but she wanted to be early.

As the train rattled through the countryside, she opened her bags and checked the contents over and over. As Ray had requested, she had brought everything that had been secreted in the hiding place in the bedroom. There were a great number of papers and she had had to split them across two canvas bags. She had contemplated putting them in an overnight case, but was paranoid about leaving the bag in a luggage rack or overhead in case it was stolen, or she left it behind in some demented moment.

The train arrived and she gathered herself together, waiting until everyone else had left the train before getting off. She walked briskly into the station and spotted a Starbucks where she ordered a double macchiato and hid herself at the back of the cafe, sipping it slowly. She checked her phone every minute, but there were no further messages. In fact, there had been no communication since

Ray had messaged her two days before to tell her precisely where to meet. She read and re-read his text and checked Google Maps to make sure she knew exactly where she was going.

They were due to meet at noon at The Holly Bush in Hampstead. It would only take twenty minutes or so to get to Hampstead on the tube, but she headed up there around ten. She was glad that she did, because the pub was not easy to find, hidden as it was off a small, steep road that led away from the tube station. She lugged her bags up the hill and found it eventually: a pretty pub with a cream exterior and green foliage outside. It was closed, but there was an old wooden bench at the front, warmed by the sun. She sat down and waited. Very few people passed by except for the staff working there, who turned up in dribs and drabs for their shifts, looking at her with pity, probably thinking it was a shame that such a relatively young woman was so addicted to alcohol that she was lurking outside a pub two hours before opening time. She was aware that she looked like a hobo: her hair unkempt and wearing sweats and dirty trainers, carrying canvas bags. It was a mercy that they did not try to move her on.

She slouched on the bench, every bone in her body aching for sleep and yet, she was hyperalert, constantly glancing up and down the street for Ray. The time passed noon and he had still not arrived. She could not decide whether to go inside or to wait for him outside, but decided on the latter. She could not afford to miss him. As she waited, the knot that was tied permanently around her stomach tightened a notch every minute that Ray was late. It reached a quarter past, and she began to wonder whether he was coming at all, and then she saw him - or at least, she thought it was him. A man strode purposefully up the hilly street. He had lolloping Ray's gait, but he was dressed completely differently in dark sweatpants and a cheap, nylon sports jacket, with a baseball cap pulled low over his face. Ray was always smartly dressed, even when he was casual. He liked his labels.

'Hi, Angie, baby.' He bent down and kissed her on the cheek. 'Let's go.' He scooped up the bags and she hurried after him back down the hill.

'Where are we going? Where's Ben?!' she shouted.

Ray stopped dead in his tracks, turning and walking back to her. 'Don't make a fuss here, OK?'

It took all of her remaining willpower to stop herself asking him more and more questions right there in the middle of the street, but she dug her nails into her palms and followed him as instructed.

They turned right and then left, winding up and down numerous small streets until they reached the entrance to the Heath, where the muddy paths were slippery under foot after the previous night's rainstorm. Ray stomped on ahead and she struggled to keep up, despite the fact she was no longer burdened with her bags. They twisted this way and that, avoiding the dogwalkers who kept to the central tracks. When they reached a densely wooded area with no one else around, Ray stopped.

'Where's Ben? I have to see him,' Angie whispered, tears cascading unbidden down her cheeks. 'You promised that he would be here.'

'We've got a few things to straighten out first.'

'You think? Fuck, Ray. What the hell is going on? Where have you been? And what are all these papers?'

'It's work stuff. I told you. It's highly confidential. You had no right to go snooping around, and now I've got to declare this as a security breach and return all these papers to MI5. My cover is blown, and you've put other people in danger by sharing it with that moronic friend of yours.'

'Why didn't you just come home and talk to me about it?'

'Because for some reason, out of the blue, you start thinking something fishy was going on. Me! And after all these years. And you told Julia. And then the two of you went around asking questions at care homes and Christ knows where else, and if I'd come back to the village I couldn't know what to expect. Julia may have reported me to the police. I just couldn't risk it.'

'But if you didn't want to draw attention to yourself, why did you kidnap Ben? I only went to the police because he disappeared.'

'I picked Ben up because he asked me to. If you want to know the truth, he's been extremely unhappy at home, and he said you were behaving very oddly, messing with my papers, and suddenly plotting with Julia. He wanted to get away for a few days without you knowing.'

'But he must have realised that I was going to panic when he didn't come home, and when I hadn't heard from him.'

'I agree. I told him to call you, but he wouldn't, and he asked me not to call either, so I respected his wishes. I realise that it wasn't my best decision, but I was flattered that he reached out to me, that he needed me. It's always been you and him and I've always felt slightly side-lined because I couldn't always be there, so it was nice to be wanted.'

'You could have been there more. You could have found a more suitable job. I've raised him single-handedly. You side-lined yourself to a large degree.'

'It wasn't of my choosing. It was work, and it was important. When I was home, you and he were as thick as thieves. It was difficult for me, and you never even noticed. So, when he called, I reacted. Not sensibly possibly, but it is what it is.'

'None of this makes any sense. I've always kept your work secret and I've always supported you and worked around your way of life.'

'Until you didn't.'

'But where the fuck were you? I needed to talk to you about Ben. I needed your help. You've never just disappeared this way. What was so important that you couldn't reply to me at all?'

'I've been very tied up on a particularly sensitive case that I've been working on for years and it's coming to a head. Much of the time I was abroad with little or no internet or phone access. It's taken up all of my time and energy. I've only recently got back. I can't tell you any more than that. I think you've screwed up the plan now anyway.'

'So, where is Ben and how's he doing?'

'Ben is fine. I wanted him to come with me today, but I don't think he could face you. He feels ashamed for putting you through so much worry. I said I'd talk to you first and make sure he was forgiven.'

'Of course, he's forgiven. It's you I'm finding it hard to forgive. What kind of a husband steals his own child away and doesn't tell his wife?! I thought he'd been kidnapped!'

'Now let's not be all melodramatic.'

'Melodramatic!' she screamed, lunging at Ray, but he grabbed her arms and held her away.

'Angie, look at yourself! You're in no fit state to look after Ben at the moment, which is much as I suspected. I think you need a good rest and maybe someone professional to talk to. I've arranged for you to spend a few days somewhere quiet where you can recuperate and then, when you're calmer, you can see Ben.'

'I'm perfectly fine! I'm in this state because you went AWOL, and then you took Ben away and I've been absolutely frantic. I've been losing my mind with worry.'

'And I'm sorry for that, I really am, but all the more reason for you to get some rest. You're not well enough to look after Ben right now. Let me help you, and in a few days when you've got some sleep and talked to someone about these weird delusions you've suddenly developed because you found some of my work stuff, we can all go back to normal.'

'Fuck off, Ray. It's *us* who need to talk.'

'We need to do that too. But until you calm down, I'm not telling you where Ben is. I'm just trying to do what's best for the both of you.'

Chapter Forty-Six

Diana buried her mother quietly. None of Marjorie's friends were still alive, and apart from the neighbours opposite, there was no one else to invite. There were no speeches at the service and very few tears. Diana was simply too tired to cry anymore. She felt like a boxer who had been hit so many times in the head by her old adversary death that her brain was numb. Now she was truly alone in the world.

She sat in the living room, nestled in Patrick's new armchair covered by a fluffy throw from her shop and sipping a large glass of Rioja. When she returned from the funeral, she slithered out of her black wool dress that had seen far too frequent service of late and pulled on her warmest pyjamas and dressing gown. Her feelings at the loss of her mother were complex. Having left home at fifteen, effectively forced out by her father for having brought disgrace on the family, she fled to London, leaving behind all hope of a brighter future. She did not take her 'O'-levels and as a result, she did not get the chance to even contemplate 'A'-levels, college, or university, settling for her secretarial qualification. But she had made her own way and life had been successful enough, marrying Patrick and owning her own shop. In the end, qualifications had been of little consequence, and she firmly believed that what ifs were a waste of time and energy.

Yet she could not help but wonder, alone as she was in her living room, what might have happened if anyone had pushed her harder about what had actually happened or shown enough compassion to help her when she was so very young. She had refused to say who the father was, terrified. Her father had posed no further questions, instead moving straight on to judgement assessing neither facts nor mitigation. Her mother, frightened of her father's temper, never once stood up to him. Once he banished Diana, there was nothing more to be said. Her mother helped her to deal with her situation, but beyond that, Marjorie had stayed loyal to her father. It took Diana a very long time to forgive her for that.

Once in London, she tried to move on, and her fortuitous meeting and marriage with Patrick had anchored her. He loved her, even though it was dispassionately, but nevertheless he protected her. He was the first person to have ever done so. She did not invite her parents to her wedding. Her father, having disowned her, would not have come anyway and Marjorie's attendance would have been forbidden. For a long time, Diana believed that she would never see either of them again.

Then suddenly, one evening, almost fifteen years after she had left home, she received a phone call.

'Hello?'

'Diana, it's Mum.'

She dropped the phone, fumbling to pick it up again from the floor. 'Mum? How did you get my number?'

'Oh, well, does it matter? I've found you, haven't I? I heard you were married, and I called directory enquiries. I've spoken to dozens of people living in London with your surname, but I'm so pleased I've finally reached you.'

Silence.

'So, Diana, the reason I'm calling is, well, it's your father.'

'What about him?'

'He's dead.'

A small sound escaped from Diana unbidden, and she lowered herself onto the floor holding the phone close to her ear.

'Yes, well, it was all very sudden. I was making breakfast in the kitchen last week when I heard this loud thud from upstairs. I thought maybe a lamp had fallen over or something like that, but when I went up to check, it was your dad. It turns out he had a massive coronary as he got out of bed.'

'I'm sorry.' She paused. 'Are you alright?'

'Well, it's been a bit of a shock, as you can imagine, and it's so quiet, you know. No one demanding a cup of tea or complaining that his collar isn't ironed straight. You know how he was.'

'Yes, I remember.'

'I'm sorry I didn't call you sooner, but it's taken me a few days to get myself organised and then I had to find you. Anyway, the funeral is next Friday. Will you come?'

'I, well, I don't know. I'm not sure he'd want me there.' Her heart was pounding like a bass drum against her chest.

'Of course he would, Diana. He loved you. I know he had a strange way of showing it, but he loved you nevertheless.'

'He definitely had a very strange way of showing it. You know, I've thought about it so often over the years, and the plain fact of the matter is that he was more concerned about his own bloody reputation than he was about what happened to his own daughter.'

'I know, and I spent all these years trying to get him to reconcile with you, but he was a stubborn bastard. I'm sorry for all of it, Diana. I really am. And I can't change what's happened in the past. But now we can talk about it openly and try to make things right, attempt to move past it. But I need you there next week. I've missed you so much and I know it will take time, but if you can bear it, let me try to be a mother to you now even if I've failed miserably at it so far.'

Diana paused for a long time. 'Let me think about it,' and she hung up.

'You should go,' Patrick urged her when she told him about the call. 'She's reached out and he was your father after all. I still don't know why you all fell out exactly, and I've never pushed you on the details, but she's held out an olive branch and I think you should take it. Two wrongs don't make a right.'

'Any other cliches you'd like to throw in?'

'No, I'm sorry, but you know what I mean. It must have taken some guts for her to find you. Maybe you can try to rebuild your relationship with her now. You did tell me that she'd been completely manipulated by your dad, didn't you, so cut her some slack. Maybe now that she is free of him, you can start again.'

'Maybe you're right. The problem with you is that you're far too forgiving. Maybe you should have been a priest after all.'

Diana had wanted to take the train, because she felt extremely wobbly at the thought of going home, but to get from Harpenden to Milton Keynes meant travelling into London and back out again, whereas driving would take her just under forty-five minutes. When she came off the M1 and began to circle around the multitudinous roundabouts, she felt as though she was in a surreal dream. Everything was familiar to her and at the same time, none of it was. And when she reached the top of her parents' street, she had to stop and take some deep breaths. She had not been back here since the argument and the events of the whole terrible evening roared back into her mind. She reverted to being fifteen again and felt completely terrified. She rooted in her handbag for some Rescue Remedy, unscrewing the top and drinking straight from the bottle before starting the car again and driving down to park outside the house.

The semi-detached was depressingly drab, with peeling paint on the windows and plants drooping in the front garden. She emptied the rest of the Rescue Remedy down her throat and stepped out of the car. Her mother opened the door before she could ring the bell. Curtain-twitching was a practiced skill of Marjorie's, her always having been able to tell you exactly what the neighbours were up to at all times and to alert the street to the sudden apparition of strangers.

'Oh, you've come. I'm so glad.'

She enfolded Diana against her soft bosom, who struggled free. Her mother looked older, soft lines criss-crossing her face.

'Hi, Mum,' she replied, her voice small.

Diana followed her inside.

'The hearse will be here shortly, and the funeral car. The crematorium isn't too far away.'

'Are there many people coming?'

'I would think so, dear. I've catered for fifty or so to come back to the house. His work colleagues will come, his mates from the Rotary Club, our other friends. I'm expecting a decent turnout.'

Diana felt a trickle of cold sweat run down her back.

'I'm not sure I can do this, Mum.'

'It's hard, burying a parent, I know. But you'll get through it.'

But that was not the part that Diana was worried about.

The car arrived and they sidled into it, the leather seats cold against their legs. Her mother prattled on about vol-au-vents and cake and whether or not she had enough cups and saucers. 'I've borrowed the tea urn from the Rotary. It's much faster than boiling the kettle a thousand times.' She patted Diana's knee. 'You look very well, Diana. I'm so pleased that you've managed to pick yourself up and move on. Maybe soon I can meet that lovely husband of yours.'

She spoke as if the estrangement of the past fifteen years had evaporated like the morning dew and that everything was now miraculously restored.

When they arrived at the crematorium, there was quite a crowd already gathered. The car stopped and Diana opened the door quickly. 'I need the toilet,' she whispered and darted out of the car. She only just made it in time before her bowels exploded with such force that she felt utterly nauseous. When she had pulled herself together and splashed her face with cold water, she re-emerged.

She spotted her mother talking to a group of mourners.

'Ah, there you are, Diana. Come and say hello to Mr and Mrs Radwell.'

But Diana ignored her, not wishing to make eye contact with anyone. She put her head down and pushed her way towards the hall, moving to the front and taking her place in the first pew. She had no wish to walk with her mother behind the coffin or to be gawped at by the attendees, who would all no doubt be gossiping about the prodigal daughter's return.

The people filed in; her mother at the rear, followed by the coffin bearers. There were a number of speeches about her father, eulogising his work for charity via the Rotary and regaling the mourners with a few funny stories about his exploits down the pub. He was, apparently, a devoted husband and father. There were several moments when Diana was forced to stifle a laugh. She certainly rolled her eyes at quite a number of comments.

And then he was committed to the flames, another life incinerated.

She helped her mother up and they walked slowly out into the memorial garden. The day was cold and grey, with heavy clouds threatening rain. They stood, shivering slightly, as the mourners filed past to pay their respects. Diana went through the motions, shaking hands, thanking people for coming. No one asked her where she had been or how she was. Diana was shaking throughout, not so much from the cold but from anxiety. If she could get through this part, she would manage. The line was dribbling to an end, and she began to relax slightly. He was not there.

Most people, thankfully not all, returned to the house for tea and sherry. Diana handed plates of nibbles around, which were eagerly gobbled up. 'It'll save me making dinner later,' she heard one woman remark to her husband. Most stayed for around an hour or so.

Diana hid in the kitchen towards the end, washing up and drying the dishes.

'Hello, Diana.'

She screamed and dropped a plate onto the kitchen tiles. It shattered into a thousand shards.

'Now, don't make a fuss.' He pushed the kitchen door closed behind him.

'Stay away from me, you bastard.'

He stepped towards her. 'Now don't be like that, Diana. You've grown into quite an attractive woman, haven't you?'

Diana pushed past him, wrenching the door open. Running into the hall, she grabbed her handbag and coat from the table, struggling to breathe. Diving out of the front door, she heard her mother chatting to friends in the hall. She knew she should stop to say goodbye, but she had lost the power of speech.

Back then, all those years ago, she had not even understood what was happening. Uncle Frank had been bothering her since she was a very small child. Everyone thought he was so bloody marvellous, a great guy, the life and soul of the party. No one noticed when he slipped up to her bedroom for half an hour. They were all too drunk by then. And when it all went wrong, she could not tell anyone who had got her into trouble. They would have simply derided her as a liar. They all loved Frank. He had a sweet wife, and they were desperately trying for a family. What would he have wanted with a skinny, young girl? They would have thought she was just making it up, covering up for some boy at school.

And so, she said nothing.

'I'm sorry, Diana, but I can't have you around me and your mother anymore after such disgraceful behaviour. I'm just very disappointed in you,' were her father's final words to her. *So very Rotary*, Diana had reflected as she listened to the words of praise at his funeral.

Chapter Forty-Seven

After several profitable years, Daniel decided that he no longer needed to sell his body to make money. He had honed his skills as a trader of stolen goods from the jewellery and the other expensive items he filched from his victims, selling them online and through backdoor deals. He had also worked hard on his social skills. He had realised from an early age that, merely by listening to people and proving to be empathetic, he could get them to reveal deeply personal things that he could use to his advantage. But now he knew how to respond to their revelations and to encourage them to tell him even more, perhaps things they had never told to another living soul before. He could achieve this pre-coitally as well as post, once he had secured their trust, which removed a great deal of the effort - and in many cases, revulsion - that he had to endure. He perfected the art of slipping in and out of a variety of personas, to which his vast collection of ID cards testified, but he began to dream that he could take it a step further. He believed that he could pass for an expert in certain professions in order to con others out of money. Man's need to offload problems was often even greater than their craving for sex.

He set himself up in a small room in Harley Street. This prestigious medical street, one of the most famous in the world, was crammed full of eminently qualified doctors who genuinely sought to cure people of all manner of illnesses. However, it was also a street where you could rent a room as a medical practitioner without anyone checking your certificates too closely. Some of the landlords were less Hippocractically minded, preferring to ensure that every room in their building was fully utilised and turning a blind eye to their renters' activities as long as they paid up in full every month.

And so, Daniel established himself there as a counsellor, helping people to deal with their anxieties and their failing marriages. In his early twenties - with a thick, dark beard which he highlighted with the odd streak of grey for gravitas - he could pass for thirty-five easily. Quite quickly, he gained a considerable reputation and established an impressive waiting list. He recorded each session with his clients' permission, making sure there were no confidentiality agreements in place. And all he needed to do was lean back in his chair and listen to their tales of infidelity, strange sexual proclivities, financial worries, and other deep, dark secrets. It was a goldmine. He believed that everyone's problems ultimately stemmed from sexual frustration or repression. He allowed them to let it all out.

Of course, he had absolutely no intention of letting go of Patrick completely, despite his newly found, respectable career. Patrick had been his cash cow and would have to be milked as such now more than ever - just in a different way. After all, he was so bored of their weekly rendezvous. They met up on a Monday night, ate, fucked. They did the same on a Tuesday and then Patrick left. Patrick was extremely generous, showering him with clothes and gifts, mostly based on items Daniel pointed out on websites and in the shops they strolled past. But in actuality, they had very little in common. Patrick did not like to hear about what Daniel got up to for the rest of his week, as it involved sleeping with other people, which Patrick had begged him to give it up on a thousand occasions. And Patrick refused to discuss his home life, apart from admitting that he had a loving wife and no children. He would not even reveal where he lived. But of course, Daniel had known who he was and everything about him for years. Naturally, he had done of all the appropriate research. When together, they would stick to discussing television programmes and Patrick's work, which was incredibly dull. If he had to listen to one more story about a retailer who had reneged on an order or failed to pay, Daniel thought he might hang himself.

'I can't do this anymore,' Daniel announced out of the blue one evening as he lay on his back next to Patrick.

'What do you mean?' Patrick asked, propping himself up on his elbows and staring at Daniel, his hair standing on end with static from the pillowcase.

'I mean this. It's over. I'm not going to see you again.'

Patrick sat up and grabbed Daniel's arm. 'But why? We've been together for years. You can't just leave me without any warning. We're partners.'

Daniel snorted, leaping out of bed and pulling on his underpants. 'Partners? You think we've had an actual relationship? You really think that's what this is?'

'Well, yes. I mean, what else would you call it?'

'Let me think.' He picked up a packet of cigarettes from the side table, picking one out slowly and lighting it. He stood up, blowing smoke towards the bed, which he knew Patrick hated. 'Personally, if I had to label it, I'd call it sexual exploitation. You've paid me for sex every time you've seen me. Initially, you had sex with a minor, which is a criminal offence.'

'You were nineteen,' Patrick whispered, his face ashen.

'I wasn't actually, but let's move on. Our relationship has been solely transactional. You pay me for sex, we have sex. That's it. In fact, you used me to bring yourself metaphorically out of the closet. You knew that I was a sex worker and have continued to be so. You know nothing about my personal life, and I know very little about yours, although truthfully, I know a great deal more than you might wish me to. So, I would conclude categorically that we are not, nor ever have been, in a relationship.'

'Is that what you really think?'

'Yes, that's what I really think.'

'But I love you, Hal. I always have. And I thought you loved me too.'

'Oh, that's very sweet, really, but rather sad, don't you think?'

Patrick wiped a tear from his eye and jumped out of bed, pulling on the bathrobe which lay in a crumpled heap on the floor. He moved towards Daniel and put a hand on his shoulder. 'What's wrong? You can't mean any of this, so something else must be going on.'

Daniel shoved him away. 'Patrick, you're not listening to me. This is over. This is the last time you will ever see me.'

'Well, if that's how you really feel, I suppose there's nothing I can do about it. I'm guessing you've met someone else, is that it? Someone who's more fun, or younger, or better-looking or richer?' He moved over to the minibar and grabbed a couple of miniatures of whisky, which he opened with a twist of his hand and swallowed down in one gulp.

'No, I just want to stop selling myself for sex.'

'But that's precisely what I've been asking you to do forever.'

'I know and I've finally taken your advice.'

'Well, that's great. So, we can carry on as we are, can't we, without all your other sordid stuff on the side?'

'No, we can't. I'm going legit.'

He stubbed out his cigarette on the ashtray by the bed and began to light up another one.

'Oh, right, and what will you do? It won't be easy to replace the money I pay you, not to mention all the nice little extras, the food, the gifts.'

Patrick hurled the empty bottles towards the wastepaper basket and missed.

'I have no intention of giving up your money.'

Turning to Patrick, he continued. 'You're going to carry on paying me just as you always have. In fact, I'd like you to pay me quite a bit more than that.'

'And why would I do that exactly?'

'Because I'm assuming that you wouldn't want your lovely wife - Diana, isn't it? – yes, I know her name, or your friends and neighbours, not to mention your work colleagues, to know what we've been up to all this time. Or would you?'

'I can't believe you're blackmailing me.'

'Well, more fool you.'

'Do your worst. They wouldn't believe you.'

Daniel picked up his phone and clicked on something. A moment later, Patrick's phone pinged with a new message.

'Go on, open it.'

Patrick opened his phone.

'Press play,' Daniel commanded.

With a shaking hand, Patrick pressed the play arrow and moments later, he threw the phone onto the bed.

'If you don't pay me, I'll send that video to your entire contacts list, which I've copied over in full, by the way. And there's plenty more of that. I've recorded every moment we've spent together, including our first sexual encounters when I was just an impressionable, young boy recently arrived in London.'

Patrick stared at him, unable to speak.

'So, I'm going to get dressed now and say goodbye, but I'll be sending you the payment amounts which I require in order to ensure my complete discretion. Miss any of them or refuse to pay in full and I'll unleash a torrent of perversion on your nearest and dearest from which you will never recover.'

He disappeared into the bathroom taking his clothes and his phone with him. When he reappeared five minutes later, Patrick was sitting on the floor emptying the contents of the minibar.

'Bye, Patrick, and thanks for everything. I'll be in touch. Don't ignore me when I do.' He smiled and walked towards the hotel room door, slamming it loudly behind him.

Chapter Forty-Eight

Angie tramped back out of Hampstead Heath, her white trainers ruined by the mud, and followed Ray back to the tube station.

'Did you know that this is the deepest station on the Underground,' Ray informed her as they descended downwards in the lift.

'Say, are you a tour guide?' an American woman wearing a gigantic bum bag and a MAGA baseball cap asked him. 'Do you do tours of Central London?'

'No, I'm afraid not,' Ray replied, turning away from the woman, and threading his arm firmly through Angie's as the lift doors opened. 'Come on.'

'Where are we going?' she shouted over the roar of the train as it rushed onto the platform.

'You'll find out soon enough. It's in the leafy suburbs.'

They boarded and then got off three stations later at Camden Town, crossing over onto the other branch of the Northern Line. The next tube took them a further three stops until they reached Kings Cross.

'This way,' he shouted over the din of the station concourse, grabbing her firmly by the hand, as if they were young lovers criss-crossing London on a day out. They followed the crowds through the tunnels leading to St Pancras station and boarded a Thameslink train.

'Don't we need to buy tickets?'

'I've already got them. I bought them this morning to save time.'

The train departed and they rattled through various, dreary London stations before the scenery altered and countryside appeared. After half an hour or so, an impressive cathedral appeared in the distance. 'This is our stop,' he announced.

They descended from the train and Ray marched out of the station, turning left.

'St Albans? Why here?'

'Why not? It's a picturesque town, with plenty of shops and a few decent restaurants and with easy access to London.' He chuckled to himself. 'I would make a rather good tour guide, wouldn't I? Something to consider in the future perhaps.'

They walked briskly along a busy street, passing all the usual chains of shops and a few pubs, which were remarkably busy for the middle of the afternoon. Suddenly, Ray dived down a side street and then down another, Angie struggling to keep pace, until they came to a nondescript block of flats at the end of a small cul-de-sac. Ray let himself in and ushered Angie inside.

'It's straight up the stairs.'

They climbed four floors and by the time they reached the top, Angie's legs were aching. She wasn't used to doing so much walking. It was a modern block that still smelt of paint and adhesive as if the builders had just finished that very day. Ray took out a set of keys from his coat pocket and opened the door of the flat. It was stark, all empty white walls and grey Ikea furniture, as if no one had ever lived there.

'Is this where you've been living?'

'No. This is where you will be staying for the next couple of days.'

'Is Ben here?'

'Obviously not. I've told you. You're going to get some rest and when you're feeling better and have recovered from your current delusions about me, you can see him. You've poisoned my son enough already with your bizarre conspiracy theories.' He moved over to the window and pulled the cord to close the blind. 'Now, give me your phone.'

'What the hell for? You're not taking my phone.'

She held onto her handbag tightly, backing away from him and as she did, she hit her leg hard on the corner of the dining table.

Taking advantage of her momentary distraction, Ray grabbed her bag and tipped the contents out onto the sofa, snatching her phone.

'I assume the code is still Ben's birthday.'

She nodded, wishing that she had thought about changing it before she saw him.

'Are you intending to keep me prisoner here? Is that the idea?'

'Of course not. There's food in the fridge and I've even chilled a bottle of white wine for you. I'm going out now, but I'll be back later on. Until then, be good.'

He pocketed her phone and keys for good measure, leaving the rest of the contents of her handbag scattered all over the sofa cushions.

'See you this evening.' He turned and walked out of the flat, slamming the door behind him.

She heard the key turn.

She ran over to the windows, but they were locked; and even if she had been able to open them, the drop was too high. She would have killed herself trying. She walked slowly over to the kitchen area, which was set out on one side of the lounge and opened the fridge. As promised, Ray had left her a cold bottle of Chardonnay. She unscrewed the top and located a large wine glass from the cupboard, filling it to the brim, before moving to place it on the kitchen table. Removing her coat and sweater, she fumbled inside her shirt and pulled a small Nokia phone out of her bra. She took a huge swig of wine and then typed out a WhatsApp message.

'I've made contact. Now in St Albans.' She messaged the name of the road and block of flats.

Two minutes later, her phone pinged back a thumbs up emoji.

Chapter Forty-Nine

Diana had been unable to find her mother's will anywhere, which was very odd because Marjorie had always been totally methodical. The rest of her paperwork was filed away neatly, including a copy of every bank statement she had received since at least 1973. Diana knew that her mother had made a will, because she had organised it for her when she moved to Harpenden a year or so after her father died.

They had slowly become reacquainted after his death, tiptoeing carefully around each other's edges, until one night they had finally opened up to each other.

As they sat next to each other on Marjorie's sofa one Sunday evening, drinking a bottle of Waitrose Merlot after sharing a roast dinner of over-cooked beef and soggy Yorkshire puddings, Marjorie confided in Diana as she never had before.

'You need to know that I begged your dad to take you back. I told him repeatedly that it wasn't right to ostracise your only child, that we should support you, but he just couldn't bring himself to do it. It was all about losing face, you see, and for him that was the most important thing. He'd worked so hard for his respectability, having come from nothing himself. He simply didn't know how to climb back down. And if only you'd told us who the father was, it might have helped. We could have got him to marry you at least.'

'No, you couldn't,' Diana mumbled into the dregs of her glass of wine. 'But *you* could have contacted me, regardless of Dad.'

'I thought about it every day. I really did. I never stopped torturing myself about it. But he told me I had a choice. I could stick with him, or I could run to you.' She picked at her nails. 'And I had to choose him. I was nothing by myself.'

Diana had held out her hand and her mother had squeezed it tight.

Diana located a copy of the will after several days. It was under a pile of unopened post in a manila envelope, which was odd as it did not have a stamp on it. She scanned it briefly, before dropping it to the floor.

'I don't bloody believe it.'

The next day Diana rang Marjorie's solicitor as soon as their office opened and made an appointment to visit him the following day.

'Mrs Whittaker,' the solicitor greeted her, 'I'm so very sorry to hear of your mother's passing. She was a lovely lady.'

'Thank you,' Diana replied, seating herself across the desk from Mr Singh. 'Yes, it's all very sad.'

'And so soon after the death of your husband. It must have all been very difficult for you. Coffee?'

'No, thank you.' She paused. 'Mr Singh, I won't take up too much of your time, as I know you're busy, but I have found a new will that my mother appears to have signed just a week before she suffered her stroke. Did you make this for her?'

Mr Singh held out his hand and Diana passed the will across the desk to him.

Having read it for a few minutes while Diana fidgeted in her chair, he placed the document back onto the desk.

'I did not make this will for her, but it appears to be perfectly legal. It has been signed by your mother and properly dated and witnessed.'

A wave of nausea passed over Diana and she swallowed hard. 'Could I possibly have a glass of water?'

'Of course.' He rose from his desk and moved over to a side cabinet, where he poured her a glass. 'Here you are.'

'Thank you.' She took a sip.

'I don't understand how or why she would have made this will. She didn't discuss it with me at any point and all she has left me are the contents of her bungalow.'

'It appears so.' He coughed. 'Do you know who this Mr Thomas Maloney is? As you can see, he's named as sole executor and beneficiary of her property and jewellery.'

'He's the man from the council.'

'I beg your pardon?'

'Well, my mother said he was from the council, but the council knew nothing about him and then before I could ask Mum about him again, she had the stroke and now it seems that he managed to make her change her will somehow. It's obviously a scam. We must be able to stop him.'

Mr Singh took a deep breath. 'I'm afraid I can't do anything. Your mother has made this will and it appears to be extremely clear as to her wishes. I suggest that if you are concerned, you should report it to the police, but I'm guessing they won't be much help. We can try to contest it through the courts, but it won't be easy.'

'But don't you have to make a will through a solicitor?'

'It's the best way to do it, obviously, but it is by no means an obligation. Anyone can write a will, sign, and witness it and it is generally completely binding. This one has been drafted using one of those forms you can download online. Unless you can find a way to stop this via the courts, Mr Maloney will be able to proceed with probate.'

'What gives him the right to take over my mother's affairs? It's ridiculous.'

'I'm afraid you have to follow the law in this matter.'

Diana slammed her glass onto the desk. 'I can't believe it's that easy to con a frail old woman into signing everything over to a perfect stranger without even checking!'

Mr Singh shuffled his papers. "You'd be surprised. There's very little protection for the elderly in so many matters.'

She stood up, knocking her chair backwards in her haste.

'Thank you for your time, Mr Singh.'

He shook her hand. 'I'm so sorry that I couldn't be of more help, and I really do wish you all the best. If I can be of any further help with contesting the will, if that's what you decide to do, please do make another appointment and we can progress from there.'

When Diana reached her car, she was shaking, barely able to press the key to open the door. Once inside, she rested her head on the steering wheel to steady herself. How she wished that Patrick was still here to help her through all of this, but he had chosen to leave her in the cruellest manner possible. It seemed that everyone she had ever loved had left her in the lurch.

Suddenly, her mobile rang. She rubbed her eyes and fumbled for her bag, which she had lobbed onto the passenger seat. It was an unknown caller.

'Hello, is that Patrick Whitlock?' a woman asked.

'No, it's his wife. I mean, his widow. Who's calling?'

'Look, I don't want to say too much on the phone, and I know you don't know me, and you probably think this is a scam, but I assure you that it's not. If you would be willing to meet me for a chat, I've found some information out about your husband which you might find useful.' The caller paused. 'Did you say widow?'

'Yes, my husband passed away a few months ago.'

'I'm so sorry to hear that. But I think in that case, you might want to hear what I've got to say even more.'

Chapter Fifty

Daniel had enjoyed an extremely successful career in Harley Street over the last few years, earning a decent amount of money in what he felt was a fairly honest way, if you discounted the recordings he made of his patients' confessions and innermost secrets. He kept all of them and used them for a lucrative bit of blackmail as and when required. In his own mind, compared to his previous employment choices, he was effectively going straight. His practice was huge success with his multiple referrals and ever-increasing fees, and at least seventy-five percent was cash in hand.

The previous week he had welcomed a new client: a woman of indeterminate age, tall, reasonably attractive, with her hair tied back in a tight bun and wearing a neat, tweed trouser suit. His initial analysis, which he had noted down as they began to chat the week before, was *career woman, single, sexually repressed*. His perfect client.

She presented herself at his practice for a second appointment on the following Tuesday afternoon. He collected her from reception himself. He liked to begin every session on a personal note, and he did not want to employ a secretary. They were far too expensive and intrusive.

'Mrs Bowen? How lovely to see you again.'

She nodded, uncrossing her long legs and rising from the uncomfortable chair she had perched herself on.

'Dr Blair.'

'I hope you're well.'

She made no reply.

'This way please.' He led her from the reception up the narrow flight of stairs into his consulting room, shutting the door behind her. 'Mrs Bowen, please take a seat.' He gestured to one of the two low armchairs, which were separated by a low, glass coffee table. 'Water?'

'No, I'm fine, thank you.' She sat back and crossed those lengthy legs over again.

'Do you mind if I recap on a few details from our last chat. It was fairly brief as I remember for a first visit.'

'Yes, I am sorry I had to cut it short.'

'So, Madeleine, or may I call you Maddy now that we know each other a little better?'

She looked at him, her eyes steely. 'No, Madeleine will do fine, thank you.'

He raised his eyebrows. 'Alright, Madeleine.'

He continued with the routine questions about how she was feeling, before laying his pen down on his notepad for a moment.

'So, let's start from where we left off, shall we?'

'Do you mind if I ask you a few questions first?'

'Of course not. I mean, it's not usual. We are here to talk about you not me, after all. But fire away.'

'Can you tell me about your qualifications?'

'Well, as you can see from my certificates,' he gestured to the numerous frames nailed to the walls, 'I studied Medicine at

Cambridge and then I specialised in mental health disorders after I qualified at Guy's Hospital.'

'That's what I thought. But Dr Blair,' she paused, having placed particular stress on the title of doctor, 'the thing is, when I checked with both Cambridge and Guy's, they had no record of you whatsoever. Strange, don't you think?'

He shifted slightly in his seat and his pen dropped onto the carpet. Bending down to retrieve it, he replied, 'That's very strange indeed. There must be a mix-up with their records. But can I ask, why were you checking up on me anyway?'

'Well, it always helps to know who you're talking to and how well-equipped they are to help patients before entrusting yourself to them, don't you think? Particularly when you discuss such personal matters.'

'I couldn't agree more. So, shall we turn our attention to you now?' His palm was sweaty, and he wiped it on his trouser leg.

She leant forward and stared straight at him. 'No, let's stick with you for a moment longer, Doctor, if you don't mind.' She smiled. 'Now, I have had a number of complaints about your unorthodox practices: some of which are unethical to say the least and others of which are extremely concerning. It's the real reason I came to see you in the first place - to see for myself what they were talking about. I must admit that even from our first session, I thought your methods were more than somewhat unconventional to say the least.'

Daniel slammed his pad on to the table and stood up. 'Who are you exactly?'

'I'm a private investigator. I've been approached by a number of your clients who allege that you have blackmailed them, or threatened to do so.' Her lips curled very slightly at the edges as she finished speaking.

'I deny any impropriety whatsoever. Who are these people who have complained? No one has ever complained to me.'

'I'm not at liberty to say. And that's not strictly true, is it? The fact is that if they do say anything, you threaten them with your video recordings. All I can tell you, Doctor or *Mr* Blair, is that I've been following you for some time and I've been compiling quite an impressive dossier. You've got away with this scam operation you've been running for some time, but it's all over now.'

'Get out of my office,' he hissed. 'You don't have a shred of evidence for these absurd allegations and if you pursue this any further, I will have my lawyer on you.'

She got up from the armchair, smoothing the creases in her trousers. 'I'm pleased to hear that you've got a lawyer. You'll be needing one. All my evidence is already with the police, including the recording I made of our meeting last week and today.' She hooked her bag over her arm and moved to the door. 'Nice meeting you, *Dr* Blair. I look forward to seeing you in court.'

As she closed the door, Daniel hurled the glass paperweight that sat on his desk. It shattered into a million pieces.

Chapter Fifty-One

There was a kerfuffle outside the door.

'Hang on, Ange. We are trying to get the door open. It might take a few minutes.'

'OK,' she called back.

There was a great deal of banging and drilling until eventually the flat door swung open. Ben raced through it and clung to his mother.

'Darling, oh it's so good to see you. Have you been alright? I've been so worried about you.' They hugged for far longer than he would normally allow.

'I've been fine.' He paused and looked around. 'Got anything to eat?'

'There's some stuff in the fridge.' She gestured over to the corner of the room.

'Hi Ange. How are you holding up?' Julia walked over to her friend and gave her another big hug.

'I'm fine, Julia. Just a bit on edge. I'm really not sure how this is all going to go.'

Julia picked up Angie's wine from the table and drank it down in one. 'It's all going to go exactly according to plan. Don't worry.' She glanced over to the flat door. 'Oh, Phillip, thank you so much for helping us out.'

'Not a problem. This friend of yours sounds like a right wrong'un. I'm more than happy to help you out, my love. Do you want me to put the new lock on now?'

'Yes please, but can you make sure that it looks exactly the same as it did before. And can we have three keys please. I'll make you a cup of tea. Sugar?'

'Right you are. Three please.'

'But Ray'll know the lock has been changed as he won't be able to get in,' Angie whispered.

'Don't worry,' Ben whispered back. 'You'll hear him coming up the stairs and you can let him in, so he won't notice. Then, when he's distracted, you can swop the key over. He keeps it in his coat pocket with a red ribbon on it. Mine is on a blue one. We've brought you an identical ribbon to put on the new key now. I did the same when we changed the locks at mine.'

'Where are you living, Ben?' Angie asked, looking up at her son with concern.

'About ten minutes away in another Airbnb he's rented. He thinks I've been holed up there all this time and that I'm more than happy about it. There's a PS5 there and he's bought me a copy of the latest FIFA game, so I tell him I'm cool with it. He brings in pizza and burgers and crisps every day.'

'Super healthy diet!' Angie commented.

'I quite like it,' Ben laughed.

'I'll bet you do!'

They all had a cup of tea, except for Ben, who had located a can of Coca Cola in the fridge, which he guzzled down followed by some impressive belching. They wittered about anything and nothing until Phillip had fitted the new lock and departed.

'Well, mission one accomplished,' Julia sighed as she closed the door behind him. 'He's a jack of all trades, old Phillip. I've known him for years and he owed me a favour.'

'He won't tell anyone?'

'I've never known anyone so discreet, and it's not as if he's doing anything other than helping us out of a dangerous situation, is he? I haven't told him the full details, but enough to know that we needed help,' Julia insisted.

'OK, as long as you're sure. But look, Julia, I have to tell you again that I'm still absolutely fucking furious with you for concocting this whole thing without telling me. I was out of my mind with worry about Ben. Why didn't you discuss it with me from the very beginning?'

'Because, Mum, we thought you wouldn't be a very good actress,' Ben sputtered, having opened a packet of chocolate digestives, and stuffed two whole biscuits into his mouth a once.

'Ben's right. We needed you to be convincing in front of the police. You couldn't have done it if you'd known the truth.'

'But why bring the police into it at all?'

'Because I was hoping that we might cut out all this part of the plan if the police took the bait and arrested Ray for kidnapping Ben in the first place. We could also have got them to examine all the papers. But they decided not to look into it, so we had to progress with Plan B. I'm very sorry that I, well that we, tricked you. I know you went through hell, but hopefully you understand why.'

'Well, I'm still very upset. It made me ill.'

'Look, it's my fault. I was very concerned when we found all those statements and especially once we'd visited that poor old guy in the care home.' She patted Angie's knee as they sat side by side on the sofa.

'Yeah, and I was bloody angry at Dad. He had been away for weeks and weeks and was totally ignoring us. When I saw you with all that stuff in the bedroom, I began to wonder if he really was totally full of shit. I had begun to think it for a while if I'm honest, even though I didn't want to. He never seemed to give a fuck about either of us and came and went as he liked. And if you think about it, he's always too cheerful unless you ask him the wrong questions. Then he ignores you or changes the subject. Have you never noticed how Dad never answers any questions? Anyway, when you were in bed, I took all the papers down again and spent days going through them. That's why I locked my door that week because I didn't want you knowing.'

'Honestly, Ange, you should be so proud of your son. He went through all of it and made comprehensive notes of names, addresses, payments, and dates. You'll make a great forensic accountant one of these days, Ben.'

'I don't want to be a fucking boring accountant.'

'Language!' Angie warned.

'A forensic is not like a normal accountant,' Julia explained. 'It's more like being an investigator of fraud and so on. Anyway, that's not the point. Ben discussed the stuff in the paperwork with Tim, who told me.' She looked down at her hands. 'Look, it's no secret that I've never warmed to Ray exactly. I've always thought there was something fishy about him to say the least. But I also realised that if he had been up to all this stuff for decades, it wasn't going to be easy to confront him. So, we had be clever.' She paused. 'Pass me a biscuit, Ben, before you scoff the entire lot.'

He passed her one, but kept hold of the packet.

In between chewing, he continued, 'So, what happened was, Tim asked me over and Julia suggested that I call Dad and tell him that you'd been snooping through his papers, just to see how he'd react.'

'And?'

'Well, he went bloody ballistic. He rang me straight away, which was a total miracle given he'd ignored both of us for so long. I was beginning to think he was dead.'

'Me too,' Angie agreed.

'Shame he wasn't,' Julia interjected.

'He told me that he'd collect me from school the next day. He said to pack a bag and that we'd spend a few days in London together. I told him I'd love that because you were being a complete cow and asking me where I was all the time and that I couldn't wait to get away, which wasn't true obviously, but that's what I had to tell him. Although, you were being a bit of a nag and it was a bit true.'

'Ben, stick to the point,' Julia warned him, her eyes boring into him.

'So, obviously I couldn't tell you what I was going to do, because you would have stopped me, but Julia thought it was the best idea and we agreed we'd tell you as soon as we could.'

'That was good of you,' said Angie, standing up from the sofa and walking over to the window.

'Look, Ange, it was the only way we could find out where he was and what he was currently getting up to. Ben was the only person he would trust because he thought he was an innocent child.'

'And he didn't think that I suspected him, because I told on you, Mum. I laid it on thick about how much I'd missed him and how appalling I thought you were going through his stuff.'

'But I've given him all the papers now, so we've got no evidence, have we!'

'Duh, we took copies of everything, didn't we, Julia. It took absolutely hours. I photo'd them and then saved them on the cloud before deleting them off my phone and Julia photocopied them all as well just to be on the safe side. We've got everything.'

'And then finally you brought me in on the plot. And for your information, I thought I acted the whole distraught mother thing brilliantly yesterday, so maybe you should have had more faith in my dramatic abilities. I could get an Oscar one day.' She laughed. 'So now do we go to the police?' Angie slumped back down onto the sofa next to Julia.

'No, not yet. There's a very specific reason he's in St Albans.'

'He's in the middle of another scam, Mum. And together, we're going to catch him in the act.'

Chapter Fifty-Two

———

Diana had arranged to meet the anonymous caller at The Grove outside Watford. It was an elegant, sophisticated hotel, the haunt of footballers and their WAGs, helpfully hidden away along a vast sweeping drive with lush golf courses on either side. They offered a staggeringly good afternoon tea at an equally staggeringly, exorbitant price to match. But Diana had been asked to suggest somewhere away from St Albans where they could eat great scones and cake discreetly. Apparently, the mystery caller did not know the area well, so would go wherever Diana suggested. As Diana was currently feeling so bruised and battered by life and had lost two stone in the process, she felt that an over-indulgent afternoon tea might be just what she needed, especially given that she had a terrible sense of foreboding as to what this woman might be about to tell her.

The waitress, pencil thin and wearing the skinniest of black trousers, led her to a corner table, handing her a menu as she sat down.

'Can I get you anything while you wait?'

'Just a glass of sparkling water, please. I'll order when my guest arrives.'

Diana had arrived early, which did nothing to quell her mounting anxiety. She had sat herself facing the entrance into the room and even though she tried to busy herself with her phone and re-reading the menu several times over, she could not stop watching every person going in and out. And anyway, the menu was so complicated that you needed a PhD to decide what to have. You could choose between the non-vegetarian afternoon tea, the vegetarian, the vegan, and the gluten-free. Children had their own menu with non-veggie and veggie options as well. There were twelve teas to choose from, including one called Margaret Hope's Second Flush. She assumed this was for the menopausal amongst the guests. It gave her a headache just reading the options. *Since when did afternoon tea become so complex? It could take you hours to make a decision, by which time it might be too late*, she mused.

She texted Ian while she waited.

How's it going at the shop today?

Alright. Sales poor. Trying to be creative.

How?

Too hard to explain. Will when I see you.

She was about to reply, perplexed and more than a little concerned by his reply, but at that moment, three people approached her table: two women in their later thirties or early forties and a teenage boy. One of the women was blonde, slim and quite attractive, if somewhat dishevelled in appearance - her shirt crumpled, her trousers creased. Diana could not help but think that she would scrub up well if someone took her in hand. The other woman had her dark, curly hair tied back in a hairband, which seemed to strain against the task. She was larger and sailed in at the head of the group wearing a floaty, floral dress. The boy was tall, gangly, with a few acne spots threatening to erupt on his forehead, twiddling nervously with the hem of his anorak.

'Mrs Whitlock?'

Diana nodded.

'Thanks so much for meeting us. I'm Julia. We spoke on the phone. And this is my good friend Angie and her son, Ben.'

'Lovely to meet you all, but I'm so sorry. I misunderstood. I thought I was only meeting you, Julia. We'll need a bigger table and I think they are fully booked.'

'Not to worry. I'm sure we can sort it out.' Julia hailed the waitress, who did her best to be unhelpful in Julia's opinion.

'I'm afraid we don't have a table for four. We are fully booked. Can you come back another day?'

'Absolutely not. Look, we can all just squidge up a bit. We just need two extra chairs.'

'Well, I'm not sure we have any spare, Madam.'

'Nonsense. I can see two which aren't being used from here. Ben, go and get them.'

'I don't think I can just go and nick them from other tables,' he spluttered, blushing crimson as he glanced at the waitress, who smiled back at him.

'Oh, for Christ sakes, I'll do it.' Julia marched off and returned first with one chair and then with another. 'There, now we can all sit down. That wasn't so difficult, was it?'

They sat and the waitress walked away defeated.

'Mrs Whitlock,' Angie began.

'Please call me Diana.'

'Diana, I'm sorry that we've come as a gang, but it's my fault. I felt that we should all come. Julia has been helping me with something, but at the end of the day, it's really my problem.'

'It's my problem too,' Ben chimed in.

'Yes, it is,' Angie agreed, forcing a short smile, 'so I felt we should all come to talk to you about it.'

The waitress returned and took their order. They all went for the straight-forward non-vegetarian option.

'This table really is too small for four,' the waitress muttered.

'We'll manage, thank you,' Julia barked.

'Alright, if you're sure.' She raised an eyebrow at Ben who almost melted on the spot.

'Talk to me about what?' Diana turned to Julia. 'You said on the phone that you wanted to talk to Patrick. Is this something to do with him?'

'Well, yes, it is. Ange, you go on.'

'So, about a month or so ago, I found some papers belonging to my husband. He had been away for a long time. He normally travels a lot, but this time he had been completely out of touch, and it was all very odd.'

'Get to the point, Mum.'

'OK, sorry. It's so hard to explain. So, anyway, as I was saying, one day I found all these papers at our house, hidden away, and they were very strange. There were bank accounts and house deeds and all sorts of things, none of which I recognised.'

The teas arrived, interrupting them again. They were all silent as the waitress unloaded an enormous, silver, three-tiered cake stand on to the centre of the table, which groaned with sandwiches, cakes, and scones. Teacups and plates were balanced at the edges of the table along with the teapot.

'Don't worry, I'll pour,' Julia scowled, shooing the waitress away.

'Can I?' Ben asked.

'Go ahead,' Angie said, as he piled his plate sky high. 'I'm sorry. He's a hoover on legs.'

Diana smiled.

'Do go on.'

'So, one set of bank accounts showed a large payment from a Patrick Whitlock. It was a regular monthly payment dating back several years.'

'It must be someone else. There must be thousands of people with that name.' Diana accepted a teacup from Julia. 'Thank you. So, why do you think it was my husband?'

'Because the bank was based in Harpenden and he was the only Patrick Whitlock we could find in Harpenden,' Ben spat, his mouth full of beef sandwich.

Diana's hand began to shake, and she put her cup down onto the floor beside her, the table being too full. 'And who were these payments being made to?'

'A guy called Hal Carpenter,' Angie replied.

A cold shiver ran up Diana's back. 'And he's your husband?'

'No, he's not. My husband is called Ray. Ray Reynolds.'

'I'm really sorry, but I'm not quite following you.'

'I know, we were confused as well. The thing is, all the papers were in different names,' Julia explained. 'Hal Carpenter was just one of them.'

Picking up a cupcake but pausing before he stuffed it into his mouth whole, Ben added, 'You see, we thought Dad was a spy working for MI5 or 6. That's what he's always told us, although he told other people he worked for the foreign office, and we thought the papers were work papers, but then we began to think they weren't.'

'A spy?'

Julia interrupted. 'Does the name Hal Carpenter mean anything to you?'

Diana hesitated. 'It may. When I was sorting out my husband's probate, I noticed that there were regular payments going out to an H. Carpenter, but I haven't been able to find out who he is. Patrick and I held a joint account for bills and so on, but we each had our own personal account and that particular payment went out from his. The name you mentioned matches, but the payments had stopped just before he died. I've no idea why.'

'I'm so sorry to hear about your husband,' Angie said, reaching out and touching Diana lightly on the sleeve. 'Was he ill?'

She shook her head. 'No, he committed suicide. I came home from work one day and he was dead. No warning, nothing. I still don't know why he did it.' A tear leaked from her eye, and she wiped it away.

'Do you know where the toilets are?' Ben asked.

'Just back the way you came in,' Diana answered in a strangulated voice.

Ben got up, dropping crumbs all over the floor from his lap.

'Sorry about that,' Angie smiled. 'I think he was embarrassed.'

'Don't worry. He seems like a lovely boy. This must all be very difficult for him.'

'And for you. You've obviously had a terrible time.'

'Yes, it's been pretty tough. I lost my mother just after Patrick passed away, so it's been somewhat of a double whammy.'

'Poor you. How awful,' Julia replied.

'Yes. In fact, the circumstances of her death are very strange as well. She had a stroke after some guy conned her into leaving him her bungalow.'

Julia and Angie exchanged glances.

'What was his name?'

'Thomas Maloney.'

They shook their heads at the same time. 'He's not one of our names, is he Ange?'

'No, I don't think so.'

'Would you like some more tea, Diana?' Julia asked. 'You've not eaten anything. Mind you, there's not much left. Ben's had most of it and I've gobbled the rest. I have a terrible sweet tooth.'

'No, I'm fine. Look, I'm not sure where any of this gets us.'

'We've got a sort of plan, but we'll need your help, if you're willing,' Angie whispered.

Diana looked down at her lap and then back at the two women.

'What is it?'

Chapter Fifty-Three

———

Daniel had cleared Dr Blair's office and left London within a couple of hours. He drove north straight up the M1, stopping in Hitchin. He thought that perhaps he should go further away, perhaps even abroad, as he often fantasised about reinventing himself as a lord fallen upon hard times and encouraging a rich American widow to gift him his fortune unwittingly. But for now, he needed thinking time. He had never been rattled before, always managing to stay one step ahead of everyone else, but now he realised that he had perhaps become a little too complacent. Establishing himself in Harley Street had given him stability and prestige, but he had lost his chameleonic ability to shapeshift and dodge. It was a model he would now have to reconsider.

He chose a small, single room at The Sun hotel, a charming pub that had originally been a sixteenth century coaching inn, checking in as Ray Reynolds. He could have afforded a much nicer room, but he was keen not to draw attention to himself. By the poor light in the bathroom, he shaved off his beard to remove any trace of his medical past. He looked ten years younger once he had completed his makeover, dressed down in a faded T-shirt and torn jeans. Suddenly ravenous, he went down the uneven wooden staircase to the bar, where he ordered fish and chips, washing it down with a pint of McMullen real ale and going all out with a sticky toffee pudding to finish. Satiated, he felt much better. He ordered one more pint, sipping it at his corner table, watching the crowd, and thinking.

He stayed for a couple of nights at The Sun, before renting a flat just outside the town. He spent his time driving around the area, visiting different pubs, restaurants, and cafes. Money was not an issue, as he had amassed a reasonable fortune in his career as a psychologist, plus he still had his monthly stipend from Patrick. He could relax for a while, but that was not really in his nature. He cruised around various pubs at night, roaming between Hertfordshire and Cambridgeshire, reminiscing about his early days in London when he did the same thing in London bars. The pubs were less classy, but nonetheless full of opportunity.

One evening, he found himself in Huntingdon at The Crown Inn, nursing a pint and nibbling on a packet of cheese and onion crisps. There was a young girl at another table, glancing nervously at the door as if she was expecting someone who was never going to turn up. She was pretty in a girl-next-door kind of way, dressed simply in a checked shirt and jeans. She wore no make-up. After watching her for half an hour Daniel went to the toilet and on the way back, he bumped into her table, spilling her drink over the surface and onto her lap.

'Oh, I'm so sorry.' He produced a clean, white handkerchief from his pocket and passed it to her.

'It's OK,' she muttered, looking down at her wet lap.

'No, really, use it to dry yourself. I'll get you some paper towels.' He headed back to the loo and emerged with a handful of tissue with which to dry the table. 'What are you drinking? The least I can do is to get you another,' he smiled.

The girl hesitated. 'I'm alright, honestly.'

'I insist. What were you having?'

'It's only a lime and lemonade.'

'OK, one lime and lemonade coming right up.' He strode off the bar and returned a few minutes later with her drink, laced with a single vodka, and another pint for himself.

'Can I join you, or are you waiting for someone?'

'I was waiting for my friend, but she's not turned up. She's just texted to say she's had a row with her mum and dad, and they've grounded her for the night, so I think I'll head home in a minute.'

'Well, why don't I keep you company while you finish your drink?' he suggested, sitting down on the stool opposite her without waiting for a reply. 'What's your name?'

'Angie,' she replied, her face flushing scarlet.'

He raised his glass to her.

'I'm Ray. This is a nice pub this, isn't it? Do you come in here regularly?'

'No, not really. My mum doesn't like me coming to pubs. She thinks I'm too young. She thinks I'm at Anita's house tonight.'

'Strict is she, your mum?' He sipped his pint, his eyes locked on her face.

'A bit. My dad died a while ago and since then she's been very possessive.'

'I'm sorry to hear that, about your dad I mean.'

'Thanks.'

'So, it's just you and your mum, is it? Do you live in Huntingdon?'

'Yes, we live just outside.'

'So, your mum's not remarried or anything?'

333

'No, she's never going to. In a way, I wish she would, because I think it would make her happier again, but she's not looking. I'm not sure anyone would have her!' She giggled and sipped her lemonade. 'This tastes a bit odd.'

'Probably just a different lime cordial. Bit of a dragon, is she, your mother?'

'Yes, just a bit. She works at the doctor's surgery as a receptionist and all the patients are scared of her.'

'Ah, poor Angie Baby. Do you know that song?'

'No, I don't think so.'

'It's one of my favourites. Look it up if you have time.' He downed his pint. 'It's getting dark outside. Can I give you a lift home?'

She shook her head. 'No, it's fine, honestly. I walk home all the time.'

'But the lanes are unlit, and it would be a shame if you got run over by some idiot. It would ruin your pretty face.'

Her pretty face was now tomato red. 'Come on. I promise you'll be safe with me. I'm on my way home anyway.'

'OK, thank you.' She reached around to grab her denim jacket from the back of her chair and picked up her bag from the floor, following him out into the car park.

'Nice car.'

He came around to the passenger seat of the Audi and opened the door for her. 'I really like it. They're great cars, Audis.'

'I don't really know anything about cars. I just know if I like the look of them.'

'Seems fair,' he replied, shutting her door, and coming back around to the driver's side. 'Shall we put the roof down as it's warm?' he asked, already pressing the button. 'Now, what's your address?'

'It's not far. I can direct you.'

Daniel zoomed out of the car park and down the road, Angie's hair flying into her eyes.

'So, what do you do?'

'I'm at school,'

'Doing your A-levels?'

'Yes, well next year. I'm in the lower sixth. Go left here.'

'What subjects?'

'English, History, and French.'

'You're obviously a bit of a brain box as well as good-looking. You've got it all.'

She made no reply, pressing her face against the breeze as Daniel sped along. Eventually, they reached her road. 'Can you stop here, and I'll walk up the road? I don't want Mum seeing the car. She'll know I wasn't at Anita's, and she'll murder me for accepting a lift from a stranger.'

'Of course, not a problem.' He leant across and brushed her cheek imperceptibly with his lips. 'I'd like to see you again, Angie, if you'd like to. Would you?'

She nodded.

'I'll be in the same pub same time next week. Hope to see you then.'

'OK, I'll try. Thanks for the lift.' She jumped out of the car and walked quickly up the road, Daniel watching to see which house she turned into. He waited until he was sure she would have gone in and then drove past the house - large, detached, with a well-manicured garden. There was some money there.

Chapter Fifty-Four

Diana had driven directly from The Grove to the shop. She had kept putting it off, bowed down under the weight of all her other problems, but she knew she had to get back to it and take control. In fact, she knew that it would do her good. It would be a welcome distraction and provide some level of stability again which might just stop the feeling that her world was spinning out of control.

She drove up to park behind the shop in her allocated space, only to find that Ian's car was in it. She felt a wave of anger pulsing at her temples, even while she knew she was being unreasonable. He had been working here for weeks, so why shouldn't he use the space. It was just that he had never asked. She reversed back out of the narrow lane and went to park in Sainsburys. She could do her shopping there on the way home, so it was not wholly inconvenient.

The high street was busy with shoppers, which was always gratifying to see and as she entered the shop, the chimes tinkling over her head, she was pleased to see that there were two customers: one browsing and another at the till, where Ian was serving. He looked up and spotted her, smiling broadly.

'Would you like a bag for that?' he asked the woman.

'No, I'm fine. I can put it in with my shopping,' she answered, nodding to Diana as she turned and left.

'Can I help you with anything?' Diana asked a younger woman who was handling the necklaces on display.

'No, I was just looking,' she replied and abruptly left.

'I think you scared her off, Diana,' Ian quipped. 'How are you? To what do I owe the pleasure?'

Diana scowled. 'Well, I thought it was about time I took over again. I've been away too long, and I need to get back to work. I think it will do me good.'

'Are you sure? You do look rather tired. Would you like a coffee?'

'Yes, I wouldn't mind. I'll go in the back and make it. Do you want one?'

'Yes please. I think I'll put the closed sign on now. It's almost five and I don't think we'll get much more traffic today,' he commented, moving to the door to swop the sign over.

'Sometimes we do get a rush about this time as people are on their way home.'

'Well, that's not been the case while I've been here, Diana.'

She pursed her lips and went through to the back to the storeroom where there was a small ledge with a kettle and a mini fridge. Emerging a few moments later with two steaming mugs, one of which she handed to Ian, she said, 'It looks very empty back there. Have the new orders not arrived?'

'Some have, but I took the liberty of cancelling most of them. You're overstocked and it's costing you far too much money.'

'But you never discussed that with me, Ian. Cancelling orders is my call not yours.'

'I know, but I really didn't want to bother you what with everything else you've had going on. I did say I'd manage it all for you.'

'Yes, and I very much appreciate it, but it's one thing working with the customers. Changing the orders is another matter.'

'You seem a little on edge. Is everything alright?' He reached across and stroked the sleeve of her coat.

She backed away. 'I'm sorry if I seem a bit snappy. I've had a weird day.'

'Weird? In what way?'

She blew on her coffee and took a small sip. 'Oh, that's hot. There wasn't any milk.'

'My fault. I haven't bought any. I take my coffee black.'

'Not to worry.'

'So, tell me. What's worrying you?'

'I found something out about Patrick today. I knew part of it already, but not the whole thing.'

'What about Patrick?'

She hesitated.

'You can trust me, Diana. Who am I going to tell? I don't know anyone round here anyway, and it seems to me that you need to get this off your chest.'

'Well, when Patrick died, I found that he had been paying a lot of money to someone. I had no idea who it was or why he was paying this person. Then today I found out who he is. I still don't know why, but I think it was blackmail of some sort.'

'Blackmail? Are you sure?'

'Not completely, but the information I was given suggested that it probably was. It's complicated to explain.'

'It sounds rather far-fetched if you ask me,' he replied, leaning back against the counter. 'Who told you anyway?'

'Some woman who thinks it might be her husband who was receiving the money. She thinks he's been conning a whole load of people using different aliases. She found Patrick's name on some bank statements at her house.'

'Right, OK, and you met this woman how?'

'She contacted me, and I met her this afternoon.'

Ian suddenly sat up straight.

'This woman. You met her today? Where?'

'Why does that matter?'

'No, I suppose it doesn't. I just wondered if she was local or not.'

'No, she lives somewhere near Cambridge. Anyway, enough of my problems, can we have a catch up on the shop?'

But Ian had slammed his mug down onto the counter, slopping coffee all over it, and was heading out to the back door. 'Sorry, I've just remembered I've got a dentist appointment. Can you lock up?'

Diana stared after him. 'He's a bloody odd bloke,' she muttered out loud.

A couple of minutes later, she heard a loud banging on the front door.

'Sorry, we're closed!' she called.

'Diana, open up. It's me, Julia!'

The woman removed her heavy hood.

Diana opened the door. 'Julia, what are you doing here?'

'I have been following Ray.'

'Ray? Angie's husband?'

'Yes. You were just talking to him.'

'That was Ian.'

'No, that was Ray.'

'Sorry?'

'That was fucking Ray.'

'Shit.' Diana wobbled and Julia steadied her by the elbow.

'I just told him about our meeting earlier. He knows I met Angie and that she told me all the stuff about Patrick and the money.'

'Fuck.' Julia fumbled in her bag for her phone and dialled.

'Ange, it's Julia. You need to get out of the flat right now. Ray knows you met Diana today and he's on his way over there now. We're coming, but he's got a head start on us. Leave immediately and call us to let us know where you are. We'll come and get you.'

She turned to Diana.

'Where's your car? And how fast can you drive? And on the way, we need to come up with Plan C.'

Chapter Fifty-Five

'Hey, Angie baby. You don't look very well. Have you been ill?'

She looked up at his broad, crooked smile lighting up his face and burst into tears.

Ray glanced around the pub. 'Hey, come on now. Whatever it is, it can't be all that bad. Let's not make a scene here, eh?' He sat down, blocking the view of her from anyone who might be looking over. He reached over and held her hand. 'Come on, tell me what's bothering you.'

Angie rummaged up the sleeve of her jumper and produced a soggy tissue. She blew her nose loudly.

Ray put his hand in his pocket and produced a pristine, white handkerchief. She took it gratefully and shortly it was stained with snot and mascara.

'Now, what is it?'

'I'm pregnant,' she whispered, her words almost inaudible. 'I'm not sure how it happened.'

'I thought I'd been careful and anyway, I thought you were going to go on the pill?' he whispered back.

She could not remember having discussed being on the pill with Ray.

'No, not yet. I have an appointment with the GP to discuss it, but I didn't want my Mum to know, so it's been difficult to arrange, especially as she works there.'

'Ah, I see,' Ray muttered. 'Well, don't worry,' he replied, his smile returning. 'This is easy to fix.'

Angie stared at him, her eyes dark-circled from lack of sleep wide. 'You want me to get rid of it?'

'No, quite the opposite. I propose that we get married and make that baby legitimate. What do you say?'

Pregnancy had not been part of the plan. He was furious with himself for being so careless, but he was damned if he was going to abandon his child like his own mother had left him. And the more he considered the issue, the more he saw it as an opportunity. Angie and the baby would be a solid base from which he could build a new life of respectability. She was young and malleable enough that he could come and go as he pleased, and she came with a big house, which he could easily take over. The mother was a bit of an issue, moaning about the age gap and his intentions, but he would win her over. In any case, he did not see her being part of the longer-term picture. She would become a complication, a drag on his freedom, so he would think of how to get her out of the way. It would not be that difficult.

He found himself oddly excited about being a father, fantasising about how he would teach his boy to be savvy like him. The baby would be a boy, of course. And the boy would be so proud of him, because Daniel had made a genuine success of his life. He had come from nothing and achieved so much. Just think what heights his son could attain if he was backed by a stable, loving family. When the time was right, he would educate him in all the important things in life; how to read people, how to dissemble, how to always come out on top no matter how difficult the circumstances. Angie could feed and house him and get him through all the dull growing up stuff, the nuts and bolts of which did not interest him, and then Daniel would take over and make him a man.

Chapter Fifty-Six

Angie grabbed her bag and raced out of the flat, taking the stairs two at a time. She ran towards the high street, figuring that she would hide in one of the cafes until Julia could get to her. She headed towards Market Place and spotted a Gail's Cafe, which was heaving with customers. There were no available seats, but she fought her way to the back, finding a small space to stand against the back wall.

She found her phone and opened WhatsApp.

Dad knows about meeting Diana. Get out of your flat now and meet me in Gail's Market Place. Urgent.

Two ticks appeared and went blue, followed by a thumbs up emoji.

She called Julia. 'I'm in Gail's on Market Place.'

'She's in Gail's,' Julia repeated.

'Who are you talking to?'

'Diana. She's driving.'

'Tell her we are fifteen minutes away.'

'That long?'

'I'm going as fast as I can, but look at the traffic. We'll be there soon. Hang on, Angie.'

'I've messaged Ben to meet me here. I was worried Ray might go after him when he finds I'm not in the flat.'

'Good idea. See you in a minute.'
'OK, thanks.'
She hung up and waited.

Chapter Fifty-Seven

Daniel backed out from behind the shop at speed, almost crashing into a car parked to the side of him in his haste. He raced down the side road and then drew to an abrupt standstill, stuck in a queue of traffic trying to turn onto Harpenden High Street. He slammed the steering wheel with his fist and sat on the horn, but nothing moved.

How the hell had Angie escaped from the flat? She seemed to have metamorphosed from a shy, suburban woman to a combination of amateur detective crossed with fucking Harry Houdini.

'This is not how it ends!' he shouted to himself. 'I say how it ends. Not them!'

Eventually, he moved onto the high street and traffic crawled along out of the town, creeping past the deserted cricket ground on his left. Once he got across the roundabout, he managed to pick up some speed, overtaking dangerously. Fortunately, the flat was on the right side of St Albans so that he did not have to drag through the town, which he thought seemed to have been created by a drunken urban planner. Eventually, he screeched to a halt and careered up the stairs to the flat. The door swung open, and it took him just a few seconds to establish that Angie was not there.

He made a calculation that she could not have gone far. She would still be trying to find Ben - and until she did, she would not leave - so she must be hiding somewhere in town. He left his car, and began to run towards the centre. He could cover more ground on foot. He glanced inside every cafe and coffee shop he passed, but could not spot her. He dived into various pubs en route, which were already filling up with jaded workers desperate for a drink after a long, hard day. He kept on jogging and that was went he ran into Ben.

Ben was wearing a hoodie and Daniel did not instantly realise it was him until he took a second glance.

'Ben? What the fuck are you doing here? How did *you* get out of your flat?' He grabbed him by his hood and held him fast.

He hesitated, 'You forgot to lock the door this morning. I was really hungry, so I thought I'd pop out to get some chips,' he answered, addressing his dirty trainers.

'Don't lie to me, Ben. You're crap at it. I locked the door. I always check it. So, I'll ask you again - how did you get out?'

No answer.

'Alright. Don't tell me. So, where are you off to now?'

Before he could answer, a phone pinged in Ben's pocket.

'Give me your phone?'

'No.'

'Give me the fucking phone.'

Ben shook his head.

'OK, have it your own way.' Daniel seized Ben by the arm, grabbing his phone from the back pocket of his jeans. It was locked.

'Are you trying to crawl back to Mummy? Where is she?'

Ben said nothing.

'Ok, have it your way.' Daniel produced a small kitchen knife and prodded it into the back of Ben's jacket. 'I'll ask again. Where is she?'

Ben gestured with his head up the street.

'OK, let's go.' He pocketed the knife and grabbed Ben hard by the arm. They marched towards Gail's. When they arrived, Daniel swung the door open, still hanging on tightly to Ben and walked towards the back of the cafe. The three women paled simultaneously.

'Ladies, what a great pleasure to see you all huddled together like the witches from *Macbeth*. Especially you, Julia, in your role as chief hag.'

'Ray,' Angie stuttered.

'Ian,' Diana cried.

'Bastard,' Julia spat.

'One and the same. Now, what do you say we take this little party back to the flat. Angie's place is closest, and we'll see if we can't all have a sensible chat. Much as I enjoy the oat cookies in here, I don't feel it's all that conducive for quiet conversation, do you?'

'I think we'd rather stay here where we have you in public,' Julia replied.

'Well, number one, my dear Julia, this is none of your business. And two, if it hadn't been for you sticking your fat arse in where it's not wanted, everyone would still be perfectly happy. Given your obvious talent for breaking and entering, I could call the police and have you arrested in seconds for trespassing on my property.'

Julia burst out laughing. 'You want to call the police to report me? We've got a file on you as long as your arm, chock full of fraud and embezzlement, so I don't think they would be too interested in me.'

'What do you think, Ben?' Daniel asked him, prodding him in the ribs.

'He's got a knife,' Ben whispered.

'For fuck's sake, Ray, he's your son. Surely you wouldn't do anything to hurt him?' Angie yelped.

'Do you really want to take that risk?'

Chapter Fifty-Eight

They walked in slow procession back to the flat: Daniel keeping tight hold of Ben and the women following behind in silence, exchanging furtive glances when they dared. Before they left the cafe, Daniel had insisted that they surrender their phones to him, all of which he put in his inside coat pocket. Once they were all upstairs, he slammed the door, shoving Ben onto the sofa.

'Stay there. Now, where's the front door key?' he demanded.

'In your pocket where it's always been,' Angie replied.

'So, how did you? Oh, fuck it. I don't care.' He fumbled in his pocket and drew out the key on a red ribbon, turning to the door and locking them all in.

'Sit, all of you,' he instructed.

'Can I get a glass of water?' Diana asked.

'Alright, but hurry up.'

She moved to the back of the room and ran the tap, fumbling around because her hands were shaking so badly, before returning to the sofa, where Angie, Julia, and Ben were all squashed up. She perched on the arm next to Ben.

Daniel drew up a chair from the dining table and sat Christine Keeler style with his chest resting on the back of the chair and his legs akimbo. He brandished the knife in his right hand.

'Now, tell me exactly what you think you've found out about me.'

No one spoke.

'Come on, don't be shy. You've clearly been discussing me amongst yourselves for some time. It's only fair that you let me in on your various conspiracy theories.'

'We know that you are not who you say you are,' Angie mumbled.

Julia harrumphed. 'That's an understatement!'

'Now, let's try to be civil,' Diana interjected. 'Clearly, you are at least two people, because I know you as Ian, and your family and Julia know you as Ray. So, which one are you?'

'I'll ask the questions, if you don't mind.'

'But you are also other people, aren't you, Dad? The papers we found. I mean, there were loads of different names.'

'But you can't trace them back to me personally, can you?'

'Except for the fact that they were all hidden in our house,' Angie retorted.

'My house, actually, Angie baby, but we'll get back to that. The papers are work aliases. That's all.'

'Bollocks!' Julia shouted.

'Keep out of this, bitch, or you'll regret it.'

'Don't threaten me, you prick.'

Before anyone could react, Daniel leant forward and slashed at Julia's shin. Blood gushed from the wide gash, and she cried out in pain. 'Now, shut the fuck up, or it'll be your throat next.'

'Can I get her a towel or something?' Diana asked, her brow knotted in terror.

Daniel nodded and Angie pointed the way to the bathroom. She returned with a couple of hand towels, which she handed to Julia, who took them gratefully, her face drained of all colour.

'I think she needs a doctor,' Angie pleaded. 'There's a lot of blood.'

'She'll live, as long as she doesn't open her trap again. Hand me one of those towels,' he demanded. 'I need to wipe the knife.'

Julia threw one over to him.

'Ray,' Angie began, her voice shaky, 'why are you doing this? I thought you loved us.' Tears began to well up in her eyes.

'Love? What is that anyway? I've never loved anyone in my whole life.' He paused, 'Except for Ben.'

'But that's not true, is it? We were happy.'

'Christ, you're such a fuckwit. Happy? You saw me for a few days a week and the rest of the time we led totally separate lives. The way we've supposedly loved each other makes a mockery of relationships. But you were too timid and naïve to expect anything else, weren't you?'

'So, why bother with us if we meant so little to you?'

'Because I was not prepared to abandon my child.'

'But you've been a crap dad,' Ben interjected. 'You may as well have abandoned me.'

Daniel looked as if he had been slapped. 'But we spent loads of quality time together when I was there, didn't we? Good old father and son stuff.'

'No, we didn't. You've been part-time at best. I was really proud of you, when I thought you were a spy and had an amazing job like James Bond or someone, but now I realise that you're just a pathetic, lying shit.'

Daniel made a low moan like a wounded animal. 'You ungrateful little git.'

Angie put her hand on Ben's leg to quieten him. 'So, why, Ray? Why have anything to do with us?'

'Because it suited me when I met you. You had money, you and your mum, and once she was out of the picture, it was my money and my house. You never asked any questions. But to be completely honest, if you hadn't got yourself pregnant, I would have scarpered long ago. Once Ben was on the way, I couldn't leave, not totally. You've both been a fucking millstone around my neck, but I took my responsibilities seriously.'

'And now?' Angie whispered.

'Well, that's up to you, isn't it. If you insist on pursuing these ridiculous allegations, then I think we have a serious problem.'

'But we just can't go back to the way we were, can we? I mean, how's that even possible?' Angie cried.

'Ian,' Diana interrupted. 'It seems to me that you are in need of help. I think that if we spoke to the police, you could get a psychiatric assessment, they could find someone for you to talk to, and you probably wouldn't be prosecuted. It seems to me that, for whatever reason, you've always felt the need to hide who you are. With the right support, you might start to feel better about yourself.'

Diana was sitting on her hands to stop them from shaking.

'Oh, listen to old mother hen here! How fucking ironic!'

'I'm just trying to find a sensible way out of the situation, Ian. Look at your family. How can you threaten them like this? One way or another, you're in a great deal of trouble. For one thing, why were you blackmailing Patrick?'

'Well, partly for the money. The silly old queen would have paid anything for me to fuck him senseless for two days every week, and I obliged him for years until I decided to switch to a more respectable career.'

Diana wobbled on the arm of the chair. 'I don't believe you!'

'Really, well how do you explain this then?'

Daniel removed his watch and turned it over. The inscription read: *With love always, Diana.*

'He told me that the watch had been stolen,' she muttered.

'Well, he lied.'

Diana took a deep breath to steady herself. 'But I don't understand. How did you meet him in the first place? How did it start?'

'We met in a bar; he thought the encounter was completely randomly, but I engineered it.'

'Why?'

'Because he was vulnerable and because I knew I could use him to get to you. I'd followed him around the London bars and watched the way he looked at other men.' He smiled. 'Did you know that he'd never had sex with a man before me?'

Diana shook her head, desperately trying to fight her tears which were clawing at her throat. 'I didn't know he'd had sex with any man at all.' She gulped and pulled a handkerchief out of her sleeve. 'Did you know that he committed suicide?'

'Of course I knew. It was my suggestion.'

Diana almost toppled off the arm of the sofa onto Julia.

'Yes, Diana. You see, he decided to stop paying me his monthly stipend which I insisted on as the price for my silence. It was only fair. I had tapes of every single time we were together, and I promised never to release them as long as he kept on paying

357

me. Then one day, he simply decided to stop: something to do with coming up to retirement and not having the funds, or some other bollocks excuse. He thought he'd paid me for long enough and that I should stop threatening him. I disagreed, obviously. He grew difficult and said that he'd rather die than pay me any more money. So, I told him to get on with it. I dared him to do it by the end of the month and if he was brave enough to go through with it, I would never show the tapes to you or to his work colleagues or anyone. I even sent him a little concoction to help him on his way and wrote a little note for him. It was a joke really. I never thought he'd have the nerve to actually top himself. But good on him, he showed some real gumption in the end and proved me wrong. I was so impressed that I kept my word.'

'Jesus, Ray. You're pure evil,' Angie gasped, reaching across Julia to take hold of Diana's hand.

'I quite like the idea of being a Bond baddy, actually. But let's move on.'

'So, you killed Patrick. I just couldn't understand it,' Diana breathed.

Daniel shifted in his chair. 'No, he killed himself. That's the definition of suicide. I was nowhere near him.'

'And all the weird stuff that arrived after he died. Was that you too?'

'Yes, that was quite cool, don't you agree? Once I realised that the old bugger was actually going through with it, I thought it might bring a bit of levity to the situation. I figured that you might like all the new household stuff. Patrick always told me how you hankered after a new kitchen and other stuff he had been too mean to buy. The sex toys were just for a laugh.'

'The sad thing is that I always knew Patrick was attracted to men. It's part of what made him safe. If only he'd told me what he'd done, I really wouldn't have cared.' She began to cry without control.

Julia groaned, the towel around her shin now totally soaked through with blood. 'She needs a doctor, Dad,' Ben pleaded.

'She'll live. And anyway, while we are in revelation mode, I may as well fill you in on a few more things that might be of interest.' He grinned at Diana. 'Thomas Maloney. Does he ring a bell?'

Diana nodded, unable to reply. She thought she might be sick at any moment.

'Yes, that was me too. Oh, she was a silly old bird, your mum. She thought she was tough, but actually she was as soft as butter once someone paid her a bit of attention. Do you feel bad about leaving her alone so much of the time, Diana? I mean she was your mum after all. You should feel bad. After all, you're not so good at this family stuff, are you?'

Diana suddenly shot up from the sofa and moved towards Daniel, speaking almost inaudibly.

'You've killed my husband and have effectively done the same thing to my mother and stolen her money and house. You're a fucking monster.'

She darted past him and pulled at the handle of the front door of the flat.

'You're not going to get away with any of this. We'll tell the truth about everything. Open the door!'

Diana began to scream, tugging at the door before collapsing in a sobbing heap onto the carpet.

Daniel swivelled around on his chair to face her. 'But that's the beauty of the whole situation, don't you see? You'll never tell on me.'

She raised her tear-stained face and stared at him. 'Why the hell not?'

'Because I'm your son.'

Her body went rigid.

'You're no child of mine!' she erupted.

'Ray, what the fuck are you talking about?' Angie squealed.

'Ask her.'

Diana remained on the floor by the door, all eyes fixed on her.

'Diana, what is he saying?'

Diana's chest convulsed as she tried to contain her crying. In between her vast sobs, she began to speak.

'When I was very young, from about the age of six, I was abused by a family friend. He was always coming over to our house, or we sometimes we would stay at his - when my parents were too drunk to drive home. This guy, he had a handgun. He used to show me how to take the bullets in and out and how to hold it properly. When I got a little older and said I'd tell on him, he threatened me with it.'

She pulled her handkerchief out of her sleeve and blew her nose loudly.

'I don't know if my parents ever suspected, but no one ever tried to intervene, and I was too frightened to talk to anyone about it. A teacher at school asked me once if everything was alright at home, but I just said yes, I was fine. I was too embarrassed to tell a stranger what was happening, and no one would have believed me if I had.'

She wiped her eyes and stuffed the handkerchief back into her sleeve.

'Anyway, when I was fifteen, this man got me pregnant.'

She was talking so quietly while sobbing at the same time that it was hard to hear what she was saying.

'My father disowned me. He assumed, or rather it suited him to assume, that I'd been sleeping around. I refused to say who the father was. I felt so ashamed and that I should have been able to stop it somehow, and that even if I had told them who it was, they would never have believed me. My mother arranged to send me away and I stayed with a family on the south coast until I had the baby. As soon as he was born, they took him away from me. I never even saw his face.'

'Oh, Diana,' Julia sighed. 'How horrific for you.'

'I didn't know where the baby went. I only know he went to a local family who couldn't have any children and were desperate for a child.' She looked down at her lap. 'I didn't see either of my parents again until my mother got back in touch after my father died many years later.'

'I'm surprised you spoke to her ever again,' Angie murmured.

'She was really frightened of Dad. He beat her and she was too terrified to leave him. Later, we resurrected a form of relationship, once he was gone.'

'And the baby?'

'I never asked, and she never mentioned it.'

'And you never even tried to find out what happened to that child from anyone else, did you? So, why don't I fill you in on the rest of the story?' Daniel suggested, rising from his chair and striding across to the window before turning to face them all. 'I was adopted by Frank.'

'Frank?!' Diana howled.

'Yes, Frank. The man who you say abused you. He took me in as a gift of charity to appease his barren wife, who then miraculously conceived a few years later and pushed me right out of the picture from then on.'

'Frank?' Diana repeated.

'Yes, Frank! He never liked me and once they conceived a child of their own, he never even looked at me. I could not get out of there fast enough.'

'How do you know he's your father?' Diana asked.

'The same way I know that you're my mother. I found my birth certificate and then I decided to find you. I searched for you because you never attempted to look for me. And I decided very early on that, once I'd found you, I would punish you for abandoning me. It just took me a while to work out how to do it.'

He looked down at the carpet and then back at Diana.

'And clearly you never felt an ounce of curiosity about me.'

'I honestly wouldn't have known where to start.'

'But you didn't even try to start, did you? Yet I managed to find out who you married and then work out how best to hurt you. I found Patrick, and then I went after your mother. I was coming for you until these two interfered.' He glanced at Angie and Julia.

Turning his attention back to Diana, he continued, 'If you'd applied just one iota of effort, you could have found me. I waited and waited for you, but you never came.'

'Ian, I'm so sorry.' Diana stood and walked over to him.

He shoved her away. 'Anyway, Mother dear, that's why you'll never tell on me. Blood is thicker, etc, etc. And now we have been reunited, you could never let me down yet again.'

'But Ian, you've lied, and you've stolen, and you've murdered. Any mother, no matter how much they loved their child, would have to tell the police. You have to answer for your crimes.'

'You continue to disappoint me, Mother.'

'You're pure evil, just like your father,' she spat back at him. 'I thought I'd got away from him, I tried to build a new life with a good man. I succeeded for so long. But then you appear, Frank's mutant seed grown into another malevolent beast. I gave birth to the devil.'

'You left me with the devil. How else was I going to turn out?'

'Ray, we can get you help. You need to stop running. It's over,' Angie screeched.

'You're right. It's over. For you guys, at least.' He twirled the knife in his hand. 'Who wants to go first?'

Silence.

'No volunteers? OK, I'll choose then. I think non-family members. It seems the politest way of deciding this. Julia, are you ready to take your leave?'

Julia moaned and shook her head.

'I seem to have shut you up anyway. Now let's try for the permanent solution.'

He leapt up from his chair and sprang towards the couch. Angie threw herself on top of Julia, but Daniel was too strong and easily pulled her away, throwing her to the floor.

'Bye, bye, Julia,' he whispered as he raised the knife.

Chapter Fifty-Nine

Article from The Times

Father and Son Found Dead in Milton Keynes After Neighbours Raise The Alarm

Mr Frank Warrender, a widower aged 81, was found dead at his home in Milton Keynes, alongside his son, Daniel aged 46. Neighbours alerted the police when they had not seen or heard from Frank Warrender for several days. They had tried to contact him, but got no response when they rang his doorbell or his telephone.

Daniel Warrender had suffered a single stab wound to the neck. Frank Warrender died from a single shot fired from a gun believed to be owned by him. Police believe that Frank Warrender stabbed his son before shooting himself.

Neighbours reported that father and son had been estranged for many years and that Daniel had not been seen in the neighbourhood since he was a teenager.

Frank Warrender lived in Milton Keynes for his entire life and was a respected member of the community. He was the head of the local Rotary Club for many years. His wife, Ruth, passed away two years ago from cancer.

Police are not looking for any further suspects in connection with this case.

Chapter Sixty

Diana carried the tea tray outside into the garden and placed it on the patio table. It was a glorious early summer day with just enough warmth to enjoy sitting al fresco with friends. The roses and peonies were showing themselves off in the flower beds, all pinks, reds, and purples. She smiled and went back inside to get the Victoria sandwich cake out of the Marks and Spencer packaging, licking the cream and jam off her fingers as she did so.

The doorbell rang. Wiping her hands on her apron, she hurried from the kitchen and down the hall to answer it.

'Julia, how lovely to see you. How was your drive?'

'Uneventful, thankfully. It's the school holidays, so most people are away. It's a gorgeous day, isn't it? I didn't even have to bring a coat.'

'Yes. I thought we'd have tea in the garden and make the most of it. Come through. Angie and Ben will be back in a minute. She's just collecting him from his football game.'

Julia followed Diana into the kitchen.

'Tea, coffee, white wine?'

'Oh, d'you know what, I'd love a cup of tea and a small glass of wine, but only if you're opening one and I'm not being too greedy.'

'I've already opened a bottle and not at all.'

She went to the fridge and brought out a bottle of Chardonnay, unscrewing the lid and pouring out a glass for Julia and one for herself.

'That's enough, thanks. I've got to be sober enough to drive home, you know.'

Diana filled the kettle and flicked it on to boil. 'Let's go outside, shall we?'

They settled themselves into two wicker chairs, Julia pulling her skirt down to cover the scar on her leg. 'The garden is looking great. Do you manage it all yourself?'

'Mostly yes. I enjoy it. It keeps me active.'

'And how's it going with the daughter-in-law and grandson living here? Have you all settled in alright together?'

'Yes, it's been remarkably easy and lovely for me to be surrounded by family I didn't even know I had. Ben is getting on very well at St Alban's Boys, and Angie has enrolled in a Creative Writing degree at the Open University, which I think is marvellous. She kept umming and arring over it, but I persuaded her that it's never too late. Ben is very proud of her.'

'That's brilliant. She's very talented, although she's never realised that she is, and I know she'd like to write books someday. It will be the making of her.' Julia sipped her wine. 'And how does Ben seem in himself, after, well you know?'

'Alright, I think. We rarely mention it, but if he does want to talk about it, we do. I think it's healthy for all of us. The most important thing is that he understands that he did nothing wrong.'

'Absolutely. Quite the opposite, in fact. He was the hero of the hour. I owe him my life. We all do.'

'I know, but I can't help feeling, when I lie awake thinking about it in the middle of the night, that if I hadn't dropped the knife out of my sleeve - the one I nabbed from the kitchen when I got a glass of water - that I would have done it. You know when Ian, I mean Daniel, lunged at you. I can't help calling him Ian, you know. Anyway, I just feel awful that it is Ben who is saddled with it.'

'But in the end, we all did it. Not just Ben. We share the agony together. But we must move on, and we do, for the kid's sake as much as for ourselves.' She drained her glass of wine. 'Did you see the article they wrote in The Times? I think it's the only national that covered it.'

'Yes, I did. Mercifully, it was a small piece. Most people would have missed it.'

'Let's hope so.'

Diana refilled their glasses and raised hers. 'Ah, here they are now. How was your game, Ben?'

Ben lurched into the garden, his socks round his ankles and his legs spattered with mud. 'We won 3-2,' he said with a grin.

'And he scored,' Angie added, bringing up the rear. 'Hi Julia.' She bent down and gave her friend a kiss on the cheek.

'Grandma, can I have some of that cake?' Ben asked.

'Yes, darling. I was just about to bring it out, and I made you a tuna sandwich. Would you like a banana milkshake to go with it to celebrate your triumph?'

'Yes please,' he nodded, plonking himself down heavily on the lawn.

'She spoils you too much.' Angie sat down at one of the free chairs around the garden table and helped herself to a glass of wine.

'And why not?' Julia replied with a grin.

'Indeed, why the hell not?' Angie agreed.

Made in the USA
Monee, IL
25 June 2025

20027975R00213